"When did you first meet Ms. Kolni—"

Before he could finish his question, Laura bolted to her feet and took off running toward the swings and her daughter. Jordan jumped up, scanning the playground. The same black sedan was on the other side of the park now, the darkened windows rolled down just enough to see a man's blond hair. Or was it gray?

Jordan jogged toward the car, keeping a low profile as he moved. The guy could be a father looking for his kid, but Jordan wasn't going to take any chances. He'd call it in.

But before he could make out the plate numbers, the car sped away. Disgusted, he strode across the grass to where Laura stood holding her daughter. "I'm sorry, Detective," she said. "We're leaving now."

ABOUT THE AUTHOR

Winner of the Daphne du Maurier Award and the Orange Rose Award for best long contemporary romance, Linda Style always dreamed of becoming a novelist, but it took a few years and several detours along the way before that dream came true. A graduate of the University of Minnesota in behavioral health, and the Walter Cronkite School of Journalism at Arizona State University, Linda has worked as a case manager, a human rights advocate, a freelance journalist, photographer, management consultant and as the director of the Office of Grievance and Appeals for the Seriously Mentally Ill for the State of Arizona. She began to write full-time in 1998, with the release of her debut novel, *Her Sister's Secret*, a Harlequin Superromance title, in June 2000.

To find out more, visit www.LindaStyle.com or write Linda at P.O. Box 2292, Mesa, AZ 95214.

AND JUSTICE FOR ALL
Linda Style

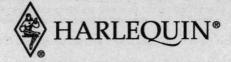

TORONTO • NEW YORK • LONDON
AMSTERDAM • PARIS • SYDNEY • HAMBURG
STOCKHOLM • ATHENS • TOKYO • MILAN • MADRID
PRAGUE • WARSAW • BUDAPEST • AUCKLAND

ISBN 0-373-71323-1

AND JUSTICE FOR ALL

www.eHarlequin.com

Printed in U.S.A.

Books by Linda Style

For my sons Timothy, Todd, Barry and Jason
My family... My heart.
You are my inspiration to write great heroes in my stories.

My deep appreciation to those
who contributed to the research for this book:
the professionals with the Los Angeles Police Department,
the City of Los Angeles Area Chamber of Commerce
and the Orange County RWA members who shared their
expertise about the City of Angels–Claire, Kim, Michele,
Aryn, Charlene and Marianne.
Since this is a work of fiction, I've taken some liberties.
Any errors are solely mine.

PROLOGUE

"DADDY WON'T WAKE UP," Caitlin whimpered.

Laura switched the phone to the other ear and glanced at the clock on the night table. Five-thirty. "It's still early, sweetheart. He's probably tired."

"He told me to wake him when I got up. Only he won't wake up...and something smells icky."

Laura sat up in bed. He'd promised! He'd vowed he'd never let their daughter see him like that again.

And she'd believed him. She always did. "Is anyone else there?"

"No. Just me and Daddy. Another man was here when I got up before, but I went back to bed and he's not here now. Can you come and get me?"

"Sure, sweetie." Standing, Laura cradled the phone between her ear and shoulder, snatched a pair of jeans from the top of the hamper and wiggled into them. "I'm on my way, but don't hang up."

"I hafta go potty."

"Okay, but then come right back to the phone." For the first time since the divorce, she was glad her ex-husband lived only a mile from the shelter. She threw on a sweatshirt over her pajama top, shoved her feet into a pair of flip-flops and hurried outside to the van.

How could he do this? She climbed inside and started the engine. "One last time," he'd pleaded.

"Tomorrow I'll be gone. Please let me see my little girl one last time."

He was going to make a fresh start in a new state, he'd said. There might be more to it, but she hadn't asked. A change might do him some good. Despite his flaws, Eddie had been a good father to Caitlin, and Laura's heart had gone out to the man she'd once loved. She'd be devastated if she had to be away from her child for even a few days. His valiant effort to stay sober for the past year was remarkable and she couldn't deny his request.

So, why would he relapse now? Maybe he *was* sick? Maybe he'd been gambling again? His drinking and gambling had always gone hand in hand.

"I'm back, Mommy."

"Good girl. I'm in the car and I'll be there in a few minutes. When I get there, I want you to unlock the side door and let me in. Okay?"

"Okay."

Laura reached the house in record time, parked, bolted from the van and took the steps in one long stride.

The door swung open and Caitlin stood there in her jammies, her strawberry-blond curls all mussed and, though she wasn't crying, a telltale streak lined her pink cheeks. Laura gathered the four-year-old into a crushing hug and nestled her face in soft, baby-shampoo-scented curls. Edging inside, she shoved the door shut with her backside.

Caitlin wiggled. "Ouch. That squeezing hurts, Mommy."

"Sorry, sweetie. I'm just happy to see you. Where's Daddy?"

"Over there." Caitlin pointed toward the living room.

The interior was wrapped in shadows, broken only by slivers of dawn filtering through the blinds. Laura flipped the switch by the door. Nothing. She tried again and when nothing happened, she glanced up. The light-bulb was missing from the fixture. Damn. With Caitlin still in her arms, she went to the window on her right and opened the blinds.

The gray-pink of sunrise was enough to see by. She glanced down the hall where light shone from a doorway, and setting Caitlin on her feet, Laura gestured toward the bedroom. "Go get your things, punkin. I need to talk to Daddy."

As Caitlin toddled off, Laura stalked across the room to the couch, hands clenched at her thighs. Eddie was lying on his side, his back to her and his face toward the cushion. An acrid scent assaulted her nostrils. Unable to contain her anger and disappoint-ment, she smacked him on the leg.

"Damn you, Eddie." She nudged him in the small of his back with her knee, this time a bit harder.

Again, he didn't move. Odd. Even when he'd been at his worst she could get a grunt out of him. But…he was too still.

Abnormally still.

The terrifying realization hit her.

Her heart pounded against the wall of her chest as she stepped closer, then leaned in to see his face. His eyes were open. A dark stain soaked the pillow under his face. She lurched back. *Oh, God!*

Covering her mouth with one hand, Laura swal-lowed back her sudden nausea and glanced toward the bedroom to make sure her daughter hadn't come out. *Think. Do something.*

Her hand shook uncontrollably as she reached out

to find a pulse at his neck. Nothing. *Oh, God!* He couldn't be... Quickly, she felt for the pulse at his wrist. He was cold. His body rigid.

Nine-one-one. She had to call for help. But she just stood there, unable to move. He was dead. Oh, God. Eddie was dead.

Her heart raced triple time, her thoughts just as fast. Was Eddie so depressed about going away that he'd killed himself? No. He wouldn't do that. And there was no gun she could see. He'd been upbeat when she talked to him last night. He was hopeful about making changes in his life. Most important, he'd never do such a thing with Caitlin there. *Caitlin.*

Oh, my God. Caitlin said she'd seen someone earlier. Had Eddie's murderer seen Caitlin? But no...that didn't make sense. If the person had known she was there...saw her...Caitlin would be—

She bolted for the bedroom. Her little girl thought her father was sleeping. She had no idea he was dead. And she could be in grave danger if anyone knew she'd been there.

"I gots everything," Caitlin said proudly when Laura appeared in the doorway.

"That's great. You said you saw a man here earlier. Did you meet him?" Laura hid her trembling hands behind her back and pasted on a smile.

"Uh-uh. I was peeking through the bedroom door 'cause I heard loud voices. Then I went back to bed because it's not nice to interrupt people."

Laura breathed a sigh of relief so deep it felt as if her lungs had collapsed. "Did you recognize the man?"

Frowning, Caitlin shook her head. She stretched her arms in the air and yawned. "I'm still tired, Mommy. I want to go home and sleep in my own bed."

She flopped back on the rumpled quilt like a limp noodle.

"We will, sweet pea. In a few minutes. You stay right here while I check for anything you might've left in the other rooms." Halfway out the door, Laura turned. "Stay where you are. Don't move. Okay?"

"Okay."

In the hallway, Laura stopped. Took a deep breath. If she called 911, then it would be on the news and everyone would know Caitlin was there.

Eddie's killer would know.

She had to get Caitlin out before anyone saw her. But what about Eddie? She couldn't just leave, could she? As she thought it, she realized nothing could help Eddie now.

Propelled by fear for her daughter, Laura tore through the small house, snatching up everything belonging to Caitlin. A red tennis shoe from the bathroom, socks, her small toothbrush…anything that would indicate a child had been there. Seeing nothing else, she went back to the bedroom. Caitlin was curled up on the bed, rubbing her sleepy eyes.

"Hey, kiddo. We're ready."

"I wanna say bye to Daddy, too."

Laura's mouth went dry. "Uh…you know…it's not even six o'clock yet, and Daddy's really sick. I think we should just let him sleep."

Without waiting for a response, Laura scooped Caitlin into her arms and ran like hell.

CHAPTER ONE

Three years later

"IT WAS A SLOPPY investigation, that's why." Detective Jordan St. James leaned forward, palms on the captain's desk. He had his reasons for wanting to reinvestigate the Kolnikov case, but he couldn't tell his boss what they were.

Captain Jeff Carlyle stood behind the oversize desk, arms crossed. A tall black man with silver hair, Carlyle was well liked by all the detectives in the Robbery Homicide Division of the LAPD.

"That case went cold four years ago. Unless you have new evidence, we have other priorities."

Yeah. He knew the drill. The murder of a prostitute wasn't important unless it could be connected to a high-profile name, politics or money. While Kolnikov's case had the potential for all that, they hadn't been able to get evidence to prove any of it.

"Frank DeMatta is still a priority, isn't he? Kolnikov worked for him for more than thirty years…and was his mistress for practically as long."

"We worked every angle on Kolnikov. If there was something to use, we would've done it. What's the deal, St. James? Why're you so interested in this case?"

LINDA STYLE   13

Jordan clenched his hands into fists. "Kolnikov also knew Eddie Gianni."

For years the LAPD had been champing at the bit to finally take down mobster Frank DeMatta, and his nephew Eddie Gianni would have been the star witness against him. Gianni's murder three years ago had been a devastating blow to the department. Without the nephew's testimony, they had no case. "My gut feeling is there's something in Kolnikov's case that will get us DeMatta. I just have to find it."

It wasn't a good answer, but it was all he had.

As he watched the captain thumb through the file, Jordan's muscles tensed. The unspoken philosophy that one person's life might be more important than another grated on his conscience. Sadly, it was a fact of life in the department. There were only so many hours in the day and some cases had priority. Anna Kolnikov was a prostitute; no one cared that she'd been murdered. She was a discard.

He hated what the woman was. He wanted to forget her, but something kept drawing him back to the file, reading and rereading, compelled to know more. He had to solve this woman's murder. If he didn't, he wasn't sure he could live with himself.

Regardless of his personal feelings about Anna Kolnikov, she deserved justice. If he had to use De-Matta's name to do it, so be it.

Carlyle eyed him narrowly. "You know it'll reach DeMatta before you leave the building." His gaze shifted to the open-space squad room, desks butted one against another in domino patterns, each cluster defined by that group's investigation priority.

"I know." They'd long suspected a mole in the department was feeding DeMatta information. Jordan smiled. "So maybe that's a good thing. We might draw someone out. Make people nervous."

The captain rubbed his chin. "Okay. You've got a few weeks to show me something. But only because I want DeMatta. Don't forget it."

Still smiling, Jordan retrieved the file and strode from the office. The captain's sanction meant a lot. He didn't like working on his own, but in this case, he would have if he'd had to.

"Yo, *paesan.*" Rico Santini's voice carried through the room, his New Jersey accent still strong even though he'd been living in L.A. for more than ten years. "What's the verdict?"

"I'm good to go." He gave his partner a thumbs-up and then sat in the gray chair that matched his gray metal desk.

"You really got a thing about this case."

"You never had a thing? I know a couple of cases you bulldogged, so give me a break."

Rico raised a hand. "You got me there, pal."

"It could be a way to get DeMatta."

"Then I'm sorry I won't be around to help."

Every cop on the LAPD wanted to nail the mobster. It had been twelve years since two of their own were gunned down by DeMatta's goons, but no one had forgotten. Sooner or later they'd even the score.

"Hey, you coming to Bernie's tonight?" Rico glanced at Jordan.

Jordan's three best buddies in the unit had a standing meet at Bernie's Sports Bar and Grill to catch a game or just hang out. Jordan's partner, Rico, hadn't been doing much hanging out since he'd married, but he still managed to show up for the most important games.

"Tonight might be the last time I'll be there for a while," Rico added. "Starting tomorrow I'm off on that belated honeymoon, besides getting the adoption thing going."

Jordan nodded. "Okay. I'm there. And by the way, I think what you're doing with the adoption is great. Billy's a great kid."

His partner and his wife, Macy, had decided to adopt an abandoned boy she'd been working with as his court-appointed attorney. Jordan knew the blessings and the pitfalls of adoption. His relationship with his own adoptive parents was both wonderful and full of turmoil. Especially when he'd told them he wanted to locate his biological parents. All hell had broken loose and they'd never talked about it again.

Eyes gleaming, Rico smiled. His marriage and the impending adoption had him smiling a lot these days.

"Okay. Later, then." Watching Rico go, Jordan felt enormous happiness for his partner and—oddly—a sense of loss. They'd been best friends for more than ten years. Now Rico's wife was his partner's best friend.

He pushed his personal thoughts aside, pulled out Gianni's file and started from the beginning. While in college, DeMatta's nephew had collected money for his uncle's business interests. It was well-known DeMatta had his fingers in every illegal activity in L.A. Gambling, prostitution, drugs, the protection racket. But there were so many levels to the mobster's network and, because his goons took care of business for him, the department hadn't been able to prove DeMatta's involvement. Not without hard evidence or someone to testify against him. But it was only a matter of time. Jordan suspected DeMatta had collected money from Anna Kolnikov, the most well-known madam in L.A., but, again, he had no proof.

He flipped pages, reading quickly. Gianni had quit working for his uncle after college and had gone into real estate. Later they'd had a falling-out over the nephew's gambling debts. The department, hearing from one of their snitches that Gianni had become a liability for the mobster because he knew too much, had swooped down. The small-time hood had been easily persuaded to testify against DeMatta—but only if he was offered protection in return.

Some protection. Their star witness had been snuffed the night before he was to go into WITSEC, the federal marshal's protection program, and it wasn't too hard to guess who'd hired the hit man. Unable to find any hot evidence, and embarrassed by the screwup, the department quickly deep-sixed the case.

He read down another page. The name Laura Gianni caught his eye. The star witness's ex-wife. She'd been interviewed after the murder, but the line of questioning was thin. Strange. The woman had been married to Gianni for two years, they'd had a child together. She must've known something about her husband's past. About his uncle.

He wrote down the ex-wife's name, then switched his focus to the Kolnikov case. DeMatta had been a prime suspect during the investigation, but he'd alibied out. With no other leads, the case had gone cold.

Yet, every fiber in Jordan's being screamed that the mob boss was involved in the woman's death—hers and every other execution-style slaying in L.A., including two LAPD undercover detectives who'd been working on a major drug sting.

Oh, he had a thing about this case, all right. He wanted to nail Kolnikov's killer, and if it turned out to be DeMatta—all the better.

MUSIC BLARED FROM tricked-out cars cruising the dimly lit street. Hookers lined the curb, ogling the slow-moving vehicles as they went by. Parked at the corner, Laura got out of the van and handed her card to a teenager hiding behind several layers of makeup and fake eyelashes. Opium-sweet perfume formed a barrier around the girl, who couldn't be more than fourteen.

"We're open twenty-four/seven" was all Laura got out before the teen sashayed toward a car that had pulled over. Counseling wasn't an option in the middle of the night with depraved men circling in their cars like vultures.

If she could get only one child to call—and they were just children—she'd feel her message hadn't been lost. *You're not alone. You don't have to live this way. We care about you.*

She nodded at her co-worker, Phoebe Patterson, in the passenger seat, as she climbed back in the van. Driving on, she turned onto Hollywood Boulevard, where four teens dressed in halter tops and microminis, showing more skin than they covered, huddled on a corner under the yellow streetlights, where they could be seen by any john passing by.

"It's time to go home." Phoebe squinted at Laura through her retro wire-rimmed glasses. "We're not getting any takers tonight."

"Just one more try here, then I'll give it up."

As they headed toward the corner, a red Corvette coasted up next to the group and stopped. A tall man in a dark suit pulled himself from the driver's seat.

"Have you seen that guy before?" Phoebe asked.

"No. But I think we should hover and maybe scare him away."

"I've seen him somewhere. He's too good-looking to have to buy it on the streets."

"Maybe he's a cop."

"Driving a Corvette. No way! I dated a cop once. He had all he could do to scrape together enough money for a movie."

Laura chuckled. "Maybe your cop was sharing the wealth."

"Yeah." Phoebe slouched against the seat. "What is it with guys who can't make a freaking commitment?"

"I'm the last person to ask." Laura made a U-turn, then drove by the red car again, both women making a point to stare at the man as they went by.

"Maybe it's time you got out a little. Have some fun for a change." Phoebe's eyes glinted with mischief.

"I have fun." Laura raised her chin.

"Not the kind I'm talking about."

Phoebe teased Laura unmercifully about her self-imposed celibacy. She had to admit, she'd also been thinking a lot about her physical and emotional needs lately. For a long time after the divorce, all she'd thought about was protecting Caitlin. Overprotecting. The only fun she ever had was with Caitlin and the girls at the shelter. Until recently, it had been enough.

"You gotta get it on with someone sometime, girl-friend. It doesn't have to be permanent."

Laura expelled an exasperated breath. "Well, I'm willing, but I haven't met anyone I want to get it on with. Besides, what kind of role model would I be if I slept around?"

"A date once in a while isn't taboo. Everyone's gotta have a life."

"I've got a life. A very good one."

"Yeah, especially when you're working all the time. You can't meet anyone that way."

"I haven't been living in a bubble. I meet people all the time. Just…not the right ones."

"That's just it. Every date doesn't have to be the *right one*. You come out with me some night. I'll introduce you to one of Adam's friends. You'll have fun. I know you will."

Before Laura had the chance to say no, Phoebe perched on the edge of her seat and pointed toward the corner. "Okay, he's leaving. And he's alone." Her voice rose with excitement. "I think we scared him off."

"Good." Laura's stomach churned as she watched the man drive away.

"Man, he's hot," Phoebe gushed. The words seemed strange coming from someone who looked like the proverbial farmer's daughter, right down to the freckles and brown wavy hair she drew back into a ponytail.

"Guys that good-looking are usually stuck on themselves. Or they have other major problems. But then you probably know that already." Phoebe's weakness for handsome men was her downfall.

"Okay, I admit I've made some bad choices, but I've learned a few things, too. And I still don't believe all the Brad Pitts in the world are narcissistic rats."

Laura hoped for Phoebe's sake she was right. After several heartbreaking relationships, Phoebe was still searching for the perfect man. And Adam wasn't him.

"Maybe not. But this guy's a sleazebag who preys on young girls."

"I don't think so. He's here for something else, I can tell."

Laura wasn't so sure. Lots of rich men in fancy cars

haunted the streets of L.A. looking for a quick trick. Some pretty famous people were known regulars. She continued driving to the corner, then stopped and rolled down the window to talk to the girls.

Ten minutes later, they were headed home in an empty van. Some nights they'd get one or two teens to come back to the crisis shelter, but tonight was a bust. Maybe they'd have better luck tomorrow night. Or maybe one of the half-dozen or so girls they'd given cards with the shelter's phone number would call the next day...or sometime. It was all she could hope for.

"Rose will be ready to go home, you know."

"I know." With three children at home, Rose Blackthorne didn't work any longer than she had to. Laura had two full-time counselors besides herself at Victory House. Three nights a week, two of them would alternate the street watch from 10:00 p.m. to 12:00 a.m. searching for children to help. In particular, Hollywood Boulevard, Sunset Boulevard—the strip—Van Nuys, Santa Monica and Long Beach, anywhere they'd find *children of the night*—runaways selling their bodies on the streets.

They brought along sandwiches and milk, fruit and bottled water, because most of the kids they met were homeless. The few minutes they spent with each child was intended to give hope and let them know they had a place to go if needed.

She gave thanks every day that her daughter was safe and secure and, God willing, would never experience what these teens went through—what she'd gone through.

Laura parked in the driveway at the shelter, and they got out and walked inside the old two-story home. Phoebe went directly upstairs to bed, leaving Laura to talk to Rose, who stood at the door holding her backpack. "Anything happen while we were gone?" Laura asked.

"That strung-out kid was here looking for Brandy."

"Any problem?"

Rose shook her head. "Not at all. Oh, and a detective was here looking for you." Rose dragged a hand through her long, black hair, a mark of her Navajo heritage.

"What time?"

"Right after you left. He didn't say what it was about, but it was probably the usual. Tracking down a missing kid."

Though the police were invited to call first, most of the time they didn't bother with the formality because it was easier to keep a kid from running again if no one knew they were coming.

"He said he'd come back tomorrow."

Laura nodded. "Okay. Now, get out of here and get some sleep."

"Uh, one other thing. I think Alysa is ready to make contact with her parents."

That made Laura smile. She liked nothing better than reconciling a runaway with her family. If she hadn't had help when she was sixteen, who knows how she'd have ended up. "Great. We'll talk tomorrow."

Laura said goodbye, locked the door and, still smiling about Alysa, traipsed down the hall to her bedroom on the first floor across from Caitlin's.

Reconciliation was the shelter's main goal—if possible. But many times it wasn't because abuse at home was the reason the teens had run in the first place. In those cases the shelter housed some girls and helped others with foster care, education, part-time jobs and gaining enough self-esteem to make it on their own. Feeling worthless was one of the biggest problems with the teens they took in.

She peeked in on Caitlin, who slept soundly, all covered up like a mummy. Cait's little-girl scent permeated the air in the tiny room…orange blossoms and bubble gum, Cait's favorite bubble bath and lotion. Cait's room wasn't a bedroom at all but an oversize pantry that Cait had insisted could be her room when she'd decided she was too big to sleep with her mother anymore. The room had one small window and was barely big enough for a twin bed and dresser, but Cait loved it. Laura felt her heart warm as she looked at her. So sweet. So innocent.

The child had no recollection of what had happened three years ago. Laura had explained that her daddy had been really sick, his death the result of an illness. It was a lie, but that was better than telling the child her father had been murdered. And whenever Cait had asked about him, Laura painted a happy picture.

Though Caitlin had quit asking about her daddy more than two years ago, Laura knew someday she'd have to tell her the truth. Someday when the child was old enough to understand.

Undressing as she went into the bathroom, Laura tossed her jeans and hoodie into the hamper, did her ablutions and then went to her own room and crawled between fresh clean sheets worn smooth by age and use. She felt an enormous sense of satisfaction. Most nights were the same; she fell into bed exhausted, but the knowledge she was helping a few kids make positive changes in their lives made it all worthwhile. She wished she could do more.

The Anaheim shelter was holding its own. She'd received more grant money to keep the place going for the next year, and they'd reunited three teens with their families in the past six months. To some critics, the numbers didn't seem like much, but they didn't know how difficult the process was. Sometimes it took months of counseling to make it happen.

She pulled up the handmade quilt and snuggled underneath. Life was good. Her daughter was safe and secure, and she intended to keep it that way.

She was just drifting off when the sharp ring of the phone pulled her back. She opened an eye and glanced at the red neon numbers on the digital clock. It read 1:00 a.m. Who would call at this time of the night? They had a twenty-four/seven crisis hotline for emergencies. She reached across the pillow and dragged the phone to her ear. "Hello?"

No answer.

"Hello, is someone there?"

Heavy breathing was all she heard. Maybe it was some kid who'd gotten her phone number and was too scared to talk? Only she never gave out her personal number. Laura pushed up on one elbow. "If you don't say something, I'm going to hang up."

Whoever it was didn't wait for her. She heard a click and then the dial tone droned in her ear.

"MOM, WHO'S THE MAN outside?"

Laura went to the door and peeked out one of the long narrow windows framing it. "I don't see anyone, sweetie."

Caitlin sidled up next to her and pressed her nose to the window. "He's gone now."

"What did he look like?" Sometimes parents came

looking for a child but were afraid to approach the house. Sometimes the police came. Sometimes an old boyfriend—or a pimp who wanted his cash cow back.

"He was big and he had on a black coat."

Laura glanced again. "Well, you're right. There's no one there. Now, c'mon. We need to skedaddle or you'll be late for school."

Mornings had been a lot easier when she'd home-schooled Caitlin the past two years. But it had been obvious for some time her daughter needed to be with other children her age. For all of her seven years, Cait's social contact had been with the teenage girls at the shelter. And it showed in her behavior.

"I'm ready already." She swung a strap of her purple backpack over one shoulder and then wiggled into the other one.

"Okay. But you have to eat first." Good grief, Cait had never been so forgetful as she had the past few days. Was something bothering her? Something with school, maybe? She made a mental note to talk with the teacher.

They went into the big country kitchen together, and once again, Laura was reminded of how perfect the old house was for the shelter. Five bedrooms, one down and four up, not counting Cait's, a living room that connected with a bright sunroom, a separate dining room next to the big kitchen and two baths. Two bathrooms were a necessity when you housed a half-dozen girls or more at one time. But sometimes, even two weren't enough.

She motioned for Caitlin to sit at the round oak table while she got the orange juice from the refrigerator, another relic from the past, but she'd been happy someone had donated the old appliance to the shelter.

She stuck a bowl of instant oatmeal in the microwave and waited.

"Here you are." Laura set the juice and oatmeal in front of her daughter, made them both some cocoa and sat.

"I've been thinking," Caitlin said, suddenly all serious. "I want to walk home with Shannon today."

Laura almost gasped but caught herself. Biding time, she sipped her drink. She really didn't need to drive Caitlin to school and back since it was only a few blocks away, but she still grappled with a tiny remnant of the fear she'd felt after…the murder. She got clammy just thinking about it. Which was silly. It had been three years.

The police had questioned Laura and accepted her explanation that Cait hadn't been at her father's in weeks.

"Please, Mom. All the other kids think I'm a baby because I can't walk home with them. It's *so* embarrassing."

Laura had to smile. "Embarrassing, huh?"

"Uh-huh." Caitlin slurped another mouthful of oatmeal. "Besides, Shannon's big sister walks with her and she's in sixth grade."

Laura sighed. She had to bite the bullet sometime. She couldn't hold her daughter's hand for the rest of her life. She wanted Caitlin to be with kids her own age. It was the reason she'd enrolled her in public school in the first place. And in the six months she'd been attending, nothing, absolutely nothing, had happened to make her doubt Cait's safety. "Okay. But you can't dawdle."

"Awright!" Caitlin made a face. "What's *dawdle?*"

"*Dawdling* is being slow. Getting sidetracked. You

have to come right home or I'll be worried. You can't stop at anyone's house and you can't—"

"Mo-om! I'm almost eight. I know my way home. Shannon walks home all the time."

Girding her resolve, Laura reached to straighten Cait's curly ponytail. "Just remember to come directly home. If you don't I'll come after you and then you'll *really* be embarrassed."

As the smile on Caitlin's face grew from ear to ear, Laura smiled, too. Such a small concession to make her daughter happy was worth the worry.

Alysa came into the kitchen. "There's some detective guy here to talk to you." The statuesque fifteen-year-old, who looked years older, had been at the shelter for six months and was doing remarkably well.

Standing, Laura said to Cait, "Finish your breakfast, sweetie, I'll be back in a minute."

Laura passed Phoebe in the kitchen archway.

"You've got company."

"I know. Thanks," she said, unable to quell her annoyance as she headed for the living room. Mornings were the busiest part of the day at the shelter and this would put her off schedule.

A tall man in a dark suit stood next to the table in the foyer, his back to her. Looking at him, she felt a sense of déjà vu. The straight broad shoulders. The purposeful stance. "Can I help you?"

He turned. "I hope so," he said, smiling, then held out a badge. "I'm Detective Jordan St. James, Ms. Gianni. I'd like to talk with you for a few minutes."

It was the man in the red car last night. Phoebe was right. He *was* good-looking. Almost too good-looking. His navy suit, light blue shirt and burgundy tie were impeccable, his brown sun-streaked hair perfectly styled. He could've been a cover model for *GQ* magazine.

Before she had a chance to answer, Caitlin skipped into the room. "I'm ready to go now." Then she saw the detective. "Hi, I'm Cait."

He reached down and shook Caitlin's hand. "Pleased to meet you, Cait. I'm Jordan."

"I get to walk home from school by myself today," Caitlin told him, her brown eyes sparkling.

Laura put an arm around her daughter and pulled her closer.

"I'm sorry, Detective. I don't have time to talk right now."

Phoebe came from the kitchen with Alysa and two of the other girls. "I can drive," Phoebe offered, her gaze traveling from the detective's head to his toes. "I've got to stop at the store, anyway."

While Cait wiggled away, Alysa held up a piece of paper.

"Can you sign this for me? It's an excuse for my last class. A doctor's appointment."

Laura glanced at the note, frowning, and lowered her voice so the detective couldn't hear. "A doctor's appointment? Do I know what this is about?"

"It's for that part-time job interview. It's only an hour before school gets out, and it's during my study hour."

"Just this once," Laura said, and quickly signed the paper. "Will you need a ride?"

"It's walking distance from school. The ice-cream parlor."

"And afterward?"

"I'll beg a ride from a friend."

That raised a warning flag for Laura. But one of

the first things she'd learned working with teens was that trust was critical. She gave Alysa a hug. "Break a leg, kiddo."

"Okay, gang. Let's get this show on the road," Phoebe announced in tour-director mode, and the group headed for the back door where the van was parked.

Laura bit her bottom lip. "You come right home, Caitlin. No detours along the way."

JORDAN WATCHED THE WOMEN leave, while two more who'd just come downstairs went into the kitchen.

"Let's talk in here." Ms. Gianni motioned toward a small sunroom off the living room. "Please have a seat."

The house smelled nice, as if someone had just baked a batch of cookies or cinnamon rolls. Sheer white curtains made the room seem full of light even though it was still overcast outside. A small white wicker love seat and two chairs with flowered cushions took up most of the room. Plants and books filled the rest of the space. He sat in one of the chairs while she took the other, a small round table between them.

He knew from her ex-husband's case file that she was the director of the shelter and also a counselor. She had a seven-year-old daughter and the only vehicle registered in her name was a ten-year-old Chevy van. Very limited information, but until he had a reason, there was no need to do a background check on her.

"This is the reading room," she said, apparently seeing him take in the surroundings. "You wanted to ask me some questions."

He nodded. "Yes, I—"

"And you know I'm bound by confidentiality in certain areas."

He nodded again. "Yes, I know. But this isn't about one of your residents. It's about a four-year-old murder case."

The woman's gaze narrowed. She had hazel eyes, but they looked green next to the tangle of long auburn curls. He could see the resemblance between mother and daughter.

"I don't understand." A frown creased her brow, underscored her words.

"An acquaintance of your late husband."

Her shoulders stiffened ever so slightly. She ran her tongue across her bottom lip.

"My ex-husband died three years ago and we were divorced at the time. I don't know any of his *acquaintances.*"

Tight. She was really tight. He had to handle this with the proverbial kid gloves if he wanted her cooperation. "Frank DeMatta. Do you know him?"

She blinked and was silent so long he wondered if she was even going to answer. Running a hand through her hair, she pushed it back, then gave a half nod.

"Your ex-husband's uncle."

"Right. And no, I didn't know the man personally. I only met him twice, once at the wedding and then at the funeral."

"Did your husband talk about him?"

She shifted in her chair. Touched her hair again.

"He told me he worked for Mr. DeMatta to put himself through school. After college, when we started dating, Eddie was in real estate."

When she didn't say any more, he asked, "Anything else?"

"If this is about what Eddie was going to say at the trial, I've already told the police everything I know."

"It's not. It's about the murder of a woman named Anna Kolnikov."

Her eyes went wide as dinner plates. Her back rigid. He'd hit a nerve. "Ms. Kolnikov was Frank De-Matta's...close friend for many years. Did either you or your husband know her?"

He thought he saw recognition in her eyes...maybe. Except she looked away too fast for him to know.

"I'd met her, but I don't know anything about her relationship with Mr. DeMatta."

"I understand your ex-husband was a gambler."

She nodded. "Part of the reason for the divorce."

"And the other reasons?"

She looked surprised, then angry. She pushed to her feet. "I'm sorry, Detective. I don't see how my divorce has anything to do with the murder you're investigating."

He stood, raised his hands in a surrender pose, hoping to put her at ease. "No, *I'm* sorry. My intent isn't to pry into your personal life. I'm trying to get a handle on your ex-husband's relationship with Kolnikov."

"There was no relationship. At least not when we were married."

Her tone was firm, her words resolute—but not altogether convincing.

"The police told me after Eddie's death that he was to be a witness against his uncle, but I don't know anything more. I don't know anything about his testimony. I didn't back then, and I still don't." She crossed her arms, eyes flashing. "But I do know the police were supposed to protect Eddie and they didn't."

That was true. Few had been privy to the information the police had used to get Eddie to cooperate and testify against his uncle, but the media made sure everyone knew the police botched the protection job. The punishment of the press for not revealing the facts of the case.

She gave a big sigh. "And, as I said, I don't know how any of that relates to the case you're investigating."

He smiled. She was forthright and wasn't going to let him get away with anything. He liked that. She was also pretty and he found himself staring at her unusual hazel-green eyes that seemed to change color with her mood. Which wasn't very friendly at the moment. "DeMatta had his fingers in a lot of pies."

"Do you think Mr. DeMatta was involved in Ann— the woman's murder? Or are you suggesting my ex-husband was involved?"

"I'm collecting information, Ms. Gianni. Trying to connect the dots. The best way to find out who murdered this woman is to find out everything I can about her. And the best way to do it is by talking to the people who knew her."

Her face paled.

"You said you met Ms. Kolnikov. What did you think of her?"

"She seemed...nice. Kind."

Just then the two girls who'd gone into the kitchen came out, harsh words flying. "I did not," the blonder of the two girls screeched.

"Yes, you did. I saw you. You're a liar!"

Gianni practically flew from the room to where the girls stood and shoved herself between them. She spoke softly so he couldn't hear, but he could tell by the teens' reactions whatever she'd said meant something. One girl's shoulders slumped. The other shifted from one foot to the other, eyes down. Ms. Gianni stood her ground, said something else, and then came over to where Jordan now stood in the archway.

"I'm sorry, Detective. I can't talk to you anymore. I have a job to do."

He smiled. "A very tough job."

She looked surprised. "It is what it is. I'm sure your job is more difficult and certainly more dangerous. I'd like to help you, but I can't. I'm sorry."

Yeah. And she couldn't wait to get him out of there. Jordan handed her his card. "If you remember anything, please call me."

She took the card, then hurried to show him out.

At the door, he turned. "Anything, no matter how insignificant. This woman's murderer is still walking the streets. I'd like to make sure he doesn't kill again."

CHAPTER TWO

LAURA WATCHED THE DETECTIVE leave, shut the door and slumped against it. Three years ago, she'd answered questions about Eddie and his uncle. She'd thought that had ended it.

But this wasn't about Eddie, it was about Anna. The woman who'd helped her during the worst part of her life, helped her get off the streets. She'd spent years trying to forget her past, and for Caitlin's sake, she wouldn't open that door again.

Besides, anything she knew about Anna was from years ago and would be no help in finding her killer. She shouldn't feel guilty about it.

The detective had caught her completely off guard when he'd starting asking questions about Frank DeMatta. A man she knew more about than she should. Eddie had known too much and he was dead. Just thinking about it made her shudder in fear.

Fear for her daughter.

She couldn't get involved and that was that.

Dakota crossed the room. "I'm sorry. I forgot there was someone here."

"I'm sorry, too," Brandy said.

Laura pushed away from the door and attempted a smile. "It's okay. I didn't want to talk to him, anyway." The teens laughed and Laura motioned for them to head for the dining room. "We've got some heavy studying to do." Laura pulled out the workbooks and tossed them on the battered walnut table. "The GED test is only a week away."

Neither girl had any desire to finish high school if it meant going to classes. A GED was the next best thing, and Laura intended to see they were prepared for the test. Both were smart but had been out of school for too long. A year for Dakota and two years for Brandy. Living on the streets had taken its toll physically and mentally.

They spent the next three hours studying and after lunch went grocery shopping. Most of the girls had few skills when it came to making a life for themselves. Learning to prepare a menu, cook, buy groceries, pay bills and do the laundry were as much a part of the shelter's program as counseling.

Back home, as the girls put away the groceries, Laura was reminded of how far the shelter had come.

Everything had worked out perfectly. But if Detective St. James kept asking questions…

She felt a tightness in her chest and took a couple of deep breaths to ward off an attack. Too late. Her hands got clammy, her heartbeat pulsed erratically. Damn. She thought she'd conquered the panic attacks, but apparently not.

"I'll be right back," she said. Holding on to the wall, she crossed to the bathroom down the hall from the kitchen, bent over the old sink, stained with makeup from the girls, and splashed water on her face. Her pulse calming, she stared at herself in the mirror.

Had she done the right thing three years ago? God knew it wasn't the first time she'd asked herself the question. She'd done what she thought best for her daughter.

Then, in one brief moment at Eddie's funeral, her need to protect her child became a desperate quest. She remembered it as vividly as if it were yesterday. Standing in the drizzling rain with Caitlin and Eddie's mother at the grave site, breathing in the scent of damp leaves. The rhythmic thud of heavy wet earth against the top of the casket decried the end of Eddie's life, and Laura's heart was filled with sadness. Sadness and regret. Caitlin tugging on Laura's shirtsleeve. *"It's him, Mommy. That's the man who came to see Daddy."*

She'd snatched her daughter's hand with the speed of light and held it in a vise grip to keep her from pointing. The man her daughter had been looking at was Frank DeMatta.

Shaking, Laura averted her gaze and ignored the man's nod of acknowledgment. But on the way to the car, he'd stopped them, reached into his pocket and handed her a package wrapped in brown paper. "It's money. For you and the child," he said. Then he added in a whisper only she could hear, "I take care of my own. Remember that."

He couldn't possibly know. Could he? And just because he'd been at the house didn't mean *he* was Eddie's murderer.

And if she believed that, she was living in a third dimension. She'd been on the streets long enough to know all about Frank DeMatta—and how he took care of people who crossed him.

Eddie had crossed him.

On the way home, she'd told Caitlin she was mistaken, explaining the man at the funeral had been out of the country for a long time. Cait had accepted the explanation and said maybe she'd dreamed it. And in the three years since, Cait had never brought it up again.

During the investigation of Eddie's murder, Laura had lived in a perpetual state of anxiety, worrying that somehow someone would find out Caitlin had been at her father's that night. And then Eddie's murderer would know. When the police closed the case, she'd nearly collapsed in relief.

Did she feel guilty that Eddie's murder would go unsolved? Absolutely. But her daughter's safety superceded everything. DeMatta said the package he'd given her contained money. The only money DeMatta had was blood money—money she would never use and couldn't give back.

They hadn't seen DeMatta again, and after a couple years, she'd been lulled into feeling safe.

But Detective St. James's questions made her realize everything could change in an instant.

"Okay, we're done!"

She heard Brandy's voice like a faint echo in her head. She composed herself, went back into the kitchen and plastered on a smile. "Thanks, girls. Dinner at six." Which meant the teens had the rest of the afternoon to themselves.

The front door slammed. "Second shift is here," Rose announced.

The three women alternated schedules every other month, so no one had to take the worst hours all the time. The changing schedule gave Laura more evenings to spend with Caitlin.

Caitlin. Laura glanced at her watch. Cait wasn't home yet and she should be. Hurrying through the living room, she checked her watch again, all senses on alert. Why had she ever agreed to let her walk home alone?

"I saw Cait down the block," Rose said, stopping Laura before she reached the door.

She heaved a silent sigh of relief.

"Hey, everyone. My mother sent brownies." Rose raised a cake pan for all to see, then turned to Laura. "Something change around here?"

It was no secret Laura was overprotective. "Nothing earth-shattering. Cait wanted to walk home with the other kids."

A knowing smile crossed Rose Blackthorne's face as she tugged off her tan leather jacket, then hung it on the coat tree by the front door. "Right."

Laura wasn't fooling anyone with her casual response. Rose knew exactly how big a deal it was for Laura.

Rose was also a mother. And one of the most beautiful women Laura had ever met. Her smooth bronzed skin and well-toned body gave no indication she was over forty and had three children.

Laura, Phoebe and Rose had worked together for three years now, and both their business relationship and their friendships were unshakable. Each evening Rose went home to her children and her mother, who stayed with her, while Phoebe stayed at the shelter a few nights a week, along with Laura. Laura wished she had another home to go to sometimes, like Phoebe, a place for just her and Caitlin. But there was no money to hire someone to stay full-time. No money to buy another place, either.

"The cop come back today?"

"He did. He was asking questions, but not about anyone here."

"Good. I hate when the police get involved." Rose headed for the kitchen, and on her way she said to no one in particular, "Keep your mitts off the brownies till after dinner."

Laura hurried to the front door to see if she could spot Caitlin through the window. If she went outside to look and Cait saw her, the poor kid would be embarrassed all over again.

She saw the two girls walking slowly toward the house, chatting and laughing, and Laura realized how much Caitlin needed the independence. As much as she hated letting go, she had to if her daughter was to live a normal life.

Laura wanted that more than anything.

"I'M NOT SURE MS. GIANNI was telling me everything," Jordan said to Luke across the table at Bailey's Sports Bar and Grill. Along with Rico Santini, Luke Coltrane and Will Houston were the best detectives in the RHD. They also happened to be his best friends. Rico, who'd convinced Jordan to come to the bar, hadn't made it after all, and Will, aka Tex, had been there earlier with Simon McIntyre, one of the newer detectives in the unit, but both had left on a call out.

"You think she's lying?"

As reruns of the best plays in last month's Super Bowl game showed on the big screen, Jordan picked up the pitcher of beer and half filled his own glass. Luke was drinking soda. The announcer's voice rose above the din of clinking glasses and the raised voices of the regulars—mostly cops—going head-to-head on the plays. "No. Not lying. Withholding. Not telling me what she knows."

"And her motive for that would be?" Luke leaned back on two legs of his chair, eyes riveted on the television.

"She seemed edgy when I asked about DeMatta."

"That slime would make anyone nervous. We all know what happens to people who get on his list."

"But why would *she* worry?"

Luke looked at Jordan. "No reason—unless she has something to hide."

Luke was familiar with the Eddie Gianni case—they all were. Luke had even worked on the case for a brief period after the botched protection job had caused several officers to be demoted.

"My thought, too. She said she'd met Kolnikov."

"Anything good?"

"No. We got interrupted and I left. I should've stayed, been persistent," Jordan said, more to himself than to Luke. His buddy's attention was back on the screen.

He should've asked Laura more questions. She'd said Kolnikov seemed nice. That she was kind. Obviously Gianni didn't know the whole story there. But he did. He tightened his grip on his glass and tried to focus on the television.

Except his mind wouldn't cooperate. The Gianni woman knew more than she was saying. He saw it in her body language, the way she avoided looking him in the eyes. He didn't know what she was withholding, but his instincts were usually on target.

For about the hundredth time, he asked himself the same question Rico had asked earlier—why was he was so interested in this case? Anyone who housed young girls and prostituted them for money was scum. A woman who'd slept with DeMatta and worked for him for thirty years had to be as amoral as DeMatta himself. Why bother?

The answer was always the same.

Because he had to.

Because it was personal.

What he knew so far was documented in three different case files. Kolnikov's, Eddie Gianni's and that of Delores Matthews, one of DeMatta's girlfriends who'd done a disappearing act. Speculation had it she was either dead or hiding out so she didn't get dead. Among the three cases he knew a few things for sure. The LAPD suspected Kolnikov housed the women DeMatta's pimps recruited. They suspected DeMatta was involved in her death, but couldn't prove either. Jordan knew Matthews had worked for Kolnikov. He knew Kolnikov's clientele were high rollers, and both women had been arrested more than once. He also knew Kolnikov had influential friends.

Combine that with the best attorneys available and you had a walk every time.

The one common thread in the cases was Frank DeMatta. And the focus of all three of the investigations hadn't been so much on solving the crimes as it was pinning something on the mobster. With good reason. If they took DeMatta down, half the illegal businesses in L.A. would crumble.

Luke suddenly launched to his feet, his arms pumping. "Hoo-yeah!" His hoots joined with a cacophony of other shouts. Then, as if just noticing him, Luke clapped Jordan on the shoulder. "Hey, man, what's with you?"

"Yeah, great play," Jordan answered.

"You still thinking about the case?" Luke grinned. "Or the woman?"

Jordan wasn't in the mood for their usual banter.

"She's a stunning woman," Luke said, his tone implying he didn't know how Jordan could resist.

Stunning, yes. Great hair and fascinating eyes. Those facts hadn't escaped him. She was tall and had more curves than the skinny model types he usually dated. She was also too classy to be married to a punk like Gianni. "Lots of pretty women in the world. Besides, she's off-limits. You know how that works."

"I know, but life doesn't always work the way it's supposed to. I might've tried for a date myself if I hadn't been going through divorce hell."

"So, what's keeping you from it now?" Jordan needled.

Luke turned away. "I've got other interests."

Jordan doubted it. He knew Luke hadn't been involved with anyone in ages because he was still in love with his ex-wife. They'd lost a child and the stress had been so overwhelming, the marriage crumbled under the pressure. Luke had spent the next two years in a deep depression.

His friend's divorce only confirmed Jordan's beliefs about the hopelessness of marriage. If a love like Luke and Julianna's couldn't hold a marriage together, nothing could.

The only thing that had kept his parents together for forty years was money. And seeing what marriage could do to two people, why bother? Particularly when he was such a lousy judge when it came to weeding out the women who were only interested in his money. He wasn't going to get burned again.

"So what now?" Luke asked. "You got another lead?"

With the game over, they headed out the door together and walked to the side of the building where their cars were parked.

"I need information from Laura Gianni and I'm going to get it."

"For what it's worth," Luke said as he reached for his car door, "she's a tough lady. I don't think you'll get anything from her."

Jordan smiled. "I've got a hundred-dollar bill on it."

Luke stuck out his hand. "You're on, bud."

They shook on it and Jordan waved Luke off before he headed for his own ride. Clicking the remote, he opened the door, slid inside and started the engine.

Thirty minutes later he'd retrieved his SUV and was turning the corner toward his town house in Brentwood, a gift to himself after he graduated Wharton Business School. The property was a good investment, even if his parents didn't think so. No big surprise. They seldom approved of his choices.

They'd expected him to invest the trust money he'd received from his grandfather in their multifaceted family conglomerate, Avecor, as his younger brother, Harry, had. But it hadn't worked out as they wanted. His decision to join the police force after earning his MBA had been another bone of contention between Jordan and his parents.

But after thirty-five years, he didn't give a damn anymore if anyone approved of what he did. He was tired of trying to be the best, trying to prove he was good enough and that he really did belong. Though he loved his parents dearly—he had to live with himself.

He pulled into the garage next to the Jag he rarely used, walked inside and went through the ritual: keys on the granite countertop, jacket on the back of a chair, over to the fridge. He wasn't particularly hungry after the buffalo wings at the bar so he grabbed a beer instead.

In the so-called media room, the *L.A. Times* was still on the end table next to his favorite chair—a well-worn, black leather lounger that every woman who saw it hated. Aside from the chair, table and the plasma TV, the room was empty. His living room had only been recently decorated because his mother couldn't stand seeing it with no furniture.

Sitting, he turned on the news. Same old, same old. He shuffled through the paper and pulled out the crossword puzzle. It didn't hold his interest, either. He kept coming back to Laura Gianni's big green eyes and how they'd sparked with recognition when he'd mentioned Anna Kolnikov.

He picked up the phone on the table, pulled a note from his shirt pocket with Gianni's phone number on it and punched it in. He'd rather stop by, catch her unexpectedly. He worked better with people when they didn't have a chance to prepare a stock answer. But it had been impossible to talk to her with so many people around. She might even be more receptive if she could pick a time and place that worked for her.

"Hello."

He recognized her distinctive voice immediately. A sleepy voice. Sexy. "Laura Gianni?"

"Who's calling?"

"It's Detective St. James. I'd like to talk to you again."

"I don't know anything more than I told you already."

"I understand. I had some other thoughts about this case, other questions I need to ask."

"Well, I don't understand why. I run a shelter for runaways. I counsel them. I don't know anything other than what I've told you, and I have no time to be answering questions I've already answered."

He'd seen her dedication to her job, how fiercely protective she was of both her daughter and the girls who stayed at the shelter. He admired dedication. In his job he saw too many mothers who didn't give a rat about their kids. Mothers who abused their children or gave them away as if they were garbage. His own biological mother had done the same.

"We could meet somewhere other than the shelter if you'd like," he added. The silence on the other end went on so long, he thought she might've hung up. "It's important."

She finally said, "I'm sorry. I can't. I don't have the time. And I really must go now."

The next thing he knew he was listening to the dial tone. *What the—* He couldn't remember the last time someone had stonewalled him, and he felt stupid he'd allowed her to do it.

But then, her refusal said a lot. His questioning made her nervous. Scared her, maybe?

Well, whether she had time or not didn't matter. He was going to see her, anyway.

When and where would now be up to him.

And Luke was going to be out a hundred bucks real soon.

LAURA SET THE PHONE in the cradle, her hand trembling. Detective St. James unnerved her, so much so, she wasn't sure she'd made the right decision.

Within seconds, she felt as guilty as she had after talking with the detective earlier today. Anna had been a friend. But Laura's personal feelings weren't going to help him solve the murder.

Apparently he didn't believe she had nothing to tell. What other reason would he have for being so insistent? Maybe he wanted information about the shelter's former residents who had history with Anna so he could talk with them? Well, if that was the case, he was out of luck there, too.

If it had just been about Anna, she might've agreed to meet him. But at his mention of DeMatta, every instinct screamed for her to run the other way. If DeMatta even suspected she knew he'd been there the night of the murder…and he found out she was talking to the police—

She rolled over and tried to go back to sleep, but the detective's words played again in her head. *It's important.* She'd heard urgency in his voice. Emotion.

She'd worked with enough cops to know they had to keep a distance or the job would eat them up. Her job was similar in that respect, but she found it difficult to remain detached. When she got involved, she got involved. Maybe she and the detective were a little alike in that way.

Another thing…why was he investigating a case that had been closed for four years?

She sighed. She couldn't let him get to her. She couldn't. No matter how convincing he was. But her resolve didn't make her feel any better.

Detective St. James wasn't going to let it die. She knew it as well as she knew the twelve-step recovery program.

If she didn't stop him, life would never be the same.

CHAPTER THREE

LAURA TOOK CAIT'S HAND as they walked through the dry Bermuda grass toward the playground at Kenwood Park, a half mile from the shelter. The late afternoon sun shone through the ficus trees, casting dappled light on Caitlin's face. A flutter of wind rustled the nearby palm fronds and feathered through Laura's hair. It was peaceful. A feeling she wished she had more often.

"I could've come by myself," Caitlin grumbled.

Letting Cait walk home from school alone yesterday had been a big step. But there was no way she was ready to let her go to the park by herself.

"I know you could. But I like to come along. It's a chance for us to have some time alone."

"Yeah, but Jenny's going to be here. I want to play with her. Can you wait somewhere where she can't see you?"

Oh, boy. "Yes, but I'm going to be where I can see you. Over there." Laura pointed to a bench half hidden behind a gnarled tree not far away. "But you can't play until I put sunscreen on your face and arms."

"Mo-om. It's winter."

"Don't complain. The sun can be as treacherous in February as it is in the summer. This is the warmest part of the day, and with your fair skin, you'll be a crispy critter without protection."

Caitlin skipped ahead, and as Laura walked closer, she saw a man sitting on the other end of the bench where she'd intended to sit. His bearing was familiar. Suddenly the hair on the back of her neck prickled. What part of no didn't this guy understand?

He sat slouched sideways, his left arm resting on the back of the concrete-and-wood bench. Wearing a black sweater and tan slacks, he could've been one of the fathers watching his child at play.

Maybe he was. She shouldn't jump to conclusions. Maybe he did have a child he was watching.

As she and Caitlin came up behind him, he turned. His eyes lit with recognition and he scrambled to his feet. "Hi."

"Hello. What a surprise," she said facetiously.

"I remember you," Caitlin broke in. "You're Jordan. You came to our house yesterday."

He smiled. "You've got a good memory, Cait."

"I'm almost eight," she said. "I remember lots of things."

"Sweetie, I see Jenny over there. Why don't you go play with her on the swings for a while?"

Caitlin crossed her arms and planted her feet apart. "I know what's going on. You want to get rid of me so you guys can be alone."

Laura pulled back in surprise and she felt heat rapidly rising to her face. Caitlin shrugged and ran off toward the swings. Too embarrassed to call her back for the sunscreen, Laura decided they weren't going to be here for long, anyway.

"I don't know why she said such a thing. I think she's been picking up a lot from the girls at the shelter."

He smiled, one eyebrow arched.

Lately Caitlin had been asking all kinds of questions

about the birds and the bees and why Laura never went out on dates. Jenny's mother went out on dates all the time Caitlin had lamented more than once, and Jenny got presents from her mom's friends.

"What are you doing here?" Laura asked as they both sat. "Do you have a child over there? Or do you just like to hang out in parks watching children play?"

He leaned back, keeping his eyes on Caitlin. "No, I don't have any kids. I'm not married." He was smiling now. "And if I hung around parks watching children, I might get into a whole lot of trouble."

His penetrating gaze caught hers. Steel. His eyes, a light steel-gray, were framed by long sooty lashes.

"So…if it's not that, why are you here?" she asked, as if she didn't know. As if it didn't annoy the hell out of her. She didn't like being tracked down. She didn't like that he made her feel like a quivery teenager.

"I called the shelter and one of the girls said you were coming here. I decided it was a better place to talk, anyway. More private. I hope I didn't interrupt anything."

"Interrupt?"

"Well, if you're meeting someone else or something."

"No. You're not interrupting." But she wished he was. She didn't want to be alone with this man. Or did she? She couldn't seem to quit staring at him, his full lips and silvery eyes.

She pulled her gaze away and glanced across the playground to where Caitlin sat on a swing. God, she hoped he couldn't tell what she was thinking. But then he was probably used to women staring at him with their tongues hanging out.

"She's a cute kid."

"Thank you. I think she's pretty special." She smiled, her love for Caitlin hard to disguise.

"That's good," he said, his voice deepening. "I see too much of the dark side in my job. One of the drawbacks, I guess."

She nodded. "But there's always hope. Which is why I do what I do." She settled back, more comfortable with the conversation.

"I saw your van on the Boulevard the other night."

"We try to reach as many runaways as possible. Sometimes we're successful, sometimes not." She folded her hands on her lap. "I saw you there, too, only at the time, I didn't know you were a detective."

He let out a burst of laughter, leaning forward, elbows on his thighs. "You thought I was looking for some action."

"It seemed that way. The car…"

"Ah, the studmobile. Not mine," he said, gesturing in the direction of a charcoal-gray SUV parked on the street. "I'm more conservative. I use the department's impound vehicles when I'm on a job and don't want to look like the fuzz."

Despite herself, she laughed. "Kind of ironic. You're out there to arrest the same people I'm trying to save."

He lounged against the back of the bench again. "I wasn't arresting anyone that night. I was asking questions. But sometimes an arrest does help. I know more than one kid who's gone into treatment and went straight because he'd been arrested."

"But then he'd have a record. I try to catch them before that happens."

His brow furrowed. "Juvy records are expunged after eighteen, unless the child is tried as an adult."

"Their records are *supposed* to be expunged, but I

think we both know that's not always the case. Many times a kid's juvy record comes back to haunt him." She knew because she'd been turned down for a job during college for that very reason.

He looked at her, surprise in his eyes. "Unfortunately it happens sometimes. But I think, ultimately, you and I want the same thing."

As she nodded her agreement, she saw a black sedan with dark tinted windows cruising slowly down the street opposite the park. She glanced to locate Caitlin. The two girls were laughing and playing tag with some other children who'd also come to play. When she looked back, the car was gone.

She had an overwhelming urge to grab Caitlin and run. But that didn't make sense. Shaking it off, she asked, "What's so important that you had to track me down?"

"Is something wrong?"

"No, why?"

"You seem edgy all of a sudden."

What could she say…that she was continually on watch in case someone discovered what Cait knew and came after her? She forced a smile. "I get nervous watching Caitlin go so high on the swings. I know I shouldn't worry so much, but I do."

His expression was hard to read, but he seemed to believe her.

"She appears to be a very capable child. I doubt you have much to worry about."

"You're probably right," Laura said, relaxing against the bench. She liked being with him, except for the way he made her stomach feel queasy. But at least she knew she was still capable of feeling something. "Okay. What questions didn't you ask?"

She thought he'd be happy she was willing to talk, but his expression turned serious and his gaze pierced right through her. Steady and searching, almost as if he could read her mind. Well, if he could, he'd know she was having thoughts that might embarrass both of them—thoughts that at once unnerved and excited her. Lord.

"So far, you're the only person I've talked to who knew Anna Kolnikov, or at least the only person willing to admit to it."

She tensed, clasped her hands tighter. If there was something she could tell him that would help him find Anna's killer, she'd do it in a microsecond. But she didn't know anything. Still, if she answered a few of his questions, maybe that would be the end of it.

"Did you know Kolnikov was a prostitute?"

Briefly, Laura closed her eyes. "I'd heard the rumor."

"From your husband?"

She shook her head. "No. I've been on the streets for the shelter since before we married. I talk to people. Word gets around."

He nodded. "It's a tough life out there for kids with no place to call home. Really tough."

"Even worse when they want help and can't get it. At the shelter, far too many times we discover the parents want nothing to do with their own flesh and blood. I had one of those today. It was heartbreaking."

"Rejection stings. I don't know why people have children when they don't want them." People like his biological mother, Jordan thought. But that was beside the point. He was here to get information.

"Laura—" he purposely used her first name to set her at ease "—the girls you've taken in over the years…do you know if any of them ever worked for Kolnikov?"

She frowned. "The shelter's information is confidential."

"I know. You'll find I ask a lot of questions I shouldn't ask." He smiled amiably. "But it never hurts to try."

She shifted her position on the bench, obviously uncomfortable now.

"Okay, getting back to the case…you mentioned that while your husband was in college he'd worked for his uncle."

She nodded. "Before we were together."

"Do you know if he collected money from Kolnikov?"

She wiped her hands on the thighs of her faded jeans—jeans he couldn't help noticing showed off her soft curves. The red turtleneck sweater she wore complemented her fair skin and auburn hair. Luke was right. *Stunning* was the best word to describe her. And he was noticing too much for his own damned good.

"He was in real estate when we met. I don't know the details of what he did for his uncle."

"How did you meet?"

She took a moment, as if weighing her response. Jordan had a knack for reading people, and Ms. Gianni wasn't very good at hiding her reactions.

"Is that important?"

"Probably not. But when I'm piecing things together, sometimes the information that seems the least important makes everything fall into place."

"Eddie and I met at the university, but we didn't date until after we graduated. I'd applied for some grants to run the shelter and had started looking for a piece of property. I discovered Eddie had gone into real estate. He helped me find Victory House. We got married a year later."

Her gaze shifted to her daughter several times during the conversation. She was still tense. She said she was concerned about her child on the gym equipment, but the look he saw in her eyes was more than concern. "When did you first meet Ms. Kolni—"

Laura bolted to her feet and took off running toward the swings. He jumped up, scanning first the playground and then the peripheral area. The same black sedan was on the other side of the park now, the darkened windows rolled down just enough to see the top of someone's blond hair. Or was it gray?

As Laura sprinted toward her daughter, Jordan jogged toward the car, keeping a low profile as he moved. The guy could be a father looking for his kid, but he wasn't going to take any chances. He'd get a plate number and call it in.

But before he could make out the numbers, the car sped away. Then he strode across the grass to where Laura stood talking to her daughter. "I'm sorry, Detective," Laura said. "We're leaving now."

She held her daughter's hand in a vise grip, but when she took a step to leave, the child didn't budge.

"Mo-om. We just got here. I don't want to go yet. And you're hurting my hand."

Laura released her hold. "I'm sorry, Caity. I…I just think it's best if we go now."

"Can't I play for a few minutes more? Please, please, please."

Jordan glanced at Laura, then at the kid. "I was going to try out the swings, myself," he said. "It's been a long time."

"Pleeease, Mom."

Laura's gaze darted to the street and back again. "Ten minutes. No more."

Jordan felt a small hand latch onto his. "C'mon, Jordan. Let's go."

He caught Laura's attention. "It'll be okay."

She nodded.

At that, Caitlin all but dragged him to the swings. "Can you push me way high?" She slipped onto a smooth canvas seat.

"Sure, but you have to hold on tight."

"You're really nice," the child said, and the appreciative smile on her face warmed him. Just then, the other child, Jenny, asked to be pushed, too. But after only a few minutes, the girls jumped off and sprinted toward the monkey bars.

"Hey, I'm too big for those," he told Caitlin. "I'll just watch."

As the girls played, Laura stood beside him, arms crossed. "Thank you for being so kind to Caitlin."

"She's a great kid. And it was fun." He couldn't suppress a big grin.

A half smile parted her lips, but he still read worry in her green eyes. "What is it? What's wrong?"

"Nothing. It…it's just time to go."

He placed a hand on her arm to keep her there. "Laura, I saw the car. Is that what upset you?"

She pulled her arm away.

"I'm an officer of the law. Remember? I wouldn't let anyone get near the kids. Have you seen the car before?"

The fear he saw in her eyes made him feel like a jerk for pushing her, making her answer questions she didn't want to answer. But he wasn't much of a detective if he didn't ask questions.

And he couldn't let this sudden sympathy for her affect what he had to do. "If you've seen the car here before, have you reported it? The department has a list of offenders in the area—"

"It...it's not that."

"What then? An old boyfriend? A pimp angry at you for taking one of his girls off the streets? I can't help if I don't know what's going on." If he was too blunt, he couldn't help that, either. She was terrified of something and he wanted to know what it was.

"If you have any other questions you want to ask, do it now, because—" she looked at her watch "—because in two minutes I'm out of here, and I'll be through answering questions." She crossed her arms over her chest and shifted her weight.

Damn, she was a stubborn woman. "Okay. When did you first meet Anna Kolnikov?"

She frowned. "Detective, I fail to see how this can help your case."

"Everything anyone knows about a victim is important. Most violent deaths among women are perpetrated by someone they know. A family member, husband, a boyfriend. The more I know about the victim, the greater my chances of solving the crime."

With her eyes riveted on her daughter, Gianni flipped her long hair behind her shoulders. "I'm sorry. Working with the girls as I do, I'm very aware of the statistics. I—I just have a lot of things on my mind at the moment and I'm not thinking clearly. She came to the wedding with Eddie's uncle."

Which meant DeMatta and Kolnikov still had a personal relationship at that time.

"Eddie also sold her some real estate. He was a good salesman."

Real estate? For another whorehouse? Realizing he'd been remiss, he took out a notepad and, turning away from the playground so Caitlin didn't see what he was doing, scribbled down what Laura had said. "What did you think of her as a person?"

Her frown lines softened. "That's an odd question."

"I don't think so. Like I said—"

"Yes, I know." This time she really smiled as she said, "I liked her. She…was kind and friendly, easy to talk to. Nice."

Nice. Kind. She'd said that before, and the words lay like a rock in his gut. "*Nice* and *kind* hardly seems an apt description for someone who prostituted herself and pimped other women."

Laura stood straighter. "You asked my opinion and I gave it to you."

"Right." And he had no business injecting his personal opinions into an investigation. "Maybe you can explain?" Because it also sounded as if Laura knew the woman better than she wanted to admit.

"Eddie told me she had a tough time of it when she was young."

Jordan felt a muscle twitch in his cheek. "Your ex must've been close to her to know that."

"Like I said, Eddie was in real estate. It was his business to collect information about people. But I still don't see how any of this is going to help you."

"It helps. One way or another. When you saw Kolnikov with DeMatta at your wedding, did they seem happy together?"

Her expression instantly switched from helpful to annoyed. "For God's sake, Detective. I didn't take notes."

"Call me Jordan, please." He smiled again, but it didn't help.

"I was getting married at the time, I was preoccupied with other things. I'm sure you can understand. I'm also sure you can understand it's time for me to take my daughter home for dinner."

She called out, "Come on, Cait. We're going now." Walking over, she took the child's hand and together they headed toward the parking area.

Jordan pressed his lips together. Yeah, he understood. He understood she knew a lot more than she was saying.

CHAPTER FOUR

CAITLIN SLAMMED THE DOOR behind them and, angry because they'd left the park so soon, headed directly to her room. "Get washed up for dinner," Laura called after her.

Laura's nerves felt as tight as harp strings. A few minutes alone to clear her head was all she needed. Her decision to talk to the detective had backfired. He kept probing deeper and deeper about Eddie and DeMatta. Whose murder was he investigating, anyway?

At the window of the sunroom, she leaned one knee on the love seat and pulled the lace curtains aside. Nothing. Still, her heart raced. Just seeing the car circling the park was an ugly reminder of what could happen. She pushed away from the window and paced from one side of the small room to the other.

"Hey, what's up?" Phoebe came in and dropped lazily into a chair.

Laura stopped pacing. "Nothing."

"Nothing? So how come you're prowling the room like a cat in heat?"

"Let me rephrase. Nothing I want to talk about."

The hurt in Phoebe's eyes took Laura by surprise. Phoebe never let anything bother her. "I'm sorry. I didn't mean to be curt. I just meant that I have a lot of things on my mind and I need to sort them out—by myself." She tried to smile, but it was a lousy attempt.

Even so, Phoebe nodded her understanding. "Yeah. I know what's wrong." She glanced to make sure none of the girls were within earshot. "You need a guy. Someone to help you get rid of all your pent-up frustration."

Laura sat in the chair next to her friend. Phoebe's solution to every problem began with a man. "I wish that's all I needed."

"What about Detective St. James? He's hot. Sizzling, as a matter of fact." Phoebe sucked air through her teeth and shook her hands as if she'd been burned.

Laura grinned. He was all that. "You're absolutely right. And getting too close to a guy like him is a good way to *get* burned." But the words belied the emotions stirring inside her. Despite her discomfort with the detective's questioning, the heat of his hand on her arm had gone directly to her core. His touch was gentle, yet firm, and the understanding in his eyes almost undid her.

Most officers who came to the shelter were all business or on some kind of power trip. While St. James was focused, there was something different about him, a sensitivity, genuine caring. And those qualities seemed to draw her to him like the proverbial moth to a flame—a perilous proposition for the moth. She couldn't for one minute let herself forget how dangerous it would be to get involved with him. A man of the law. Yet he was exactly the kind of man she'd want.

If she wanted to be with someone.

And if she had the choice.

"So this thinking you need to do," Phoebe said, getting serious. "You want to bounce something off me?"

Laura knew her friend would do anything for her, but there were some things that couldn't be shared.

"Thanks, Pheebs. But no. I just need a little time alone." She pushed to her feet. "But now it's time to make dinner. The rest of the girls will be back soon."

They went into the kitchen together and checked the menu posted on the refrigerator. "It's my night," Laura said.

"You up for it?"

"I'm always up for food."

"Which is another thing I can't figure out. If I ate as much as you do, I'd be rolling across the room instead of walking."

Laura couldn't help but laugh. Phoebe was good at raising her spirits. Thank heaven.

"As it is, I'm a chub."

"You're just right for you. Self-respect, remember. You teach it to the girls all the time."

"Yeah, I have self-respect—but it doesn't mean I'm not fat."

"Okay, have it your way. Now, let me get to work on this." She glanced up at the other woman. "Alone."

"All right. I'm outta here, anyway. I need to do some paperwork I didn't get done earlier."

As Phoebe left, Caitlin pranced into the room and out of the blue she said, "Do you like that man?"

"What man?"

"The one at the park. Jordan."

Laura's stomach lurched.

"*I* like him. And I think he likes you." There was no uncertainty in Cait's voice.

Laura took a package of chicken out of the fridge and brought it to the sink while Caitlin boosted herself up on a stool at the center island—really an old wood chopping block.

Cait eyed Laura. "So, do you like him?"

Um. "I think he's nice."

Laura tore off the plastic wrapping, took the chicken to the sink and ran some water over it, rubbing the cold slippery meat with her fingers. Junk-food junkie that she was, she'd rather have a cheeseburger. It was hell having to keep up a healthy diet for the girls, Cait included.

"If you think he's nice, then you should go out with him."

The thought appealed to her—if only circumstances were different. "Well, it's not so easy. When he's talking to me, he's working. And you shouldn't go out with people you work with." Though that wasn't the case with some, it was as good an excuse as any.

"Do you *want* to go out with him?"

Laura put the chicken on a plate, brought it back to the island and blotted it dry with a paper towel. "It's been a long time since I've been out with anyone." And it didn't matter what she wanted. The other person had to want it, too.

"Jenny's getting a new dad and I don't even remember my daddy."

A change of subject was most welcome, but not *this* change. With any mention of her father, Laura heard the need in Caitlin's voice…almost a plea. Laura's heart went out to her. She knew that need, felt it every day as a child. Like Cait, she'd longed to have a normal family like other kids. But nothing in Laura's childhood had been normal.

"I know, sweetie. But in your heart, you'll always remember how much he loved you." Laura hadn't even had that much.

"I don't want him in my heart. I want a real dad, and you could get me one if you wanted to."

Laura sighed, picked up a piece of chicken and dipped it in flour. "It's not easy, honey. I'd have to find someone I really liked, who liked me and who would also be a good father to you. That's a tough act."

Caitlin became quiet.

"Sweetie, can you get me the big skillet from the bottom cabinet. Please." Laura held up a sticky hand full of flour.

"Yuck." The child scooted off the barstool. Handing the pan to her mom, she said, "I saw the other man at the park before."

Laura's swung around. "The other man?"

"The one in the car. I saw him yesterday in front of the house. Remember?"

"I CAN'T MAKE IT, DAD." Rain drummed on the roof of Jordan's Pathfinder. Holding the cell phone between his ear and his shoulder, he tried to make out street signs through the sheets of water his wipers slapped off the windshield.

"Your mother will be disappointed."

"Harry will be there."

"It's not the same."

"I'm sorry, Dad. I'm on a job. I can't leave." When his father didn't answer, Jordan added, "*You* wouldn't leave a company business meeting for a social event, would you?"

Harlan St. James paused for a moment, during which Jordan thought he heard a muffled laugh. Finally his father said, "Okay. I'll make some excuse."

"Thanks, Dad."

"But you'll be at the stockholders' meeting next week."

It wasn't a question. While Jordan hadn't any personal interest in the corporation, as a family member, he still held major shares. His grandfather had made sure of that. "I'll be there."

Jordan hung up knowing he'd been manipulated again. His father had given him something to turn down to make sure he'd feel obligated to come to the stockholders' meeting. He chuckled. Got to give the guy credit. He was a shrewd businessman and knew how to get people to do what he wanted. Especially his sons. Despite Jordan's inability to meet his parents' expectations, he had enormous love and respect for them.

He squinted at another street sign through the pelting rain. Over the past week, and after interviewing a half-dozen women who "might've" worked for Anna Kolnikov, he had little new information. He'd retrieved two pieces of paper buried in the case file without a single notation in the file on either one. A scribbled date on a piece of paper and a name on a birthday card sent to the victim wasn't a lot to go on.

The windows started to fog, so he switched on the defrost. He checked for addresses again. A few blocks later, he found Thirty-Fifth Street, turned the corner and drove halfway up the block to a dilapidated apartment building, then directed his flashlight at the sign in front. La Mariposa. The infamous La Mariposa.

The building was a magnet for prostitutes who couldn't make it on the streets anymore. Living at the complex, they made themselves ready for any pimp who could supply them some business—which he'd heard was poor because there were so many young women out there willing to practically give it away. Some were just barely teens.

Laura Gianni came to mind again. She was doing a

good thing trying to help kids whose lives had gone down the toilet.

He parked curbside a half block away and jogged to the building. Cautiously going inside, he stopped by the stairwell. Rain dripped from his overcoat onto the cracked tile floor. He brushed the water off and finger-combed his wet hair. He'd probably get the same run-around he got from everyone who'd supposedly worked for Kolnikov. No one knew anything, even when they'd known the woman for years.

But he had to try. It wasn't a waste of time if he got even one clue—one piece of information he didn't have before. Finding the first apartment number on his list, he knocked. Once. Twice. He heard a harsh voice—couldn't tell if it was male or female—shout out, "Hold your freaking horses!"

Before the door opened, the disembodied voice yelled, "Who the hell's there?"

"LAPD. Please open the door."

The door creaked open and the sweet scent of cannabis wafted out. It was so thick he thought he might get high just standing there. A plump woman with dyed blue-black hair studied him with rheumy eyes.

"Ms. Rita Valdez?"

"That's me. But I haven't done nothing. I'm clean."

Jordan pegged her to be in her midforties, but the hard lines in her face made her look years older.

He flashed his shield. "I'm Detective St. James. I'm only here to talk to you."

She hesitated before letting him in.

The room was dimly lit, the curtains drawn, and another sweet scent stuck in his throat. Incense. Used to cover other smells, except it wasn't working now. "I have some questions for you about Anna Kolnikov."

The heavy mascara on the woman's eyes had seemed to weigh her eyelids down, keeping them at half-mast, but at the mention of Kolnikov's name she snapped her eyes fully open. "I don't know anything."

"You worked for her before she died."

"You can't prove it."

No, he couldn't. And he didn't want to. He was on a fishing expedition. Jordan sat on the arm of the ragged brown couch, indicating he wasn't leaving until he got his answers. "I only want to know more about Anna Kolnikov."

Rita, dressed in a red silk Oriental robe, sat at the other end of the couch and stretched out her legs, skin showing up to the thigh. A seductive pose just for him. He knew the drill.

"Why do you think I know anything about that woman?"

"Because you sent her a birthday card the month before she died. She kept it in her personal belongings. People don't send birthday cards to people they don't know."

"Well, maybe I knew her, but my memory ain't so great."

Jordan pulled out a twenty. "Maybe we can jog it a little."

Rita snatched the bill. "Maybe."

"Did she have friends?" He pulled out a notepad and a pen and another twenty.

"Everyone liked Anna," Valdez said, snatching the bill. "She was a business lady through and through. She had lots of friends."

"Were these friends outside the business?"

"I don't know."

"Got some names?"

"Me. I was a friend. She helped me when my daughter was in the hospital."

"I'm sorry your daughter was ill," he said, hoping to put her at ease, get her to relax and open up. Fact was, if she'd had a real job she'd probably have had hospitalization to cover a sick child. But he wasn't there to lecture or dole out advice.

"Thanks."

"How did she help you?"

"She gave me money, and she helped me get off…the junk so the welfare wouldn't take my girl away."

From the tracks on the inside of her leg, Jordan guessed the rehab had only been temporary. "Where's your daughter now?"

The woman looked down. "She's gone. Foster care. But I'm going to get her back."

Again, Jordan fought the urge to give advice and say something about needle diseases and responsibility. It wouldn't make any difference, anyway. "So, give me some other names. You know Delores Matthews?"

She nodded. "Dee was Anna's friend. But I heard she disappeared."

"Anything else you know about her? Did Matthews have friends who might help her?"

"Nope."

"She ever talk about going anywhere?"

The woman squinted at him with uncertainty, as if deciding whether to say anything more. He took another bill from his pocket and fingered it.

Rita sighed heavily. "She used to talk about starting over in Hawaii or somewhere exotic. She was a dreamer. She wanted to get out of the business. I think Anna was going to help her, but then she died and Dee disappeared."

He had a theory that the Kolnikov murder and Matthews's disappearance might be related somehow. What Valdez said fit perfectly. But theories only went so far.

"What about other friends of Anna's?"

"There was a guy Anna took up with the year before she died. Handsome man. Younger than she was. But I never got introduced."

"Were they dating?"

"I couldn't say for sure, but they were mighty friendly."

Jordan stood, too impatient to sit for long. "Anything else? You must remember something else." He handed her the other bill.

"He was blond and...um...he was around all the time." Furrows on her forehead proved she was thinking hard. She pushed at the front of her lacquered hair. "I heard he came from the town where she grew up."

Jordan's skin prickled. *The town where she grew up.* Kolnikov had a life before she came to L.A. A life that could provide more clues about the woman, clues that might lead to her murderer. He didn't recall seeing anything in the case file about it. Nothing about a younger boyfriend, either. Odd.

"What town was that?"

The woman shrugged. "I don't know."

"Getting back to Delores. Did you know her well?"

She shook her head. "No, but I bet they dumped her body in the ocean."

"They? Who do you mean?"

She frowned, then shrugged.

Jordan was just about to ask another question when they heard a loud double knock along with a short one at Rita's door.

The woman stood. "I'm having company, Detective. And I really don't think I can entertain you any longer."

"Sure." He pulled out a card and gave it to her. "Call me if you remember anything more."

She smiled as she fingered the money she still had in her hand. "Maybe. If I think of anything."

"You see that pothead friend of Brandy's around here lately?"

Laura stopped dusting and looked up at Rose. "No. Why?"

Rose shrugged. "I saw him twice in the last week."

"No one has said anything."

"Well, maybe it's nothing."

Maybe. Or maybe not. They'd had stalkers at Victory House before—a junkie boyfriend of one of the girls, a pimp one of the girls had worked for. "I'll keep a watch for him."

"Good." Phoebe headed for the kitchen just as Caitlin came in the front door with Alysa on her heels. Cait had walked home from school on her own all week, and Laura could see her daughter's confidence growing. Cait needed to feel capable, every bit as much as the girls staying at the shelter. And with each day that passed, Laura had felt less worried—until now.

She started to ask Alysa if she knew anyone who might be hanging around, but with Cait right there, she decided against it. "Hey, ladies. How was your day?"

Alysa tossed her bag down. "Great. I got an A on my last midterm exam."

"Wonderful," Laura said. "I didn't expect anything less."

Alysa smiled proudly.

"And how about you, squirt?"

Cait waggled her hand in a so-so gesture.

"Do you have homework?"

"I have tons of homework. I always do. My teacher sucks."

Laura swung around to look at her daughter, who was now heading down the hall to her room. "You love your teacher. What's this all about?" Laura said, following Cait, arms folded across her chest.

"Shannon got busted for talking and sending me notes. Now her mom probably won't let her walk home with me anymore."

"Maybe. Maybe not. You'll have to wait and see. But there's no reason to be mad at your teacher. Shannon was at fault, and I think you know it."

Cait chucked her backpack on the desk and dropped onto the bed. "Yeah. I guess, but I can still walk with her sister, Kayla."

"We'll see." Laura sat next to her. "So, what else happened today?"

"Nothing."

"Nothing?" Laura pulled back, giving Cait her I-don't-believe-you look.

"Nothing much. But I saw the car. The black one at the park. It was by the school playground."

Laura's heart stopped. Her mouth went dry. But somehow she managed to push words past her lips. "Are you sure it was the same one? Lots of people have black cars." Something she had to remind herself of.

"Uh-huh. But it wasn't doing anything, it was just sitting there."

"Did you see someone inside?"

Cait shook her head.

"Did you tell someone? Your teacher?" The schools were always on watch for anything unusual.

"No."

What to do? Laura couldn't think. Was someone stalking Caitlin? Some deranged pervert waiting for an opportunity to present itself? "It's okay, honey. I'll call the school. I think the principal should know, and if you see the car again, you go right inside and tell someone. Okay?"

"Okay. But maybe it's just one of the parents. Jenny says her mother watches everything she does. It's *so* embarrassing."

"Like me watching everything you do," Laura said, and gave Cait a quick hug, hoping the child didn't sense her panic. It could be nothing. She didn't want to scare Cait over nothing.

"Maybe not *that* much."

"Does Jenny's mom have a black car?"

"No, hers is white."

"Okay. Well, this isn't getting your homework done." Laura stood. "Call me if you need any help."

Cait rummaged in her backpack and took out some wrinkled papers. "I want to do it in the dining room like everyone else."

More independence. "Okay. I don't see anything wrong with it—if you get the work done and don't pester everyone else. They have their own work to do."

Cait beamed as she hurried off. "Way cool!"

A black car. Rubbing the gooseflesh on her arms, Laura walked across the hall to her room and immediately picked up the phone and called the school. She got the damned answering machine.

After leaving a message, she started to call the police, then hung up. She'd called the police before when a couple of the shelter residents had boyfriends stalking them...and the police never did anything.

They needed proof someone was being threatened. She made another quick decision and pulled Detective St. James's card from the drawer on the nightstand. Hands trembling, she punched in his number. She didn't know if she was scared or angry. Probably both.

"St. James."

"Detective St. James, this is Laura Gianni. Do you have a minute?"

"Sure. Has something happened?"

"I don't know. I—I think someone might be stalking us."

"Us? You and Cait? Someone at the shelter?"

"I don't know who."

"Do you think you're in danger right now?"

"No. He's gone."

"Where are you?"

"At home. Victory House."

"Well, stay put. I'll be right over."

He hung up before she had a chance to say anything else. She felt a knot in her stomach as she replaced the receiver. Walking quickly to the dining room, she felt better when she saw her daughter working hard at the same table as Alysa, Brandy and Dakota. The child wanted so much to be like other kids, wanted so much not to have her mother hovering over her all the time.

It wasn't as if Laura didn't understand how Cait felt. She understood only too well. Still, she had good reason to be watchful of her daughter. Very good reason.

JORDAN SCOUTED THE FEW blocks around Victory House before he pulled into the driveway, and then he did a quick three-sixty of the grounds.

Laura opened the door just as he reached it.

"That was fast."

"I wasn't far away. Are you okay? Cait?"

"We're fine. In fact Cait doesn't know I was upset about anything. She doesn't know I called you."

Given she'd been trying to get rid of him ever since they'd met, he figured she'd have to be extra nervous about something before she'd call him. The worry in her eyes confirmed it.

"So, let's call this a social visit."

"Come in. I'll make some coffee."

They went into the kitchen, where Laura closed the thick oak door into the dining room and then scooped some Folgers into the pot. He shrugged off his leather jacket and hung it on the back of a chair. Sittting at the table, he waited while she set out some cups.

"Why don't you tell me everything that's happened. From the beginning."

Laura leaned a hip against the counter and crossed her arms. "I don't want to scare Cait or the girls. And maybe I overreacted. I probably shouldn't have called."

She kept her voice barely above a whisper, and if the look he saw in her eyes was any indication, she was one very scared lady. Every time he'd seen her he'd noted what a strong woman she was, but right now, she seemed vulnerable. He wished he could say something to make her feel better. He might if he knew what was wrong. "But you did call, and you had a reason. Why don't you let me be the judge if you overreacted or not."

The coffee stopped percolating, and when she reached for it, he saw her hands shake.

"Okay. You be the judge." She poured them each a cup, then put a sugar bowl and a milk carton on the table. "No fancy stuff here."

"Good, I don't like fancy," he said, and then dumped a spoonful of sugar into his cup. He waited for her to continue.

After a sip, she managed to say, "The car at the park the other day—Cait has seen it before. Outside here a few times and today she saw it at the playground of her school. At least she thinks it was the same car. I called the school and left a message."

"Did you call the police?"

She gave him a strange look. "Yes. I called you."

He noticed her gaze drifting over his jeans and sweater.

"You're not on the clock, are you?"

"No."

"I'm sorry...I didn't mean to take you from anything."

"Not a problem. But I'd like to know why you didn't just call the local station so they could send someone out."

She sighed. "We've had people hang around before, old boyfriends and...such. But the police never do anything, and the old boyfriends usually go away once they know it isn't going to do them any good. But this feels different...and you saw the car before, too."

"Can you think of a reason someone would want to harm any of you?"

She rubbed her hands together in her lap.

He sensed she had more to tell him, but nothing was forthcoming. "Anything you say is between you and me. I didn't come here in any official capacity. I came because you called."

She closed her eyes. Whatever it was weighed heavily on her.

Finally she blurted, "I'm worried Caitlin might be in danger."

Right. She'd not be as worried about herself as she would be her daughter. "Not one of the girls?"

She shook her head. "No. I don't think so."

"Because of the car or something else?"

Instead of answering, she stood and looked out the window. "Because the car was here *and* at the school *and* the park. I think that's enough for me to be worried."

"If you call the police, they'll check out any known criminals in the area."

"I know. But I don't want everyone…the girls to know about it. I just want it to stop."

She was afraid for her daughter, thought she was in danger, but she didn't want to involve the police— except for him. It didn't make sense. Unless she thought talking to the police would make things worse. He decided to take a stab at it. "I've got to notify local law enforcement. They'll put a watch at the school. All anyone will know is that someone reported a car prowling the playground. No one will know you said anything."

"No one? If you notify them, you'll have to say where you got the information, and that stuff always gets out."

"I'll make sure it doesn't," he said, placing a reassuring hand on her shoulder. Though, he wasn't sure how he'd pull it off since most police reports were public information. But looking at her, knowing how scared she was, he'd figure a way. Maybe call in a favor if he could.

"Thank you," she said softly. "I appreciate whatever you can do."

As she stood there under his touch, he felt a need to pull her closer, to physically comfort her. The contact and the invitation in her eyes made him suddenly aware of how long it had been since he'd felt this way with a woman. Too long.

And he sensed something had changed between them, that she'd lowered her protective barrier. Not much, but a little.

The door swung open and Caitlin came in. "I'm done, Mo—" Seeing him, the kid stopped in her tracks. Her eyes brightened. "I didn't know anyone was here."

Laura stepped back.

"Hello, Cait. I was in the neighborhood and thought I'd stop by," he said quickly, hoping the excuse would work so Laura didn't have to lie to explain his presence. Already he knew that lying to her daughter would bother her. Other lies he wasn't so sure about.

"I got a star on my papers today," Cait announced.

Laura placed her hands on her hips and looked at her daughter. "You didn't tell *me,* Caitlin."

"But you know I always get stars. Jordan doesn't know."

"Oh," Laura said, closing her mouth.

Just then Phoebe peered into the kitchen. "Sorry to interrupt the party, but it's my day to start dinner." She glanced at Jordan, her eyes big. To match her smile. "Do we have a dinner guest?"

Before Laura had a chance to say anything, Cait piped up, "Please, Mom, can Jordan stay for dinner? Please."

He glanced at Laura.

Laura looked at Cait. "Uh…Jordan's a busy man. I'm sure he has other plans."

She was giving him an out—and he could tell by the way she shifted from one foot to the other, she really wanted him to take it. Sweet. "No. Except for a few phone calls, I have no other plans at all. I'd love to stay for dinner."

CHAPTER FIVE

WELL, THAT HADN'T GONE the way she thought it would. Laura watched Cait and Jordan from the window in her bedroom. After Jordan had made his phone calls, Cait immediately dragged him outside to show off her new scooter and Phoebe had shooed Laura out. They both knew too many women in the kitchen was a recipe for disaster.

Laura glanced at her image in the bureau mirror. Her unruly hair sprouted in all directions and her jeans and orange T-shirt were smudged with dirt after her efforts to shovel out a spot for a spring garden in the backyard. But Jordan hadn't seemed to notice.

Laura felt a twinge of embarrassment. When he'd touched her, she'd jerked away as if he'd had the plague or something. Stupid. He was a gentle, caring man. And she even liked the way he smelled. Woodsy, as if he'd been outside in the fresh air. She didn't recognize the scent, but then why would she? It'd been nearly four years since she'd been so close to a man.

She took another look at herself. Cait would probably monopolize Jordan until dinner, so maybe she'd freshen up. Quickly, she turned on the shower, pulled the grungy T-shirt over her head and sloughed off her jeans.

As she stepped inside the stall, she heard Caitlin

laughing. She didn't know what had possessed Jordan to say yes to dinner, but she was glad he had.

Standing directly under the shower nozzle, she tipped her face into the fine, hard spray, reminding herself Jordan wasn't really there for a social visit. She'd called him because she was scared.

But, oddly, she wasn't so frightened anymore. Jordan exuded confidence and she, in turn, had confidence in his abilities. A male presence in the house had all kinds of effects on her psyche. She felt very much alive again.

Within ten minutes, she'd washed and toweled dry. She quickly blew dry her hair and then put on a clean pair of blue jeans and a green hoodie. She didn't have much else in her wardrobe but jeans and T-shirts. For the first time in ages, she wished she had something more feminine. She dabbed on a bit of lip gloss and blush. That was about as dressed up as she got these days.

A knock on the door startled her. "Mom, are you going to come out? Dinner's almost ready."

Laura opened the door. "I was just coming."

"Yum," Cait said. "You smell good."

"I took a shower." She passed Cait in the doorway and headed for the kitchen.

"It doesn't smell like soap. It smells like perfume."

Oh, the honesty of kids. "Okay, I'm busted. Now, let's see if we can help Phoebe in the kitchen or set the table or something. Where's Det— Jordan?"

"He's with Alysa and Claire."

The apprehension she thought she'd stifled surfaced again. She didn't think he'd question the girls, but she really didn't know him and couldn't be sure. "See if you can help with the table. I have to talk to Jordan for a minute."

Cait grumbled something as she went into the kitchen.

Laura found Jordan in the sunroom with the two girls, their eyes wide in rapt attention and hanging on his every word. He had his back to her and neither girl looked up when Laura came in. She waited for Jordan to finish. At the end of his story, the girls laughed and Jordan turned, almost as if he knew she was there all along.

"Hey. You look great in green," he said.

"Oh…thank you. I was dirty from working in the yard so I…cleaned up a bit."

"Well, you clean up nice."

Claire and Alysa giggled and Laura felt heat rise to her cheeks. She cleared her throat. "Can I get anyone something to drink?"

"We already got Mr. St. James something," Alysa piped up.

Laura saw a glass of lemonade on the table next to Jordan. "Oh. Good."

"He's telling us stupid-crook stories," Claire said. "It's unbelievable how dumb some people are."

"Please, call me Jordan? It works better for me," he said to the girls, and they giggled again.

Laura had wondered how her charges would take having a guest for dinner. A detective in particular. Some of her residents didn't have a high opinion of the police. She needn't have worried.

"Tell her the one about the bank robber and the deposit slip," Alysa prompted.

Laura sat next to Jordan on the love seat since the others had the chairs. "Please do. I'm all ears."

An hour later, after they'd finished dinner and a fruit dessert, the girls shooed Laura and Jordan out of the kitchen, volunteering to clean the mess. Phoebe and Rose claimed they had work to do and even Cait went to her room to finish some homework.

On their way into the TV room, Jordan grinned at Laura and shrugged. "Was it something I said?"

Laura laughed. "It's a thinly disguised plot to leave us alone."

"Really?"

He stood next to her, near the old vinyl sectional. Neither made a move to sit.

Having dinner with Jordan had been delightful. He was an easy conversationalist, charming and surprisingly funny. He made everyone around him feel at ease, including her. When any of the girls spoke, he gave his full attention, as if she was the only person in the room. He made the teens feel important. She knew because she'd felt the same. "Yes. They've all been bugging me to get a social life for a while now."

He arched an eyebrow. "And what do you think?"

"About what?"

"Do you think you need to get a social life?"

His eyes, the color of quicksilver, held hers. Her stomach fluttered like a schoolgirl's. Without answering, she set her cup on the table and turned to sit. He stopped her with a hand on her arm. The teasing look in his eyes said he already knew the answer.

She moistened her suddenly dry lips. "Maybe. A little. But this isn't the time."

His playful expression faded. "Right." He let her sit, then sat next to her. "I think you need to tell me what you're afraid of."

The warmth and concern in his voice compelled her, and right then, for a fraction of a second, she wanted more than anything to tell him everything.

Wanted to relieve herself of the horrible secret hanging over her head like the sword of Damocles. Because as long as she kept the secret, she'd live with the fear of discovery. She'd never stop watching. Waiting. Never be free to have a relationship.

But protecting her daughter was more important than her comfort level or any social life she might want. She shrugged. "I was afraid Caitlin was in danger because of the car. That's it. Really."

His head bobbed. "I could help."

When she didn't answer, he added, "I'm asking as a friend. A concerned friend."

A friend. Could he really be? If she told him, he'd have to report it. She knew that as well as she knew what DeMatta was capable of doing. And what kind of friends could they be then? She almost reached for his hand for reassurance, but thought better of it. "I'm truly grateful for everything you've done tonight, Jordan, but please don't read anything more into it. It was the car. If he goes away, we'll be fine. I'll be fine."

He frowned, clearly puzzled, then took her hand. "Okay."

His touch was gentle, but she could tell he didn't believe her. Not for a second. Well, whether he did or not didn't matter. He was just going to have to accept it.

DRIVING HOME, JORDAN returned a call to Luke on his cell phone. "What's up?"

Luke grunted. "Shit. A lot of shit."

"Something I can do?"

"Where are you?"

"On my way home."

"You want to stop by? I'll buy you a beer."

"Sure. Any hint on what it's about?"

"I'll tell you when you get here."

"Give me twenty."

Intrigued, Jordan clicked off. Since his divorce, Luke never invited anyone over. It had to be important.

He took the exit to Highway 10 and headed west toward Luke's place in Venice, but his thoughts veered in another direction—where they always seemed to go these days—to Laura. She was right to be upset about the car. And he was glad she'd called him. He knew the police would put a watch on the school, but he doubted they'd put one at the shelter.

He felt he should do something else, but he didn't know what. It made him even more determined to find out what she was hiding. It had to be something with catastrophic effects if it was revealed—hurting her or someone she loved. Otherwise why hide it?

The traffic congealed, a mass exodus from downtown L.A. Slowed to a halt several times, it took him longer than he figured to reach Ocean Avenue. He drove past the beach houses, funky shops and streets crowded with the usual tourists, vendors, artists and jugglers still out even though it was late. He turned onto a strip of road leading to Luke's.

Luke's grandfather had willed Jordan's buddy the old home, now hidden among the palms on one of the old Venice canals. The area had seen a rebirth since the beatnik days of the fifties and hippie days of the sixties, and now Venice boasted some of the most expensive homes in West L.A. Luke's property was worth a bundle, but his friend couldn't care less.

Jordan parked, got out and filled his lungs with the salty sea air to clear his head. He strode to the door. It was late, 10:00 p.m., and he'd had a long day. The highlight being dinner with Laura and her daughter. He smiled at how much he'd enjoyed himself—despite the reason he was there.

The door sprung open. Luke stood there, his shirt unbuttoned, his jeans wrinkled even more than usual. His sandy hair looked like a pile of hay. He motioned Jordan inside.

"Hey, what's up?" Jordan said. "You look like hell."

Luke ignored the comment.

Jordan followed Luke into the kitchen and took the beer his friend handed him. "Nothing, I guess."

"Have a seat," Luke said.

They sat at the wooden table. The place was small, but well laid out. Everywhere Jordan looked he saw signs of Julianna—things Luke hadn't bothered to get rid of. Some of the black-and-white photographs she'd taken were still tacked to the corkboard next to the refrigerator, most of them discolored and hanging at all angles. But no pictures of Michael. "What's with the old stuff?" Jordan waved a hand at the pictures. "It's been how long—four years since the divorce?"

"Four and a half."

Jordan nodded. He doubted Luke had called him to talk about his broken marriage.

"Where've you been? I tried calling."

"I had dinner at Victory House tonight."

Luke's head came up. "How'd you manage that?"

"Ms. Gianni called me." He waited briefly for the response he knew he'd get.

"No kidding."

Jordan took a swig of beer, then studied the label, drawing out the suspense. After all, they had a hundred-dollar bill riding on Jordan's success or failure in getting information from Laura Gianni. Jordan held up the amber bottle. "Fat Tire. What kind of name is that for a beer?"

Luke crossed his arms and gave Jordan the evil eye.

"Actually, she called me for my law-enforcement expertise and her kid invited me to stay for dinner."

"What kind of expertise is she interested in?"

Jordan lifted his beer, frowning. The whole thing still bothered him. "She thinks someone is stalking her daughter."

"Is it valid?"

"I don't know. The kid saw a car hanging around the school, and that's enough for me."

"Why would someone stalk her daughter?"

"You got me. They've had old boyfriends hang out before. Could be some pervert preying on her daughter or an old boyfriend of her own. Could be anything. She didn't seem to know a whole lot."

"You get anything else from her on Kolnikov?"

Jordan leaned back on two legs of the chair. "Nope." He smiled. "But I will." No way was he going to admit defeat.

"Well, while you're figuring it out, I've got something else for you to chew on."

"It must be good, or you wouldn't have dragged me here."

"I found a bug under my desk, so I checked yours." Luke pulled a tiny computer chip out of his pocket. "Someone knows everything we're doing."

"Which is?"

"The Kolnikov case and the Gianni murder, and apparently we're ruffling some political feathers. Both cases have mob overlap, so I figure someone's making enough noise to get the mayor involved. Which funnels down to the captain, and he isn't too happy about it."

"You think DeMatta's got the mayor under his thumb?"

Luke shrugged. "Pressure does funny things to rational people."

"A bug, huh?"

"Yeah."

"Anyone else know?"

"Not yet. And I'm thinking maybe we should keep it quiet."

Jordan shook his head. "I don't know. Whoever our mole is, he's got major cojones."

"CAITLIN? IS THAT YOU?" Laura thought she heard the back door open and shut, but the older girls had gone to the mall with Phoebe, and Cait had gone to Shannon's house for a birthday party. Maybe Cait had forgotten something.

"Cait," she called again, and when there was no answer, she passed it off as her imagination and went into the family room. She so rarely had time to herself that it felt strange being alone. After the noise level a house full of people generated, she found the quiet unsettling. Every sound seemed magnified. The hum of the refrigerator, the fan clicking on and off, the wind rattling the windows as rain threatened again. She could almost smell the electricity in the air. Clouds had dropped like a thick gray blanket over the city and the silver-gray sky made late afternoon seem like twilight. She hoped it wouldn't rain before Cait came home.

She should call Shannon's mother and tell her she'd bring an umbrella over for Caitlin. But it was only three houses away and Cait would be mortified.

It was hard always hiding her concern from Cait, but if she didn't, she could make Cait afraid of her own shadow. The incongruous image made her smile. That would probably never happen. At seven, almost eight as Cait always insisted, her daughter was decidedly her own person. Laura felt a sense of achievement in that. She wanted Cait to be strong, to trust in herself and know she could accomplish anything she wanted if she worked hard enough.

Sitting on the navy-blue sectional, another donation, along with all the furniture at the shelter, she picked up the television remote and turned it on. An old *Seinfeld* rerun was playing. She rarely watched television, preferring a good book when she had a moment to herself—but not this afternoon. She had other things to think about, questions to be answered. And Jordan St. James was at the heart of each and every one.

He seemed to be interested in her. But was he interested in her personally, or did he simply want to pump her for more information? She'd wanted to tell him more about Anna, but if she got into too much detail, her own tarnished past might be exposed. Caitlin didn't know about Laura's days on the streets. No one knew—except a few people in her past she'd lost track of over the years. She saw no reason to make it an issue.

Her daughter knew Victory House was a shelter for troubled girls and the girls stayed there because they needed help and a place to live. The first rule for the residents was no discussion of street life except in counseling sessions. The shelter had a limit on the number of beds, so anyone who couldn't live by the rules didn't get to stay.

Just then, a bold headline scrolled across the bottom of the screen. Breaking News: Officer Involved Shooting, Hostage Situation In Progress. Laura perched on the edge of the couch, her heart suddenly in her throat. Did Jordan work in that part of the city?

"We have a hostage situation in progress," a news reporter interrupted the program. "One officer down and one inside with the suspect. SWAT teams have surrounded the small home believed to be the target of a drug sting gone bad. Stay tuned for more on this event as it unfolds. KTTV. First with the news."

Laura didn't want to wait. She wanted to know now. This was why she didn't watch news on TV. Everything that happened was entertainment, no matter how devastating. Hearing an officer was involved suddenly made it personal. She had to know what happened. *Who* was hurt and who was in the house?

Just thinking it could be Jordan made her anxious. Her eyes were riveted on the screen as she waited to hear more.

A deep rumble of thunder shook the sky, then there was a blinding flash, followed by a crack of acoustical energy that rattled the house. The lights dimmed, the TV fizzled to gray then black. The lights went out. Another release of thunder was quickly followed by more lightning and rain that pelted the windows so hard she thought the glass might break.

Laura got up from the couch and hurried into the kitchen to call Shannon's house and find a flashlight. As she picked up the phone, she felt a breeze and, turning, saw that the back door had blown open. Though she had enough light to see, she took out the flashlight and scanned the room. Everything looked okay. She walked to the door and pushed it shut. Nothing out of place that she could see. She was still looking around as she punched in Shannon's number and lifted the phone to her ear.

Dead. And if her phone lines were out, all the lines in the neighborhood were probably out. She went back to the family room and fished her cell phone from her purse to try again. She didn't care what Cait thought. If they were in the dark over there with a half-dozen eight-year-olds, they might need some help. She punched in the number again. Surprisingly the phone rang.

"Robin," Laura said when a woman answered. "This is Laura. My electricity's out and I wondered if yours is out, too?"

"No, it's not," Robin responded. "We're fine here. We're in the middle of a game. The storm is awful but the girls aren't paying any attention. They're having fun."

Relieved, Laura said, "Can you tell me what time you'll be done? I'll bring an umbrella over for Cait."

"Don't worry. My three older children will walk everyone home when it's time."

Laura hung up and took the phone with her into the living room. Out the window, she saw lights glowing in all the houses down the block. Had her home been the only one affected? A fuse, maybe? Or had something been struck by lightning?

Another crack of thunder shook the rafters. She jumped, then felt foolish for being so skittish. It was just rain, for God's sake.

Still, there was no way to know how long the power would be out, and though it wasn't too dark to see, she went in search of some candles and a sweater. As she walked toward her bedroom she heard a loud thud, and then another. Heart racing, she eased down the hall, her back against the wall. Reaching her bedroom, she slowly opened the door. A powerful gust of wind hit her. The French windows were open and banging in the wind. Rain blew in, soaking the chest of drawers under the window and the rug underneath.

She ran over and slammed the windows shut, getting soaked in the process. *What the…?* She'd secured the windows tightly last night and the locking handles were on the inside. The wind couldn't possibly blow them open.

Maybe Caitlin had opened the window and forgot to close it tightly…. But why would she do that? It didn't make sense. Uneasy, Laura crossed the hall to her daughter's room. The old oak floor creaked as she stepped inside. The window, the kind that lifted from the bottom, was open, too.

Had Cait left it open?

Or had someone jimmied it from the outside?

Her heart lodged in her throat when she saw the cloisonné music box Eddie had given Cait on her second birthday scattered on the floor—in pieces. Laura knelt and picked up a shard of the delicate china. If Cait had accidentally broken it and didn't want Laura to know, she'd have picked up the pieces.

More important, Cait didn't lie or deceive her mother. She would've told her about it. Laura was as certain of that as she was of her ability to help the kids staying at the shelter.

Maybe the wind coming through the open window had blown it to the floor? No, it was too far from the window. Something else had happened here. But what? Quickly she picked up the pieces and dumped them into the wastebasket in the corner. Turning, she stopped cold. Her breath caught.

The quilt, the one Eddie's mother had painstakingly made by hand for Cait, was sliced to shreds. Laura felt a sickening knot in her stomach. Cait cherished the quilt, almost as much as the music box from her father.

The phone in Laura's pocket chirped and she

jumped. Nerves on edge, her hands trembled as she pulled out the cell. The numbers were lit, but she didn't recognize them. "Hello."

"Hey, it's me," Phoebe said, sounding far away. "We're still at the mall. I don't want to drive back in this rain, so we're going to wait until it lets up a bit."

Though she didn't like to think it, the possibility that one of the girls had done this loomed in the back of Laura's mind. She swallowed her concern and managed to say, "Okay. You know what's best."

"I didn't want you to worry."

"Thanks. Uh…I won't."

"How about you? Everything okay?"

"Don't worry about me. I'm fine."

But she wasn't fine. Someone had destroyed Cait's things. Someone had been in both of their rooms.

"Okay," Phoebe said. "See you when we get there."

Her mouth dry, Laura mumbled, "Okay. Bye." She clicked off, then touched the torn fabric, a silky piece of taffeta that had come from one of Cait's old dresses. As the fabric slipped through Laura's fingers, the reality of the situation hit her square in the gut. If someone had come in while she was there, he could easily have come for her, too.

She took a step toward the bed, and reached out to steady herself against the wall. Why? Why would anyone do something like this? *Who* would do something like this? She felt violated. The act was vindictive, personal. They'd destroyed keepsakes. Whoever did this had an agenda.…

She should call the police. But if it was one of the girls… No, she had to talk to them first. But what if it wasn't? Moving like a zombie, she crossed the room, closed the window, and then took a towel from the bathroom and started wiping the wet floor. Just as she finished, she heard the front door open. Her heart stopped.

"Mom, it's me. I'm back."

Laura snatched the quilt off the bed, rolled it into a ball and held it in her arms along with the towel. She eyed the wastebasket, then grabbed it and set the quilt on top. Turning, she found Caitlin standing in the doorway, her expression bewildered.

"How come the lights are out?"

"The storm, I think. Maybe lightning. I don't know. Good thing we have a couple of flashlights and candles if it gets too dark."

"What are you doing?"

"Well, I'm just doing some…uh, cleaning." Laura tightened her grip on the bundle in her hands. "The quilt needs to be washed. I'll bring you another one."

"You're supposed to be relaxing." Cait sounded like a mother reprimanding her child. "That's what you said you were going to do."

Laura forced a thready laugh. "Well, you know me. I like to keep busy."

"You weren't snooping, were you?"

The question caught Laura by surprise. "Snooping? What do you mean?"

A strange look of defiance glittered in Caitlin's eyes. "You know. Looking at my stuff. My private stuff."

The question was almost laughable. What kind of private stuff could a seven-year-old have? Laura tried to look serious. "Of course not. I wouldn't do that any more than you'd go looking through my things." She studied Cait's face for a reaction, to see if she'd gone into Laura's room and opened the window. But Cait's expression was innocent.

"I am upset that you left your window open."

Cait looked up. "I didn't open it. It's too cold outside."

Laura felt a chill and it *wasn't* coming from outside.

"I'm going to find the candles."

Cait's eyes lit up. "Can I help? Then I can tell you about the party and we can pretend we're camping and roast marshmallows on the stove."

They could do it since the stove was natural gas…and it would take her mind off other things. "You bet," Laura said, hoping her voice didn't give away her fear.

CHAPTER SIX

JORDAN SHRUGGED OFF HIS suit jacket and hung it on the back of his chair. He pulled out the Kolnikov case file, surreptitiously taking note of anyone looking his way.

Tex was on a call out along with his new partner, Simon McIntyre. Jordan didn't know Simon at all, but Tex seemed to think he was okay. Apparently Simon had a few run-ins with a couple of officers in his last job and had a reputation for being a troublemaker. Rico wasn't due back for another week and Howie Ralston, who'd only been on the team for a year, was eyeing Jordan from the captain's office. Who was the mole? One of them? Or someone who had access to the office but only came in occasionally?

That would cover a lot of people, including the mayor and his staff.

Rico and Luke, he'd trust with his life. Tex, too, though he didn't know him as well as the others. The rest of the unit was fair game. Even Mary Beth, the admin assistant. Okay, now he was losing it. Mary Beth had been the one person most willing to help on every case they had. She'd helped Rico a lot in the Ray case. He crossed Mary Beth off his list.

He glanced at the file, searching once again for something he might've missed…any mention that

Kolnikov had had a new boyfriend. Nothing. He flipped pages, searching for Anna Kolnikov's death certificate, something he'd looked at more than once. While he'd scoured the file, he hadn't paid particular attention to the woman's place of birth. Maybe he didn't want to know.

He found the certificate, but it was of no help. She was from Poughkeepsie, New York. Her DOB and parents' names were listed as unknown. Hadn't anyone bothered to find out if she had a family to notify?

The thought disturbed him. If she had a family…and she must've had one at one time…did they even know she was dead? Did they know about her life? He dismissed the thought. Anybody in L.A. would know she'd died. Four years ago, the media had gorged themselves on speculation about Kolnikov's clients, making thinly disguised references to particular California politicians. Kolnikov's name made the front page of the *L.A. Times* for longer than most people cared to read about it. It was probably on the national news, as well. If she had family somewhere, how could they not know?

Checking again, he saw zero notations about anyone contacting the LAPD about her death. Her body had remained at the morgue for several days after the autopsy. There'd been no memorial service and no visitors. Kolnikov was subsequently buried in Los Angeles' equivalent of Potters Field. Alone.

What puzzled him was that no one had even acknowledged her existence. Both Laura Gianni and her ex knew Kolnikov. Why didn't they make an appearance? If the woman who'd sent the birthday card, Rita Valdez, was such good friends with Kolnikov, why didn't she pay her respects?

What difference did it make? Kolnikov belonged to

the dark underbelly of society. People who exploited other people. Like DeMatta. The world was better off without them.

"St. James." The gravely voice came from behind him.

The scent of cheap cologne and stale tobacco preceded Ralston as he rounded his desk. "Captain wants to see you."

A conversation with the captain wasn't first on Jordan's list this morning. With all the flack from the mayor's office, Jordan knew it was only a matter of time before Carlyle put the kibosh on the Kolnikov investigation.

Engrossed in some papers on his desk, the captain didn't look up when Jordan entered. "Have a seat."

The tension in the air was so thick it was almost palpable. Just as Jordan was about to ask Carlyle what he wanted, the captain looked up.

"You better have something for me," he said. "Something worth all this crap I'm getting from the mayor's office."

Jordan cleared his throat. "It's not huge, but it's a lead. A boyfriend who seemed to have been overlooked before." *Or ignored.*

"Where'd you get the information?"

"From a woman who, while she wouldn't admit to working for Kolnikov, did admit to being a friend. Another lead left hanging."

"Who screwed up?"

"I don't know anyone did. But some leads weren't followed up. Or if the leads were ruled out, it's not documented."

The captain leaned back in his chair and rubbed a hand over his chin. "Anything to implicate DeMatta?"

"Not yet."

"What about the Gianni woman?"

Jordan's gut twisted. *What about the Gianni woman?* He'd asked himself the same question more than once. "She's got a tough job."

Carlyle frowned. "*I've* got a tough job. You've got a tough job. Lots of people have tough jobs. Does she know anything or not?"

Jordan thought she did—was almost certain. But he had no proof and the captain wanted evidence, not speculation. "She said she met Kolnikov a couple of times. But there was no documentation in the file."

The captain slammed a hand on the desk and bolted to his feet. "Dammit. I've got the mayor's office breathing down my neck on the Matthews case, there's a serial killer roaming the streets and now I find out I've got a bunch of incompetents working for me."

The Studio Killer. So named because his victims were all porn actresses and had been killed near or at the setting of their movies, which was usually a third-rate motel.

"Luke's on the Matthews case." Jordan didn't have to say that Luke was the best detective they had.

Carlyle clenched his teeth. His right eye twitched. It was obvious he was under a lot of pressure. "Yeah, well, Coltrane worked the whore's case, too."

The hair on the back of Jordan's neck bristled. "Briefly," he said. "He uncovered one of the leads before he got transferred. Ralston and Vargas finished it up."

Carlyle glanced toward where Ralston was sitting at a computer. Vargas had been transferred out a year ago. "Right. And we can't change what they didn't do. But if something doesn't happen soon, we're going to quit wasting time. We've got other priorities."

"What's more important than taking down DeMatta?"

"The good citizens of our thriving community get freaked out when a cold-blooded killer is on the loose. They call the mayor's office and he calls me."

"I'm sympathetic, but I need to finish this one, boss." The lives DeMatta had destroyed, the number of people he'd hooked on drugs and then exploited for prostitution couldn't even be counted.

Carlyle became pensive. "Okay," he finally said. "What's the plan?"

"I'm going to lean on DeMatta."

The captain chewed on the inside of his cheek. "That's a dangerous proposition."

"I know. But he knows what I'm doing, anyway."

Carlyle looked surprised. "You know that for sure?"

Jordan nodded.

The phone rang and Carlyle picked up. Listening, he silently indicated that Jordan could leave. But before Jordan got to the door, the captain said, "Hold it."

Carlyle covered the phone. "Rita Valdez?"

Jordan tensed. "She gave me a lead on Kolnikov's case."

"You got her address?"

He nodded.

"Get out there. We've got another homicide."

LAURA WAS STILL REELING when the sharp ring of the phone startled her. She couldn't bring herself to answer it.

"Mommy?"

"Uh…it's probably just a phone solicitor, honey. They kept calling the whole time you were at the party and I'm tired of them."

The electricity had miraculously come back on, the rain had stopped, and sitting with Caitlin in the family room watching an old Disney DVD as they waited for the rest of the group to come home had a calming effect.

Keeping her cell phone at the ready, she thought about what had happened and always came back to the same thing. If the intruder had wanted to hurt her, he could easily have done it when she was there alone. And if he didn't want to hurt her, the destruction had to be meant as a warning. For her? Caitlin? One of the residents? Realistically, it could be anyone at the shelter. She needed to talk to the girls—without Cait around.

"Shannon's mom is getting married," Cait said out of the blue.

"Really. How wonderful."

"He's got lots of money, too."

Laura glanced at Cait, who'd pulled her legs to her chest and wrapped her arms around them. She rested her chin on top of her knees. Cait had never mentioned money before. But the child was aware they didn't have much. "Well, money doesn't make a person happy, sweetheart."

"Shannon gets lots of presents and she's happy."

Laura frowned. "You're happy, aren't you?"

"But presents would make me happier."

Laura laughed, giving Cait a noogie. "Well, you'll get presents on your birthday and that's not too far away. In the meantime, you'll just have to suffer."

Just then, a car door slammed outside. Then another and another.

"Oh, I hear them," Cait shouted, jumping up. "They're home."

Laura heard a cacophony of female voices as the women came inside.

"I'm starved," Brandy said. "Who's got dinner tonight?"

"How can you be hungry with all you ate at the mall?" Claire demanded.

"It's no one's turn for dinner," Laura said. "It's pizza night. I've already ordered."

After the girls went to their respective rooms, including Cait, who wanted to play with her prizes from the birthday party, Laura pulled Phoebe and Rose aside. "We have a situation. After you left, we had a power outage and someone broke into the house."

Phoebe's eyes grew big and Rose looked aghast.

"When you were here?" Rose asked.

"I don't know who it was and yes I was here. I heard a noise early on, but ignored it. Later when I went into my bedroom and Cait's, both windows were open. Someone had slashed Cait's quilt and smashed her music box."

Both women stood there, speechless. Finally Phoebe said, "Why would anyone do something like that?"

"We'll know the answer if we find out who it was. Do either of you know anyone who might have a grudge against you or any of the girls?"

Rose shook her head, but Phoebe's eyes lit up. "There's that wacko guy I dated. The one who kept calling and told me I'd be sorry I didn't go out with him anymore. He sent me a dozen rambling letters, but then he quit. I thought it had ended. Only if it was him, he'd probably destroy things in my office."

"Maybe. But if he didn't know whose room it was—and he knew I was in the house and he'd have to pass me to go upstairs…" She shrugged.

"Brandy had an argument with her old boyfriend a week or so ago," Rose injected. "She said it was nothing and assured me he was harmless."

Laura remembered the incident.

"What about Cait? Does she have any friends who're jealous of her? Kids can get really nasty sometimes."

"I hadn't thought of that. But I also can't think of anyone who doesn't like Cait. Besides, I doubt any seven-year-old could've opened those windows and come in."

"And then the electricity just came back on?" Phoebe asked.

"It does seem coincidental, doesn't it?" Laura frowned.

"Yes," Rose said. "But it's not the first time the power has gone out in a storm. We all know the old wiring needs to be replaced."

"We should call the police," Phoebe said.

The doorbell rang. "It's the pizza, and no, I don't want to call them yet. I want to talk to each of the girls first. In the meantime, keep an eye out and your ears open."

ONCE HE GOT ON THE FREEWAY, Jordan floored the gas. Six o'clock and it was getting dark. He hated California winters. It was dark when he got up and dark when he went home. And that was when he was on the day shift.

He swerved to avoid a vehicle going so slowly the car was a danger to others. The rain had stopped, but the roads were still slick.

Jordan reached the crime scene as quickly as possible, arriving in concert with three squad cars, the scream of overhead sirens and blue-and-red flashing strobes lighting up the graffiti on the outside of the building. The entry to the place was cordoned off and a couple of blues held the gawkers at bay. There were always gawkers. People whose morbid curiosity couldn't be contained.

"Detective St. James," Jordan said to one of the officers, flashing his shield. "First officer on scene?"

"Officer Hansen. He's upstairs."

Jordan took the stairs two at a time, clipping his badge on the pocket of his suit jacket as he went. The closer he got to the top, the worse he felt. His heart hammered in his throat and he started to sweat. Fifty freaking degrees and he was sweating. More than a hundred homicides and his reaction was always the same. Whoever said you got used to seeing dead bodies was crazy.

Upstairs, crime-scene tape surrounded Rita Valdez's apartment, but the door was open. A couple of techs from the Scientific Investigation Division followed directly behind him. The SID was alternately referred to by detectives as the CSU or CSI because of the television show—a joke the techs didn't appreciate.

"Hansen?" Jordan said to the first officer he met.

"That's me."

"Detective St. James."

Hansen glanced at Jordan's shield and nodded.

The officer looked as if he'd barely graduated high school. "Give me a rundown," Jordan said.

"We got a call. The guy wouldn't give his name. Said he came to see her and found her dead. Probably one of her customers who doesn't want to be identified."

"Or her murderer."

"She's in the bedroom."

"Anything else I should know?"

"No signs of a break-in, so she probably knew her killer."

Nothing new there. "Maybe. Maybe not. She opened the door for me last week and she didn't know me. And I doubt she knows all the johns sent her way."

Hansen cleared his throat. "Uh...right."

It was obvious the kid was green. Jordan smiled, sympathizing.

"My first," Hansen said. "I didn't expect it to be this bad."

"You'll get used to it," Jordan lied, then crossed the room.

The coppery scent of blood met him at the bedroom door, a precursor to the ugliness inside. The fact that he was there to see justice done was the only thing that kept him going.

"Anything jump out?" he asked a tech who was dusting for prints. Another was bagging the woman's hands.

"Nope. No gun. No bullets or casings. Yet."

Blood pooled under Rita's black hair. The woman's partially naked body and the way all the drawers were half-open, the contents spilling out, fit the usual MO for a robbery-rape-murder.

But the way everything was laid out so perfectly seemed too obvious for him.

Hansen came up beside him.

"Rape and robbery," the tech said.

"Or cold-blooded murder." Jordan studied the body. "Look at the ligature marks around her wrists. The red marks on her knees. And where the bullet entered."

Hansen shifted from one foot to another, his eyes

bugging out, as if it'd just dawned on him that his quick leap to judgment wasn't necessarily correct. "You think the crime scene was staged?"

"Always a possibility," Jordan answered. Murderers had good cause to throw suspicion in another direction. What bothered him the most was that the crime scene was eerily familiar.

"So what do you think?" the younger man asked.

"I think someone wanted her dead. And we need to find out why. Anyone contact her family yet?"

"I don't think she has anyone."

"She has a daughter," Jordan said. And someone had to tell the kid. His stomach rumbled. "I'll take care of it."

"St. James," someone called from another part of the apartment. That grating voice was too familiar.

Howie Ralston. Ralston was talking to the ME when Jordan reached him. "Gentlemen."

"I'm your backup while Santini's gone," Ralston said. "What've you got?"

Jordan gritted his teeth. He didn't know Ralston very well, and what he did know, he didn't like. The guy was an arrogant bully on a power trip. Always looking for a way to promote himself. But if the captain had assigned Ralston to take Santini's place, there had to be a reason. Maybe so Jordan could keep an eye on him?

"Take a look," Jordan said. He'd see just how close they were in their assessments.

LAURA GLANCED OUT THE front window to see if Cait was walking home. No kids. She checked her watch. It was too early. She shouldn't be watching and waiting. She needed to get a grip.

But she couldn't get last night out of her head and hadn't slept a wink. She'd gotten up and checked on Caitlin probably a dozen times, checked the doors just as many.

She'd debated all night whether to call the police—or Jordan—but decided to give it one more day. Everyone at the shelter was on red alert. Except for Cait. She was too young to know what was going on, and God knew Laura didn't want the child watching over her shoulder every minute.

Laura had long ago cautioned her daughter about talking to strangers and she'd participated in the Stranger Danger program the police gave at the school. But knowing what to do and doing it were two different things.

Rose had already arrived for her shift and was in the kitchen with Brandy and Claire. Alysa wasn't home yet but would be soon.

"Need some help?" Rose said, coming up behind Laura.

"Oh!" Laura jumped. "I didn't hear you."

The other counselor put a hand on Laura's shoulder. "She'll get here. Give the kid some slack."

Laura sighed. "You can say that after last night?"

"Well, worrying isn't going to change anything. Besides, if someone wanted to hurt any of us, they could've done it already."

This was true. But it didn't stop her from worrying.

"Someone wanted to scare us, and it looks as if they've succeeded." Rose twisted her long hair into a knot and fastened it with a clip. "We've had things like this happen before and you haven't wigged out. What's different now?"

Laura closed her eyes, felt the burn behind her lids.

Lack of sleep was making her punchy, even paranoid.
She drew a long breath, then looked at Rose. "It's different because…I feel violated. Someone was in my
room. In Cait's. And destroying Cait's quilt, a keepsake
from her grandmother, and the music box from her
father…those things seem personal."

"Do you know anyone who might be carrying a
personal grudge?"

"You mean other than the usual suspects?" Laura
gave a wry laugh. "No. I don't know anyone who has
it in for me, or Cait. Especially not Cait."

Just then the phone rang. "Hello."

"Hi. It's me, Alysa. I just wanted to tell you I'm
going to be late coming home tonight."

"Is something wrong?"

"No," Alysa answered practically before Laura got
out the question.

"What's going on?"

"I—I'm going to check on the job at the ice-cream
place."

"Did you get a call from them?"

"No, but I want to make sure they remember me. I
won't be too late."

"Okay," Laura said reluctantly. Alysa sounded
nervous, edgy. But she wasn't going to push the issue.
Most of the girls at Victory House had trust issues
going both ways. "We'll see you when you get here,
then. Good luck with the job."

"Thanks." Alysa disconnected immediately.

Laura looked at Rose. "It was Alysa. She's going to
be late." She paused, thinking. Something in Alysa's
tone said she was in trouble.

"Is there a problem?"

Going back to the window to check on Cait, Laura

said, "No. Not with her being late. But she sounded…preoccupied."

"Well, it's only been two weeks since the confrontation with her parents. She's probably still upset."

Laura felt Alysa's pain as if it were her own. Alysa had been devastated when her parents had told Laura they weren't interested in reconciling with their daughter. Only they hadn't said it so nicely. As far as they were concerned, when Alysa started working the streets, she gave up her birthright. They no longer had a daughter.

Even though Laura had advised and counseled Alysa afterward, she knew Rose was right. It would take time for the wound to heal. Alysa had to work through the rejection, the abandonment. If that was possible.

The cold indifference made her angry. She'd buried the heartbreak of her own experience deep inside, but she knew exactly how Alysa must feel.

Laura felt a lump in her throat. She'd been so wrapped up in her own worries, she hadn't been paying attention to the obvious. When she thought back, she realized Alysa had been too quiet. Many nights she'd gone directly to her room after dinner. Though she still got good grades, her interest in school had waned these past few weeks.

"Rose, I need to go out for a bit," she said when she finally saw Cait coming up the walk. "If I get Cait set up with her homework, can you keep an eye on her for an hour or so?"

"Sure. What's up?"

"That's what I'm going to find out."

Ten minutes later, Laura was in Rose's car and headed toward the ice-cream store. Alysa had said it was near the school in the small strip mall. As she pulled into the parking lot, she saw a group of girls standing in a huddle and was reminded of her night duty, combing the streets for runaway teens prostituting themselves.

An odd comparison. These were high school girls, dressed nicely, hanging out in the middle of the afternoon and having a good time.

She'd obviously been in the field too long.

Alysa wasn't with the other girls, so Laura decided to wait. If Alysa was inside talking to the manager, she'd be out soon enough.

Just then a small BMW pulled up and one of the girls leaned down to talk to the driver, an older man. Seconds later, she climbed into the passenger side and the car took off. Probably the girl's father.

But as the girls stood there, Laura felt her uneasiness grow. The teens stood in seductive poses, preening and watching the street, as if waiting for someone to come. And where was Alysa?

She pulled out her cell phone and called the shelter. "How's Cait doing?" Laura asked when Rose answered.

"She's fine. And she'll be fine until you get back. So, don't be calling every five minutes."

Laura laughed, reprimand taken. "Okay, okay."

"Did you find Alysa?"

"Not yet. I'm waiting outside in the parking lot. I don't want to embarrass her by going in."

"You'll probably embarrass her just by being there. What are you going to say?"

"I'll let her know I was concerned about our conversation. I felt she needed some support."

"Right."

Laura watched another girl get in another car. "This is really weird, Rose. I'm sitting here watching some high school girls standing on the sidewalk...then a car pulls up and after a brief conversation, one of them gets in a car. It's happened three times."

"Boyfriends?"

"Not the ones I've seen so far. These guys are old enough to be their fathers."

"Maybe they are?"

Just then a BMW, same color as the one before, pulled up, stopped and the same girl who'd gone off before climbed from the car. Laura's mouth fell open. "I don't want to think the worst, but damn, it looks like they're hustling."

"Nothing we're not familiar with."

"Yes, but these aren't street kids."

"Not the kind you can tempt with some food and a warm place to sleep, huh?"

"Not a chance. Judging from the clothes they're wearing, these girls sleep in better places than the mayor."

"So, how long are you going to wait?"

"I'll give it another fifteen or twenty."

After she hung up, she watched a big black sedan cruise up to the curb. The car was so much like the one that had plagued them at the park—and at Caitlin's school—cold fear shot down her spine. Was it the same car? She should get out and go over...see who's driving. That was ridiculous. There had to be thousands of black cars in the city.

Still, she kept watching the car like an onlooker at the scene of an accident—she didn't want to look, but couldn't pull herself away. Then the passenger door opened.

And Alysa stepped out.

CHAPTER SEVEN

"HI, PHOEBE, IS LAURA around?" Jordan switched the phone to his other ear.

"No, but she should be back soon. Can I have her call you?"

"Sure." His disappointment because Laura wasn't home was greater than it should be.

"Does she have the number?"

"Yes, but I'll give you another one. If she calls within the next couple of hours, I'll be here." He gave Phoebe the number.

"It must be important. I can tell her what it is if you want."

It was important. To him. Still shaken about Rita Valdez's murder, he needed to talk to someone. No, that wasn't true. He wanted to talk to Laura. "It's not important, but thanks."

"It was nice having you here for dinner last week," Phoebe quickly injected before he could hang up. "We don't have dinner guests very often."

He shifted in the lounge chair. "Well, I'm flattered to be one of them. I don't get to spend the evening with a household of beautiful women very often, either."

"You'll have to come again."

He'd like that, too. But if Laura wanted him there, for dinner or anything else, she'd ask. "Thanks. Nice talking to you, Phoebe. And thanks for relaying my message," he said as a way to break off the conversation. Phoebe seemed like a nice person, but last week, she'd looked at him as if *he* was the main course.

He heard a slight hesitation in Phoebe's voice when she said goodbye. As comfortable as he was around most women, he wasn't around Phoebe. He didn't know why.

He sat there a few moments, watching the people on the TV screen mouth their words, as the set was on mute. Finally he took out Laura's cell phone number and stared at it. He could call and ask some questions about Kolnikov or DeMatta, or even her ex—and he would have to—sometime. But not tonight.

The truth was, he simply wanted to talk to her, get to know her better…. He hadn't felt that way about a woman for a long time.

She made him smile. He liked being with her. He liked her honesty. She was a strong person to do what she did every day. And she was just as strong in her refusal to give him any information. He hadn't been able to weasel more than a few tidbits out of her.

He couldn't help wondering what pushed her buttons. She was great with the teens in her care, and with her daughter—a little spitfire. He rested his head against the back of the chair. The kid had a streak of independence a mile wide. Laura was going to have her hands full in a few years. Maybe sooner.

The phone rang and he was immediately on alert. He hoped it wasn't dispatch. He didn't need another call out so soon after the last. "St. James."

He heard a click and then the dial tone. Odd. But at least it wasn't another homicide. People who thought cops were hardened to the stuff they saw every day were crazy. It all took its toll.

When he was on the job, he had to act, take care of business. There was no time to think about the victims or their families. No time to think about himself. But at night when he was alone, everything coalesced into one ugly nightmare. There weren't too many nights when he didn't wake up in a sweat. In a way, he envied his married friends. They had another world to escape to.

And tonight was even worse. He couldn't shake the thought that his visit to Rita Valdez may have led to her murder. The method, the timing of the killing, only a few hours after he'd been there, seemed more than coincidental.

The phone rang again, this time his cell. He glanced at the number but didn't recognize it.

"St. James."

"Hi."

He might not have recognized the number, but it didn't take a millisecond to recognize her sexy voice.

"Laura. I guess Phoebe gave you my message."

"Uh…no, she didn't. I called because I need to talk to you…can you meet me?"

"Anytime, anywhere. What's going on?"

"I saw the black car this afternoon. I've got a license number for you to check out, but I can't talk here."

"Okay. Where?"

She gave him the name of a café not too far from the shelter. "I've got a couple of things to do, so it'll take me about an hour to get there."

"Okay," he said. "It'll probably take me that long, too." As he hung up, Jordan's adrenaline was pumping. Where had she seen the car in order to get the license number? Quickly he changed into jeans and a black sweater, grabbed his leather jacket and headed for the garage.

Close to an hour later, he pulled up behind Laura's van, parked in front of a place called Java the Hut. He got out, and as he walked around the vehicle, he saw she was still in the driver's seat.

He knocked on the window and she jumped so high he thought she'd hit her head. "I didn't mean to scare you."

She didn't answer as he helped her out, and they went inside the café together. "I'll get the coffee," he said. "What's your preference?"

"A large vanilla no-fat latte."

He smiled. "That'll keep you awake all night."

"It's okay. I've got tour duty at ten."

Back at the table, he slid one cup to her and then sat across the table where he could see the door.

"Thanks." She clutched the cup in both hands. "I appreciate your coming so late."

"No problem."

She moistened her lips, which made him wonder, not for the first time, what it'd be like to kiss her. As far as he could tell, she wore only lip gloss, and her unadorned lashes were dark in contrast with her auburn hair.

"I saw the car and got the license number," she said without preamble.

"The same vehicle?"

"Yes."

"Are you sure?"

"Ninety-nine percent."

He leaned back in the booth. "There are lots of black cars out there."

"I know. Trust me on this." Her voice was a bit shaky.

"What's the number?"

She handed him a piece of paper.

"California?"

"I think so. I was too focused on the numbers."

"Did you notice the make?"

"A Cadillac, maybe. You saw it before, what do you think?"

"What I think doesn't matter. What matters is what you saw today." When she didn't answer, he continued, "Where did you see the vehicle?"

"Uh…at the mall near the school."

"Was it parked?"

"No, the car pulled up, someone got out and then he drove away."

"He? You saw the driver?"

"The windows were tinted, but I could see the driver was big, definitely male."

"What about the person who got out…male or female?"

"W-what difference does it make?"

"The more information I have the better."

She sighed heavily. "A girl got out of the car. A teenager." A second later she added, "I was so upset about seeing the car, I didn't get the best look."

"Are you okay now?"

She nodded. "It just shook me up."

That was obvious. And seeing her this way made him feel even more protective. "I'll get a DMV check tomorrow."

"Then what?"

"If I get a name, we'll run it through NCIC, the National Crime Information Center, and see what shows up."

"How long will it take?"

"Barring any problems, a few hours."

"I really appreciate this, Jordan."

He shrugged, smiling. "I'm here to serve. It's my job."

"Will you let me know what you find out?"

"Sure. I'll call as soon as I can." He wanted to keep her here, to talk about other things, personal things. "How's Caitlin?"

She hesitated, then said, "She's fine."

"Did the scooter stay together after I fixed it?"

"I didn't know it was broken."

"Well, it wasn't, not exactly."

"Oh, my." She rolled her eyes upward.

"Hey, it was my pleasure. She's a great kid."

"Well, thank you. I think so, too, though she can be difficult when she wants to be."

"Can't we all?"

She laughed. "Yes, I suppose."

Her laugh came from deep in her throat, natural and sexy. "You should do that more often."

"Do what?"

"Laugh. You have a nice laugh." He couldn't seem to take his eyes off her.

She fidgeted under his gaze, making him think he'd gotten too personal for her. He hoped not because he really wanted to get even more personal. "I had a tough day and laughter always takes the edge off," he added.

She took another sip, then licked the moisture from her lips. Her momentary self-consciousness seemed to slip away. "For what it's worth, I enjoy a good laugh, especially when *I've* had a tough day." She fiddled with her cup, turning it in circles. "I'm a good listener if you want to talk about it."

If only he could. If only he could tell her one of Anna Kolnikov's friends had been murdered—and that he might be responsible for her death. But what kind of confidence would she have in him then?

His phone rang. "Thanks," he said, pulling the cell from his pocket. "I appreciate the offer. Can I take a rain check on it?"

"Sure. Anytime I'm available."

He got up, answering the phone at the same time, then took a step away from the booth for privacy. "St. James here."

He heard heavy breathing. Then after a few seconds, a whining drone.

As he stood there, he heard another phone ringing. Looking over his shoulder, he saw Laura answering her cell phone. He moved closer to hear.

"Hello. This is Laura."

Her mouth turned down at the edges. "Hello?" she repeated. "Is someone there?" A second later, she disconnected.

Jordan sat across from her again. "Something important?"

She looked at him, puzzled. "No. It must've been a wrong number because whoever it was hung up."

Jordan's pulse rocketed.

"It's odd because I've had a couple other hang ups recently. I wonder if the black car and the calls are related?"

He clenched his cup then slugged down the rest of his drink. "Well, with this new information you gave me, we may soon find out." Two hang ups between them, only seconds apart. A coincidence? He didn't think so.

Someone knew they were together and wanted to send a message. Only Laura didn't know about his hang up, and it wouldn't be wise to tell her.

AFTER MEETING WITH Jordan, Laura picked up Phoebe and they did their stint on street duty. 10:00 p.m. to

2:00 a.m., since it was a Saturday night. They had no takers on their offer of a warm place to stay for the night, but managed to talk to quite a few teens and handed out cards with their hotline number.

At nearly two, Phoebe said, "Time to call it quits, don't you think?"

Laura sighed. "Yep. I'm heading home."

"So, how's it going with the detective?" Phoebe turned in the passenger seat to look at her.

She knew what Phoebe was getting at, and she wished she had a good answer. She couldn't deny she wanted to get to know Jordan better. She couldn't deny she was attracted to him. And she felt the same vibes coming from him. But even if she'd fantasized about him once or twice, he was a cop. She had to remember that, stamp it in the forefront of her mind. "He's checking on the black car for me."

Jordan St. James had pulled no punches regarding his feelings about Anna Kolnikov and those in her profession.

If only she could go back to the womb, start her life all over again. But she couldn't. And now she had too many secrets to ever share a life with anyone. The thought of never having a close relationship with a man—with Jordan—left her feeling hollow. And the more she wanted what she couldn't have, the larger the void inside.

"Great. But is there anything else? I get the feeling he likes you."

"No, there's nothing else. And I'm not in the market for a fling."

"You sure?"

"I'm sure."

"So, why don't I believe you?"

Laura laughed, and reaching the driveway to the shelter, she glanced at Phoebe. "Maybe because I'm still trying to convince myself. Damn. You know me too well."

After she parked, they both went inside. "Well, it's good to know…for two reasons. One, you're finally getting some sense, and two, I won't try for him myself."

Laura stopped. "My interest doesn't mean anything is going to happen."

"Does that mean he's fair game?" Phoebe perked up.

Laura didn't answer.

"Well?"

Even though she knew Phoebe was pushing her buttons, Laura felt suddenly and overwhelmingly proprietary. While Jordan wasn't exactly a close friend, she had to admit she wanted him to be. And she sure as hell didn't want to see him with Phoebe…or anyone else, for that matter. "It doesn't mean anything."

She shook her head as she started down the hall. What a liar she was. She wasn't only lying to Phoebe, she was lying to herself.

She wanted Jordan. She'd wanted him from the moment she'd laid eyes on him.

"Good night, Pheebs," she called, and, after checking on Caitlin, went into her bedroom, closed the door and flopped on the bed. She should be tired, but she wasn't. Jordan's face materialized in her mind and along with it, she felt intense longing. At that moment, she also felt the sting of her solitary future more than ever.

The night she'd left Eddie's and said nothing to the police about what Caitlin had seen, her fate had been sealed. She'd done it to protect her child. And to continue to protect her, she had to keep her silence. If she didn't…

A soul-deep fear gripped her every time she thought about it. So...she wouldn't think about it. She would keep her silence, no matter what.

She got up, undressed and went to bed. But just as she slipped under the covers, the phone rang. Her stomach lurched. Oh, God. *Not again.* Whoever it was wanted to terrorize her, and she wasn't going to give him the satisfaction. Finally, she snatched up the receiver. "If you think you're intimidating me, you're wrong. Whatever it is you want, you won't get it this way."

"You have no idea what I want." The voice was deep, obviously disguised.

Laura's heart stalled, but she knew she couldn't back down. "Then you'd better tell me."

"Stay away from the police."

Laura couldn't breathe. Her head started to throb. *The police?*

"Your daughter's life depends on it."

MARY BETH STOOD AT Jordan's desk, hands on her hips. "Here's the social worker's number on Rita Valdez's kid. She arranged the foster care."

"Thanks." He'd asked her to get the information because he was pressed for time, and Mary Beth had always volunteered to do things before, but this time he got the feeling she felt put out. Her long dark bangs hung half over her eyes, eclipsing her expression. "Sorry if it was any trouble. Is something wrong?"

"No." Mary Beth dropped into the chair next to him. "But I would like it if some of the extra things I do around here were appreciated more."

He hadn't been giving her his full attention, but he did now. Was that a reprimand? He grinned.

She clasped her hands in her lap and kept twisting

the ring on one finger. "What I mean is…if someone told the captain about the extra things I do, it might help."

"Sure. I'll be happy to let him know. What's it supposed to help with?"

"Me—getting a raise. And a good gig once I'm through the academy."

Jordan couldn't disguise his surprise. "You're going to take the test again?"

She nodded. "I've been working out. This time I'll pass the physical test. It's the only one I missed."

"Well, I'll be happy to let the captain know how indispensable you are."

She rose from the chair. "Thanks. I appreciate it."

As Mary Beth walked away, Jordan had a strange feeling something else was going on with the administrative assistant. He didn't doubt her abilities on the clerical end of the job, but he wasn't convinced about her emotional stability. She sure wasn't the kind of person he'd want covering his back in a dangerous situation.

"She having more problems?" Luke asked as he passed Mary Beth on his way in. He sat at his desk. "Take my advice. Don't get involved."

"I'm not. All she wanted was a little recognition to reach the captain. She does do a lot of our research and paperwork." Jordan felt as if someone was watching him and looked up to see Mary Beth staring his way. He turned his back.

"You got anything on the Valdez case?" Luke asked matter-of-factly while pulling out a blank report.

"Nothing except the number of the foster care agency so I can find the daughter and tell her about her mother." Jordan swallowed a wave of regret.

Luke was quiet for a moment, his blue eyes dark like coal. Then he went back to his papers.

Luke was probably remembering when the captain had knocked on his door, Jordan didn't know how Luke could continue to work in the field afterward. But his friend had been dogged about it, never once saying he couldn't do the job.

"I talked to Valdez yesterday," Jordan said. "She gave me some information that might help on the Kolnikov case."

Luke's head came up. "You saw her the same day she was killed?"

Jordan heard the implication in Luke's tone, that his visit might have something to do with Rita Valdez's murder. "Yeah. I'm wondering the same thing myself." He shook it off. Couldn't do his job if he was second-guessing himself. "The MO is strikingly similar to Anna Kolnikov's murder."

"Can I help?"

Jordan snorted a laugh. "You've got enough with the congressman, don't you think? Besides, Carlyle put Ralston on it with me."

"No shit." Luke glanced to Ralston's desk. The man wasn't there. "I don't trust him."

"Any particular reason?"

"Just the rumor mill. You've heard it."

Howie Ralston, a power-hungry snitch with an attitude, a guy who'd do anything to save his ass—even rat out his own partner. "Yeah. I heard. But I figure the captain has his reasons."

"Uh-huh," Luke said. "Take my advice. Watch your back."

"I always do," Jordan teased as his gaze slid to the DMV information on his computer.

What the…? The plate number Laura had given him was registered to a corporation. What the hell was the Belzar Corporation? Without an actual name, he couldn't get anything from NCIC or III, the Interstate Identification Index. Damn. He did a quick Web search. Nothing. He got up and went to Mary Beth's desk. "I'm going out, but I need a favor."

She raised an eyebrow.

"I'd really appreciate it if you would call the Corporation Commission and get the name of the president or owner of this company for me." He handed her the note he'd jotted down.

"I'm glad someone needs me."

"Thanks," he said, and headed for the door. First on his list, the social worker, then Rita Valdez's daughter and last, he'd go to Laura's to see if the name of the corporation was familiar to her—or her ex.

By the time he arrived at the foster care home, it was 10:00 a.m. Valdez's child wasn't exactly a child anymore. She was a sixteen-year-old with a grudge against the world. A girl who didn't give a damn about her mother and couldn't care less if she was dead or alive. He saw the attitude every day, and every day it made him wonder whether the job was worth the chunks sliced from his soul.

But he had to hold on to his beliefs that people were intrinsically good. Victims deserved justice, and bad guys deserved to go to jail. There was a whole lot of deeper stuff in between, but that's what it boiled down to.

Then, affirming his beliefs, the teen had stopped him on his way out to ask a question. As she stood there trying to get the words out, tears formed in her eyes and he realized her earlier bravado couldn't mask real emotion. The loss of a mother was tragic. Even though he'd never known his own mother, he felt the loss. Still had the never-ending questions.

"If you call the morgue, they'll let you see her. I can take you if you want."

She shook her head. "I can't."

"Well, let me know if you need help with anything." He handed her his card. On the way out he said, "You should be in school. Your mother would've wanted you to have an education."

He'd left feeling somewhat better. Someone cared about Rita Valdez. No one should die alone and without acknowledgment.

The next stop was Laura's. When he turned the corner and saw the van in the driveway at the shelter, his spirits lifted. He was anxious to see her...so what else was new? He'd felt that way since their second meeting.

Rose answered his knock but held the door only partway open. She didn't invite him in.

"Detective."

"Hello, Rose. Is Laura here? I'd like to talk to her."

The woman's dark eyes narrowed. "No, she's not. I—I don't know when she'll be back, either."

He peered inside. "Really. You mean she went away and didn't say when she'd be back?" That was hard to believe.

"Yes. She said it would be a while."

"What about Cait?"

"She took her along."

"Did she say where she was going?"

"No."

He put his hand on the door to make sure she didn't shut it. "How about a phone number? It's important."

Rose shrugged. "I'm sorry. I can't help you. I really

don't know where she went. She said she couldn't tell me because she didn't want any trouble for the shelter."

Jordan's blood ran cold. "What kind of trouble?"

"She didn't say."

"What about the van? Doesn't she usually drive the van?"

As if to solidify her position, Rose squared her shoulders. "We need the van here, so she…made other arrangements."

The woman was lying. He knew it by the way she wouldn't look him in the eyes, the crossed arms. Anger tensed his jaw. He didn't like what he was hearing. Laura wouldn't just leave the shelter on a whim and not tell anyone where she was going or when she'd return.

Something was wrong. He felt it in his gut. "I repeat, it's extremely important."

"I have to respect Laura's wishes." And then Rose shut the door.

"Dammit." He slammed the butt of his hand against the door frame, then stomped to his vehicle. As he reached the car he heard someone call his name. He turned to see one of the girls waving at him from the side door. It was the blonde, the fifteen-year-old who looked twenty. Alysa. He loped across the grass.

"I think I know where she went, Mr. St. James." She bit her lower lip. "I could get in trouble for saying anything."

"Where'd she go?" Jordan gritted his teeth.

"I don't know, but I heard her on the phone to Amtrak. She sounded scared about something."

"The train station? How would she get there?"

"She got a ride."

"How long ago?"

"A half hour, maybe."

"Can you tell me why she left?"

The girl shook her head, and Jordan didn't have time to pry out more information. He might not know Laura very well, but he knew her enough to know she wouldn't leave the shelter for any length of time unless it was urgent. He mumbled his thanks and took off.

On the freeway, he jammed the accelerator to the floor, considered clipping on the ball and running hot through traffic, but decided against it. Why announce his arrival? If she didn't want him to know where she was going, she'd likely try to avoid him.

A half hour later, he pulled into the parking lot at the Gateway Center, a transit hub for bus passengers and riders of Amtrak and local commuter trains. It was raining again, and he wished he'd brought an overcoat. He dashed inside, stopping in the entry to scan for Laura's auburn hair and a seven-year-old girl with strawberry curls. Small boutiques, cafés and souvenir shops lined the perimeter. Several freestanding kiosks and generous clusters of vegetation prevented a clear view. The place was unusually crowded for a non-holiday weekend. He scanned the room several times, then glanced toward the East Portal to the railroad station, and to the elevator shaft with a waterfall twisting around it.

If she was here, she wasn't anywhere he could see. But then she could be in a shop or café or already on a train. He started toward the station portal scanning inside each store on the way. At Starbucks he saw a woman with a child standing at the cashier, and though their backs were toward him, he recognized Laura. She'd tucked her hair under a funky black hat and wore a raincoat that looked two sizes too big for her.

Cait was in a yellow rain parka, wearing her insepara-
ble tennis shoes with their blinking lights. Laura
turned, her hat pulled down so her face was half
covered. What was she doing? And why the corny
costume?

He waited outside the door until they came out.

They both saw him immediately.

"Jordan," Cait said. "What're you doing here?"

"Hey, kiddo." He smiled. "I'm here on business. I
didn't expect to run into my two favorite people."

A humongous smile spread across Cait's face.

"I didn't expect to run into anyone, either," Laura
said pointedly, anger flashing in her eyes. She glanced
at Cait and back to him.

He understood…not in front of the child.

"I need to talk to you," he said, anyway.

She pursed her lips, then looked at Cait. "Sweetie,
can you sit on the bench over there for a couple of
minutes? Jordan and I have something private to
discuss."

The child frowned and crossed her arms.

"For just a minute. Please."

Cait stomped off, sitting where they could see her
but not close enough to hear.

"What are you doing here?" Laura spat out.

"I was worried about you."

"Well, there's nothing to worry about."

"I don't believe you."

She crossed her arms just like her daughter.

"I can't help what you believe or don't believe. I
wish to be left alone, and I'd appreciate it if you'd
respect my wishes." She turned, started to walk toward
Cait.

He pulled her back by the shoulder. "I don't think

it's wise. If something is so wrong that you need to run away and hide, then you're making the wrong choice."

"We're taking a vacation, going to my father's. That's all."

Dammit. She was stubborn. "If I found you this easily, so can someone else. Think about it. A ticket is easily traceable, especially if you're going to a relative's."

Laura looked at Cait, chewed on her bottom lip.

"What are you afraid of? Is it the stalker?" He was only guessing, proposing scenarios to see if she reacted. All he really knew is that she was leaving town and had to have a reason. And it wasn't to visit relatives.

Indecision warred in her eyes. Finally she let out a long breath. "All I want is to keep Caitlin out of harm's way."

"Is she in danger?"

Her eyes darkened and she didn't have to say a word for him to know the answer. Obviously she believed even telling him might make it worse. "It's okay," he said softly, gently taking her hand. "I can help. If you'll let me."

She stared at him. "How? How can you help?"

"I know a place where you'll be safe."

Her jaw tensed. "Eddie was supposed to be safe."

"This is different. It's not a department operation. This is personal. No one will know. I promise."

She looked at Cait again before she said, "Okay. What should we do?"

He drew her to the side of the nearby kiosk where they were partially hidden but could still see Caitlin. "Have you bought a ticket yet?"

She shook her head.

"I want you to buy a ticket to someplace far from

here. Then go to the ladies' room down the hall from the ticket counter. But instead of going inside, go a few steps farther and take a quick left. The hallway leads to an exit, a loading zone. Go outside immediately and I'll be there to pick you up."

She looked hesitant. "Do *you* think I'm being followed?"

"It's a precaution. If anyone is watching, they won't follow close enough to know you didn't go into the bathroom. Don't worry."

He could tell from her pinched expression she wasn't used to someone else making the decisions, but finally she agreed.

Ten minutes later he was drumming his fingers on his steering wheel, waiting in the loading zone. No sign of Laura. Where the hell was she?

Another ten minutes and she still hadn't shown. He fidgeted, couldn't sit still. He should go look for her, but he couldn't get back inside from here, and if she was on her way, or coming from a different direction, he'd miss her—and then what?

Another thought smacked him between the eyes. Had she ditched him? Had she only agreed to do as he said to appease him—when she'd had no intention of doing what he wanted? He banged the steering wheel. No, she wouldn't. She wouldn't lie and send him on a wild-goose chase. He trusted her enough to know she wouldn't do that.

He trusted her. The thought came as a surprise…and made him realize what he'd said to her was true. This was personal. He wasn't there because he was on a case, he was there because he cared about her. And Cait.

And the longer he waited the worse he felt. He pulled at the collar of his shirt. His nerves felt like jumping beans under his skin. Damn. He should've stayed with her. Should've made her come with him instead of this stupid decoy maneuver. If something happened…he'd never forgive himself.

CHAPTER EIGHT

LAURA JERKED CAIT TO the side, pressing the child flat against the wall.

They'd just turned the corner after passing the restroom and she thought she saw a man's shadow loom from behind. Was someone following them? That man in the ticket line had looked strangely at her…out of curiosity or was it something else?

She had to admit, though, she probably did look weird in a hat half covering her face and a Dick Tracy trench coat. For all she knew, she *was* overreacting. She'd panicked. But she couldn't take any chances when it came to Cait's welfare.

"Okay, let's hustle." She grabbed Caitlin's hand and pulled her along, clinging to the wall in the loading area as they headed for the door. God, she hoped Jordan was waiting.

At the door, she grabbed the handle…then noticed the padlock. *Damn.*

"Can I help you?" The deep voice came from the shadows behind some stacked boxes on her left.

A man approached them. He was dirty and unshaven.

Her heart hammering against her ribs, Laura tightened her grip on Caitlin's hand. "I—we're just going outside for some air. I'm feeling sick."

"There's a bathroom on the other side." His voice was gruff, his tone suspicious.

"No…I really need some air." She reached a hand to cover her mouth. "Do you know if there's another door? This one is locked."

He stepped closer, his hand jutted out.

Laura flinched and pulled Caitlin behind her, before she realized the man had grabbed the lock and released it.

"Stupid lock doesn't work," he said. "Be careful on the stairs out there."

He was walking away before she managed a strangled "Thank you." Still holding Caitlin's hand, she thrust open the door.

Rain slashed across her face, but when she saw Jordan's car, she literally sighed with relief. She helped Cait down the wet metal steps and as they reached the bottom, the back door to the SUV flew open.

"Get in and duck down," Jordan said.

Laura shoved their duffel bags in first. The next thing she knew, they were moving.

"Why are we ducking down?" Cait grumbled.

"It…it's a game, honey."

"What kind of game? I don't have enough room with this thing in the way."

"Just a few more minutes," Jordan said. "Then I'll put the luggage in the back and you can get comfortable."

"I still want to know what kind of game we're playing."

"Remember when I said we're going on a vacation to visit Grampa?" Laura said.

"Uh-huh."

"Well, we're really going someplace else. It's a

surprise and Jordan doesn't want us to see which way we're going because it could ruin the surprise."

"I like surprises. But I wanted to see Grampa, too."

Laura cringed. The only reason she saw her father at all was for Cait. He was the only family she and Cait had. "We will, sweetheart. Just not now."

With her cheek pressed against the suitcase, Laura felt the vibration of the engine, like a soothing massage, and her tension eased. Jordan was taking them to a place where no one could find them. *And then what?*

She hadn't thought that far ahead—she'd thought only about getting Cait to safety and buying herself time to think of what to do.

"Is Jordan going to stay with us?"

"No," Jordan answered for Laura. "I'd like to, but I'll have to go back to work."

Laura felt the car swerve, speed up, turn another corner and then come to a slow stop. She heard a noise outside, like metal scraping metal. Then the car moved slowly, stopped, and she heard the grinding sound again.

"You can get up now."

Laura lifted her head.

"Where are we?" Cait asked beside her.

"We're in an airplane hangar." Jordan opened his door and a man wearing a baseball hat walked up. "Hey, Har, how's it going?"

Jordan got out of the car, leaving his door open. The two men shook hands and talked under their breath. When they finished, Jordan transferred the bags to the back of the SUV.

While he was busy, Laura surveyed their surroundings. They were indeed in an airplane hangar, and the place was huge. Two small private planes took up most of the space next to them. "This is Harry," Jordan said. "The planes belong to him. Harry, Laura and Cait."

Harry tipped his hat. "Nice to meet you, ladies."

"Wow!" Cait said. "Are we going to fly somewhere?"

Jordan laughed. "Not today, kiddo. I thought it was a good place to switch the luggage around without getting wet."

"Oh." She slumped back, disappointed. "I never went on a plane before. It would be fun to fly someplace."

"It sure would," Jordan said. "But it's raining and we have other plans. Maybe another time I can get Harry to take you up."

Laura got out, pulled off her trench coat and tossed it into the back along with the luggage. Jordan and Harry stood off to the side, deep in conversation. The other man was shorter and stockier than Jordan, his hair darker, his features coarser, but handsome nonetheless. "Give me your raincoat, Cait. You won't need it in the car."

Taking the coat, Laura went to put it in the back of the vehicle. Apparently finished talking, Jordan came up beside her. "So, Jordan," she said. "Can you tell us now where we're going?"

He grinned. "It's a surprise. I'll tell you once we're out of the city." He pulled a pillow and an afghan from the back and tossed them to Cait.

Jordan motioned for Laura to sit in the passenger seat up front, got in himself and started the engine.

The other man waved and said, "I'll wait to hear from you." Then he walked to the opposite side of the hangar and shoved open first one side of the heavy door on rollers and then the other.

Signaling to the man, Jordan gunned the engine and they were off. "You okay back there?"

"Yeah. But I'd be better if I had my CD player."

Laura picked up her backpack, which also served as her purse, pulled out Cait's CD player and, smiling, held it up.

"You brought it," Cait exclaimed. "You're the best mom ever."

"Oh, sure. You got what you want and now I'm wonderful," Laura teased.

Laura felt warm inside even though the compliment was practically purchased. From the moment she'd known she was pregnant, her goal was to be the kind of mother she'd never had.

Except now...last night...everything had fallen apart and she didn't know how to fix it.

They drove for an hour in silence, and with Jordan continually glancing in the rearview mirror. Cait, headset on, hummed along with the music on her CD. Laura checked the highway signs. They were heading east toward San Bernardino. And when they were definitely out of the city, she asked, "Can you tell me now where we're going?"

"A cabin not too far from Bear Lake. It belongs to...some friends. It'll be perfectly safe."

Safe. It was true, no one would expect her to be with him going anywhere, and no one could possibly imagine she'd be at his friend's place. "Bear Lake. That's in the mountains, isn't it?"

"The San Bernardino Forest, to be exact. You'll be comfortable there."

"Your friends won't mind if Cait and I stay there?"

"No. Not at all. I have carte blanche...and they're out of the country at the moment. It's okay. Trust me."

She did, she realized, or she wouldn't be here. He gave her a sense of security that all would be well. How ironic. Jordan was a threat and yet she felt safe with him. But getting Cait out of town was only part of the solution—an immediate fix to a much bigger problem. "Do you think the roads will be okay? I heard there's snow in the mountains."

"I checked the weather. We're good." He turned briefly to look at her. "It would be much easier if you told me what this is all about. I could help."

She closed her eyes and felt the burn of the last few sleepless nights behind her lids. "I wish I could, but I need time to think." To make a plan. God knew what the plan would be.

"Okay. I can understand needing time."

She liked that he didn't probe. Maybe he knew all it would do was alienate her, and it seemed he didn't want to do that. So what was he getting out of helping her? She'd answered his questions already. They'd had dinner, but the dinner was more Cait's doing than anything. It wasn't social. His helping her now was personal...so he'd said. Or did he suspect she knew more about his case than she was telling? Did he think that because he helped her she'd spill her guts? "What's in this for you?"

His head jerked to the side. "What do you mean?"

The sharpness in his tone took her aback.

"Do you think I have some ulterior motive?" he insisted.

"Well, taking all this time to help me must be inconveniencing you. You have a job...a social life."

He frowned. "It's not an inconvenience. I called the station. They know I'm out. What's in it for me is knowing you and Cait will be safe."

She felt a tightness in her chest. Was it true? Did he really care?

He looked at her again. "And you will be, so quit worrying."

"Aye, aye, captain." She couldn't help smiling. Noticing the humming had stopped, she glanced back and saw Cait had fallen asleep.

"So, tell me," she said to change the subject. "How did you get into law enforcement? Was it something you always wanted to do?"

He snorted. "No. And it certainly wasn't what my parents wanted. As an undergrad, I couldn't decide between business or law school. I took lots of law classes and eventually the law won."

"You went to law school? A detective with a law degree?"

"No, I got the MBA." He adjusted the air vent on the dash. "Can't hurt to have a backup. Not to mention it's what my parents wanted and paid for."

She nodded as if understanding, but she didn't. It had taken her so many years and several student loans to get her master's. How could he brush it off so lightly?

"So, you got the MBA and then decided to be a cop?"

"Exactly."

"Do you think you made the right choice?"

"Most of the time I can't imagine doing anything else. But there are times…"

"There are times when the job takes a toll?"

"Ah, the psychologist is coming out." He gave her a sideways glance. "Trying to find out my innermost secrets?"

She felt heat rush to her cheeks. He was right on there. She wanted to know all about him. "Of course. It's what I do. Seriously, though, doesn't it…all the bad stuff you see…doesn't it affect you?"

His grip tightened on the wheel. He expelled a long

breath. "Sure. But I have to let it go or I couldn't do my job. It's just one more job hazard."

His light tone belied the emotion in his face. She'd bet the job affected him far more than he let on. "And the rewards?"

"Knowing I've helped get the bad guys off the streets is a pretty good reward," he said without hesitation. "Knowing I've put a murderer or a rapist or child molester in jail, so a victim's family can find closure of some kind—and feeling justice has been done, even for the people no one cares about—those things make it worthwhile."

She heard the conviction in his voice and she wondered if Anna Kolnikov was one of the people he meant. Anna was someone the world would rather forget.

"But your job isn't too different," he said. "Seeing so many kids throwing their lives away, doesn't it affect you? Shock you?"

The answer was easy, but not easy to admit. Yes, she hated to see the children on the streets, hated to see what that kind of life did to them. But it wasn't a shock. "Sure, it affects me. But like you, I have to put it away or I couldn't do my job."

"Are we there yet?" Cait's sleepy voice came from the back seat.

Laura was glad for the reprieve.

"Not too long," Jordan said.

"How long?"

"About the length of a CD," he answered.

Laura liked how matter-of-fact Jordan was with Cait. So easy, as if he'd had a lot experience with children. He'd said he wasn't married, he didn't have a family.

Her thoughts drifted and she wondered what being married to Jordan might be like.

"We'll make a rest stop soon. Pick up some supplies."

"All right," Cait said, and clamped on the headphones again.

"You seem so relaxed with Cait," Laura said. "One would think you had a brood of your own."

He laughed. "I like kids a lot—as long as they're someone else's. My way of life wouldn't be good for anyone, a wife or kids."

"Really. Lots of cops have families. It can't be all bad."

"True. But it's tough on everyone involved. Marriage is hard enough without all the extra stress."

His response puzzled her. What would make him so adamant? "Bad experience?"

His frown told her she was analyzing him again. But after a moment, he said, "More than one."

Well, that rid her of any little fantasy she'd entertained.

"So, how about you? How come you've never married again?"

Oh, boy. She'd asked for that one and now she was sorry she had. She shrugged. "It's never come up."

"Really?"

"Really."

"You do date, don't you?"

Laura's heart pounded. She hadn't dated since the divorce, but she sure as hell wasn't going to admit to it. She wasn't that stupid. "Occasionally."

"I see mountains," Cait piped up. "And snow!"

Laura had been so absorbed, she hadn't even noticed the scenery. "I see them, too," she said.

"There'll probably be lots of snow where we're going," Jordan added.

"I never saw snow before. It's so beautiful. It's so

white. Like clouds on the ground. Is it soft? Can I make a snowman?"

Laura smiled. Cait hadn't been this excited in a long time. "It would be fun, wouldn't it? But I'm afraid we don't have warm-enough clothes, sweetie. And I don't know how long we're going to be here, either."

"No problem," Jordan injected. "There are warm jackets at the cabin. Maybe even some boots. And you can stay as long as you want."

"Cool!" Cait bounced up and down on the seat, her excitement gaining momentum.

Despite the reason they were going away, Laura felt excited herself. Except for taking Cait on short trips to see her grandfather, she and Cait had never gone anywhere. The thought brought with it an awareness of what a narrow life they'd been leading. But then, taking vacations took money. A rare commodity in her household. They had their fun in other ways.

"I see some cabins!" Cait shrieked.

"Yep. We're coming into the town of Big Bear. I'm going to gas up and get a few things at the grocery store."

When they finished in town, they headed up the mountain going north, or at least Laura thought it was north. It was hard to tell since the road twisted and turned and, after getting off the main road, they took one small road after another.

Giant snowflakes fell on the windshield, melting as they hit. As they drove on, the drifts at the edges of the road grew higher and the roads, clear at one point, were now packed solid with snow. Tall pines lined the narrowing road, their boughs sloping downward with the weight of the wet snow.

At the end of the road, if it could even be called a

road anymore, a log cabin loomed. Only it didn't look like a cabin at all. The place was huge and more resembled a ski resort.

"This is it," Jordan said, pulling up to a four-car garage.

"It's amazing. Your friend must be very wealthy."

Jordan opened the door and got out. "More money than any one person should have. His family uses the place for business entertaining as well as pleasure. Wait here while I open things up. I have to get the garage door from the inside."

Laura felt the bite of fresh, crisp air on her face before he shut the door.

"This is way cool," Cait said. "I'm going to make a snowman right away."

Laura turned. "Don't get ahead of yourself. We have to get settled first and I don't want you bugging Jordan until we are. Okay?"

Cait's bottom lip protruded.

After what seemed an extra-long time, more time than necessary to simply open a door, it slid upward. Two snowmobiles and a huge snowblower occupied one side of the garage. A small pickup truck was parked in the last space beside an array of boxes piled in the corner.

After Jordan pulled inside and they gathered the luggage, they entered the cabin through what seemed to be a coatroom. Puffy down-filled jackets and parkas hung on one side and several pairs of boots were set neatly in square shelves along the wall below. As they moved into the kitchen, Laura's mouth fell open.

"Wow!" Cait said.

Exposed beams slanted across the lofted ceiling, black granite countertops, pine cabinets, shiny oak floors and stainless-steel appliances all said the owner had a taste for nothing but the best. The epitome of rustic elegance.

"The guest bedrooms are all upstairs." Jordan gestured in another direction. "Come on. I'll show you up." He took the luggage and headed through a huge room past a slate fireplace that soared two stories high.

A rustic wood dining table at least ten feet long sat at one end of the large room, a giant chandelier made of deer antlers suspended over it. The smell of leather permeated the air.

"It's cool in here right now," Jordan said. "But I've turned up the heat and it'll be warm soon enough."

They walked upstairs through a loft with a television set and a pool table. "Mom, I can see all the way downstairs," Cait said.

"It's beautiful."

"There are bedrooms on either side." Jordan shifted one of the duffel bags to his shoulder. "But let's go this way. I think Cait will like the last bedroom the best."

When they entered, Cait's eyes enlarged like moons. "Awesome!"

The room was all pink and white and ruffled, with Barbie dolls prominently displayed on shelves extending from floor to ceiling on one wall.

"I never saw so many Barbie dolls. They're even on the bedspread. Whose room is this?"

"It's a guest room, just like I said. Decorated especially for young ladies."

Jordan seemed to know an awful lot about the place. "I guess you come here often?"

He cleared his throat. "I used to. But not so much

anymore. My friends are gone a lot and it's not the same without company."

Was that a note of wistfulness in his voice?

"Cait, why don't you get settled in, and I'll take your mom to her room."

He and Laura walked back down the hall, stopping at another room. "This okay? If not, there are others."

"How could it not be okay?" The room, bedspread and curtains were all ivory with warm golds as accents, complemented by rich dark furniture. A mountain of fluffy pillows at the head of the bed covered the embroidered spread. "To quote Cait, it's awesome!"

He set her duffel bag on a wood chest at the end of the huge sleigh bed and then sat next to it. He motioned for her to sit, too. She took the end of the bed.

Looking at her, his expression turned serious. "I know you need to get settled, and I know you need time to think, but at some point, we should talk."

She picked at the embroidery on the bedspread. "Yes, I know." But she didn't know what she was going to say. As far as Jordan knew, her only worry was the stalker, and while she was worried about him, it wasn't the whole story. But she couldn't tell him the rest. She couldn't tell him she'd received threatening phone calls, that someone had sneaked into her house and destroyed Cait's things. She couldn't tell him she was worried that somehow Frank DeMatta had found out her secret—and that hanging out with Jordan might even be the cause of her recent problems. "I need time to come up with a plan."

Jordan shifted on the bench. The worry in her eyes made him want to hold her, protect her. He'd hoped being out of the city and in a secure environment would give her the confidence she needed to tell him what was really wrong. But if she needed time to feel comfortable enough to trust him, he'd give it to her.

A sharp jab of conscience pierced his detective's veneer. She already trusted him somewhat or she wouldn't be there. But his own motives were a bit murky. First and foremost, he wanted to protect her and Cait. But he couldn't deny he also hoped to get information from Laura. The thought made him feel like a creep.

"I agree. You need a plan. Because no matter how protected you are here, there are other considerations. How long do you think you'll stay?"

"I told the school Cait would be out two weeks when I called about getting her homework. The shelter is fine with Rose and Phoebe holding down the fort for a while. If I get worried about them, I can always call. And they have my cell phone number. Is that too long to stay here?"

"No, of course not."

She smiled and seemed to relax. Jordan knew they had issues to discuss, but watching her talk, he had difficulty focusing on anything but her amazing eyes. From the first day he'd met her, he'd been entranced by those eyes. Though right now he had to admit her mouth was just as intriguing. He felt a pull toward her, an urge to kiss her. Instead he said, "I hope your cell phone works better than mine does. This place is right between the mountains and sometimes my phone works and sometimes it doesn't. When the weather's bad, you can forget it. I had to call the station from the store where we stopped."

"Well, good. At least there's an option if I need to call someone." She thought for a moment. "But if you're gone, how would I get there?"

"Do you know how to drive a snowmobile? It's the alternate mode of transportation up here—along with cross-country skis."

"I'm a quick study. It can't be all that difficult."

He laughed, enjoying her self-confidence. "It's not. But the keys to the pickup are here if there's an emergency. And I'll show you how to operate the snowmobile before I go…in case you want to try it out."

"So, when *are* you leaving?" she asked.

"The roads are treacherous at night, so I'll have to wait until morning. There's a security system you can activate whether you're inside or out. The video monitor will activate instantly if there's a break-in and automatically alert the police. I'll show you how to use that, too. Then I'll come back in a day or so."

"We'll be fine."

"Good. Why don't you get settled while I bring in the groceries and put them away. I don't know about the two of you, but I'm starving."

"Can we make snowmen now?" Cait stood at the doorway.

Jordan looked at Laura.

"In a bit, sweetie. We have to unpack and have something to eat first."

"But then it'll be too dark!"

"Not to worry," Jordan said. "We— Uh…there are lots of outside lights, so no matter how dark it is, it'll seem just like daytime."

Cait's smile was huge as her gaze circled the room. "Mom, your bedroom rocks! Where's your room, Jordan?"

"I'm sleeping downstairs." But he knew where he'd rather be sleeping. The thought didn't come as a surprise. He'd been feeling that way for a while now.

Feeling things he knew could come to no good. "You two have the upstairs all to yourself."

Cait spun around, arms spread as if she were a ballet dancer. "I feel like a princess."

Jordan smiled. "You look like a princess, kiddo. Except you're even prettier."

CHAPTER NINE

"I DON'T KNOW HOW TO MAKE a snowman," Cait explained once they were outside.

For dinner, they'd had the pizza Jordan bought at the store in Big Bear, which Laura had warmed in the oven. By the time dinner was over, and with both the heat and the oven on, the place was toasty warm. She'd almost hated to go outside.

"Quite frankly, I've never made one before, either," Laura admitted. She had to laugh at how bundled up Cait was. They couldn't find a jacket her size and the blue parka she'd picked out came down to her knees. To Cait's delight, they'd found a small pair of women's boots on the shelf, and they were only a little too big, she'd said.

"It's easy as pie," Jordan said, grabbing a handful of snow. "First you make a snowball. Actually, you'll need three snowballs."

"We can each do one." Cait's voice echoed in the crisp mountain air. She held her mouth open to catch the light flakes of snow, which seemed to be falling more rapidly now.

"Sure, I'm game," Laura said, scooping up a handful.

"Okay, once you've made a hard-packed snowball, you start rolling it through the snow, stopping once in a while to pat it down. We'll need a large one for the bottom, medium for the middle and a smaller one for the head."

"Like Frosty the Snowman," Cait added.

"Yes." Jordan laughed. "Just like Frosty."

Soon they were all concentrating on their own part of the snowman, rolling and pressing and patting as they went along to make perfect balls. As Laura finished the middle section, she stood up to show everyone…and a glob of snow hit her on the side of her face. She sputtered and turned to Cait. "Did you just throw a snowball at your mother?" she said indignantly.

Cait backed away, giggling like crazy. "I never threw a snowball before and I missed."

Practically before Cait finished her sentence, Laura felt another splat against her back. She turned to see Jordan egging Cait on. "Well, that does it," she said, and scooped up a handful of snow, packing it into a hard ball. Within seconds a flurry of snowballs hailed around her and she was in the midst of a full-on snowball fight. The missiles flew, one after the other, pelting her time and again until her jacket was white with ice.

She'd managed a few well-placed hits herself, but finally Laura crumpled to her knees, exhausted. "I give up. I give up." She fell back in the snow and stretched out her arms. "I'm going to make a snow angel instead."

Cait dropped to her knees next to her. "Me, too."

Standing above her, Jordan tossed one last snowball from hand to hand. "Don't you dare," she said firmly, but couldn't hold back her laughter. "Oh, I'm so out of breath. Either I'm way out of condition, or that was a lot of work."

"It was lots of fun," Cait countered.

"It's the altitude." Jordan sat in the snow next to her. "If you're not used to it, you can get altitude sickness. Be sure to drink lots of water."

"But we didn't finish the snowman," Cait said.

Jordan tossed his snowball to her. "Let's get busy, then."

Two hours later, Laura had changed into a sweat suit, tucked Cait into bed and watched her drop off to sleep immediately. Playing in the snow was more exercise than either of them had had in ages.

Pulling the door ajar, Laura felt a sense of peace. She couldn't remember when she'd had so much fun. It was good to forget about her problems, and it even felt good to forget about the shelter for a while.

But forgetting didn't make her problems go away. She had to figure a way out of this mess she'd gotten them into. She went downstairs, and halfway down, she saw Jordan kneeling in front of the huge fireplace, coaxing a few flames into a blaze. He'd changed clothes, too, probably into one of his friend's shirts and pants since he hadn't brought anything with him.

He turned as she descended the last step.

"Hey," he said.

"Hi."

"I thought I wore you out."

She walked over to him and stood with one hand on the mantel. "What…you think I'm a wimp?"

He smiled. "Not a chance."

"All the fresh air did take its toll on Cait, though. She's already asleep."

"Too bad. I thought some cocoa by the fire would be fun."

Cocoa by the fire. Laura didn't know what to say.

This was a Jordan she hadn't seen before. The take-charge guy had a softer side. Playful, too. "I'm sure she would've liked that. Maybe tomorrow."

"Well, no reason we can't do it, anyway—unless you'd like something stronger."

"Actually, I would love something stronger." She rarely had the opportunity at the shelter since she was gone several nights on street watch, and when she wasn't, she had to be a good role model for the girls.

"Okay." He got to his feet. "What's your preference?"

"Did you buy something at the store?"

"No. There's a well-stocked bar here. A wine cellar, too. Well, it's not really a cellar, just a small room."

He was awfully free with his friend's property, but then, if it was okay with his friends that she was staying here, she guessed it must be okay if he drank their liquor. "A glass of wine would be great."

"Come with me, you can pick out what you'd like."

Together they went into the kitchen to a small stairway—three steps—leading down to a rustic, hand-carved door that looked as if it was direct from Tuscany. "The wine room," he said, and gave the door a shove.

The room was a small square closet with shelves on three sides, all filled with bottles. The space was so close, she felt the heat of Jordan's body, smelled his cologne. An earthy all-male scent that made her pulse thrum. "I've never seen anything like this before."

"You've never seen a wine cellar?"

"Not in person…or in someone's home." The only wine storage she'd seen was for her mother's empty bottles—strewn around their trailer and overflowing the trash can outside.

"How about a nice merlot?" He held up a bottle.

"Sure."

They went back into the kitchen where he uncorked the wine and poured some into two delicate glasses with wafer-thin stems. He handed one to her, then took her other hand and drew her back into the living room in front of the now crackling blaze. Standing only inches apart, he raised a glass. "Peace."

She raised her glass to his. "Peace and happiness."

As they stood there in the firelight, his steel-gray eyes seemed to shimmer. His gaze locked with hers, so intense she felt as if he could see directly into her soul. God, she hoped not. He wouldn't like what he saw.

She shifted her stance, took a sip of wine and felt the rich liquid slide slowly down her throat, heating her from the inside out. As if her insides weren't heated enough. "Mmm. That's good."

"It is, isn't it."

His suggestive tone said he wasn't talking about the wine. Desire stirred low in her stomach. She ran her tongue across her lips, savoring the dry wine.

"Come on." He tugged her hand. "Let's sit." He grabbed two pillows off the couch and tossed them on the floor.

She had the oddest feeling he was seducing her. But then she wasn't sure she'd recognize seduction if it bonked her on the head.

He seemed so relaxed, as if having wine in front of a blazing fire was something he was used to doing all the time. Perhaps he was. And perhaps *she* was letting her imagination, her wishful thinking, get out of hand. Four years of celibacy might do that to a person.

But just because she hadn't dated for a while didn't

mean Jordan hadn't. He probably had women all over the Valley.

She sat next to him all the same.

"I've forgotten how nice it is up here in the winter." He leaned back on one elbow.

She plumped the pillow behind her and nestled into it. "I'll bet it's nice in the summer, too. I love the smell of pine."

He was still watching her, she realized, studying her.

"What else do you love? What are your passions?"

The question gave her pause. She hadn't thought about herself for a long time. She stretched out facing him, her weight on one elbow, too. "Lots of things. Cait, for one. My friends. Helping teens…the ocean, walking on the beach, music, dancing…" She raised her glass to her lips and smiled. "A glass of good wine."

He laughed. "One of my favorites, too. When was the last time you went dancing?"

She looked away. "Too long, I think." She wasn't going to admit the only dancing she'd done lately was with Cait or the girls at the shelter when they cut loose. On the other hand, they kept her on top of the latest dance crazes and she was pretty good at most of them.

"Okay. It's your turn. What are *your* passions?"

He grinned and, keeping his gaze on hers, said, "I love being in the moment. And sitting by a great fire with a beautiful woman is about as in the moment as it gets."

Her heartbeat quickened. He *was* coming on to her. Feeling the heat from both the fire and the inferno suddenly blazing inside her, she took another sip of wine. It didn't help. In fact, it had been so long since she'd had a glass of wine, it made her woozy. "Good," she finally managed to say. "That way you don't waste a lot of time living in the past or looking to a future that's uncertain at best."

His brows arched and he looked puzzled, as if he was still trying to figure out what to make of her.

Okay. That was too serious. "I'm sorry. I'm not used to drinking wine. It makes me too…moody and unpredictable."

He reached over and trailed a finger down her cheek, then lifted her chin so her eyes met his. "I like unpredictable. I like you."

Time suddenly stopped. His lips met hers, soft and warm and tasting of wine. It was a quick kiss, only a few seconds long. She touched her mouth with her fingertips. "What was that for?" she said, her voice almost a whisper.

His pupils were dilated, making his eyes seem charcoal instead of gray. "Because I've wanted to do that ever since I met you."

She blinked. Her heart raced. On impulse, she leaned forward and kissed him, only she made it longer, deeper—more urgent. And this time, they shared the kiss, passions suddenly unleashed. He wrapped his arms around her and she melted into him, need engulfing her. He traced her teeth with his tongue, she nipped his bottom lip. It had been so long…so long since she'd felt a man's strong arms, so long since she'd felt…desired.

When they moved apart, both breathless, she said, "I've wanted to do *that* for a while, too."

They fell back, smiling, both a bit befuddled. Well, at least she was. What *was* she thinking?

After a moment, he said, "Well, now that we have that out of the way, why don't you tell me more about yourself?"

Her guard came up. But her passion—the need—still pulsed inside. She felt as if the curtain had fallen at the end of a great play—and she didn't want it to end. She wanted more. So much more.

What would it hurt to enjoy herself for once?

"My parents divorced when I was two. I grew up in a trailer park in Modesto with my mother. I never knew my father until I went to live with him in Sacramento when I was sixteen. I stayed there for two years until I graduated high school, and then I moved out and went to USC." She shrugged. "You know the rest."

"Any sisters and brothers?"

She shook her head. *Not that she knew of.* "No, and it's a good thing. My mother wasn't the nurturing type. We weren't very close."

"Weren't?"

"She died a few years ago."

"I'm sorry."

She shrugged. "Like I said, we weren't close."

"Is that why you went to live with your father?"

"Partly… How about you?" she asked. "Do you have any siblings?"

"One brother."

"Really. For some reason I pictured you as an only child." She smiled at how little she knew about him. "Does your family live in California?"

"Uh-huh. Right in L.A. There's no escape."

His tone was joking, but his eyes weren't. "My parents and I have our differences, but they've given me a lot. Sometimes I forget and take them for granted."

In the next hour, the conversation drifted all over the place. They talked about her job, his job. She talked about Phoebe and Rose, and he talked about his partner, Rico, and some other detectives on the force,

Luke and Tex. She got the feeling his job weighed heavily on him most of the time. Dedication had that effect on a person.

By the time they said good-night, she felt she really knew what kind of man Jordan St. James was. Honest and caring, a man whose integrity and sense of justice directed his life. Men like Jordan had been few and far between in her world.

As she climbed the stairs, he said, "I'll be leaving in the morning."

FOR JORDAN, MORNING CAME too soon. And too often. Once at 2:00 a.m., again at 3:00 a.m. and now at 6:00 a.m. And each time he woke up, all he could think about was Laura. She was an admirable person, someone who cared more about others than herself. He liked her sense of humor, her forthright personality. No wondering where you stood with her. Then there were her eyes, and her soft lips, and how perfectly she fit into his arms. He probably shouldn't have kissed her, but he was glad he had. He liked her; she obviously liked him. What could be the harm?

Yeah, right. No harm at all. If he wasn't deceiving her. If he wasn't trying to get information from her about Kolnikov and DeMatta.

He hadn't actually lied to her, but he hadn't been fully truthful, either. His motives for solving a murder and taking down a mob boss were one thing. His reasons for helping her, another. He cared about her. Cared about her and Cait. Knowing they were in danger—and not knowing why—made him feel helpless. A feeling that burned like acid in his gut.

Finally he got up, went to the kitchen, made some coffee and flipped on the small TV on the counter.

"Unrelenting rains in the Valley are causing major backups on Highway 10, at the El Toro Y at 5 and 405. Mud slides have occurred in the Malibu Hills and farther north. It may become necessary for residents to evacuate their homes. There are reports of heavy snow in the mountains above six thousand feet. Roads are closed on Highway 330 at Redlands and on 18 through Lucerne Valley. Don't travel if you don't have to."

Damn. He walked to the window and peered out. Snow blanketed everything, the white so bright it hurt his eyes. The pines were so heavy with snow, he couldn't see the green. He couldn't even see the snowman they'd made.

Grabbing a jacket, he headed for the garage, then opened the side door. Snowdrifts. Five feet tall. One stab at the button to open the garage door told him either the mechanism was frozen, or there was too much snow against the door. He picked up a shovel, intending to cut a path from the side door, but after a couple of swipes, he realized it was futile.

Great. His only option was to call for a snowplow, but if he couldn't get one, he wasn't going anywhere for a while. He pulled out his cell phone and surprisingly got a signal. After contacting headquarters to let them know he was tied up, he left a message for Mary Beth to call him if she'd had any luck getting a name for the head of the Belzar Corporation. He went back inside to look up the number for someone to plow him out.

"Good morning," Laura greeted him as he walked into the kitchen.

"Good morning. How did you sleep?"

"Like a baby. Caitlin is still asleep."

"Understandable. It's early." He indicated the cof-feepot. "Would you like some?"

"Thank you."

"We had a snow dump last night. The road is closed and the drifts are covering the doors."

Her eyes went wide. "What will you do?"

He handed her a mug as well as a half-gallon milk carton from the refrigerator. "I contacted the station to let them know I'll be gone another day. If I can get a snowplow out here, or the sun melts some of the drifts so I can use the snowblower, I can get out."

"But if the roads are closed…"

He shrugged. "We'll see."

Taking her mug, Laura walked to the table in the breakfast nook. "That means your cell phone works."

"So far so good." He punched in the number for the plowing company and left a message. "I guess I'm not going anywhere for a while."

She glanced out the bank of windows. "Well, last night you said you wanted to talk. I guess this gives us the opportunity, doesn't it?"

He sat next to her. "About last night…"

She looked directly at him. "I'm fine with last night. Forget about it."

Okay. That was good. Especially since he'd come to the same conclusion. A relationship between them would only hurt her in the end. Apparently she felt the same. So why did he feel disappointed?

"Anything else?"

"Yes, I'd like to make sure you have everything you need to stay here. And…I'd like it if *you* could give me more information so I can do further investigation while I'm gone. I really do want to help you resolve whatever it is that's hanging over your head."

She stiffened.

He placed a hand on hers. "This is a great place, Laura. It's safe and secure, but you can't stay here indefinitely. What about Cait's school? The shelter? The reality is that you can't stay anywhere long enough to make this stalker go away. Stalkers aren't like other criminals. They keep coming back."

Her expression hardened. "I know. I've dealt with stalkers before at the shelter. But once you find out who the car belongs to, you can do something about it. Right?"

"That's the problem. I haven't found out anything. The license number you gave me wasn't traceable. We're still working on it, but there's no guarantee we'll get anything. I want to help you, and to do that, you've got to tell me what's going on."

Her face paled. Slowly, she rose to her feet, and in a low, firm voice, she said, "I can't. I can't tell you anything more."

"You can tell me who threatened you."

She didn't answer.

"I brought you to this place because I knew no one would ever think to find you here. But no place is safe forever. You can't run forever, either. Think of Cait."

She whirled around, anger flaring in her eyes. "I *always* think of Cait. I wouldn't be here if I wasn't thinking of her." Her hands on the counter, she bowed her head in frustration. Her voice cracked when she said, "She's my life."

"W-what's wrong, Mommy?"

Both Laura and Jordan turned.

Cait stood in the doorway in her jammies, clearly terrified.

"Nothing's wrong, honey. Nothing at all," Laura

said, hurrying to her daughter. "Jordan and I were simply having a discussion, and sometimes adults get loud when they discuss things."

"Good morning," Jordan said with a salute. He hoped the kid hadn't heard too much. "How'd you sleep?"

Laura knelt down and hugged her.

"Good. I'm hungry."

Jordan walked to the fridge and peered inside. "We've got Cocoa Puffs, Cheerios, oatmeal and eggs."

"Cocoa Puffs. They're my favorite."

He glanced at Laura for her okay. She nodded.

"Cocoa Puffs it is."

"Can we make another snowman today?"

"It snowed a whole bunch last night," Laura told Cait.

The child's eyes lit up. "Then we can make lots of snowmen."

Jordan laughed. "If we can shovel ourselves out the door, we'll make a whole family."

"And an igloo. Eskimos live in igloos, so snowmen must live there, too, because they like the cold."

"Makes sense." Jordan nodded. "Whatever you want."

"Oh, boy," Laura said. "You'll regret you ever said that. She'll hold you to it."

Glad to see she'd lightened up, he poured a bowl of cereal for himself. "Not bad," he said after his first bite. "I may have to put Cocoa Puffs on my grocery list in the future."

Cait giggled. "Cocoa Puffs aren't as good for you as oatmeal. My mom says so."

"You've got a very smart mom," he said, eyeing Laura. "She knows what's best for you."

She just didn't know how to let someone help her.

But before he left, he was going to find out exactly what was going on.

LAURA SIPPED HER COCOA as she watched Jordan and Cait play Monopoly on the floor in front of the fire. She'd been the first one out of the game and wasn't too proud of it. But her heart warmed seeing Cait have so much fun. It was obvious Cait idolized Jordan. She couldn't help thinking how much fuller life would be for Cait if they were a real family. For her, too.

They'd spent most of the morning watching DVDs and playing games. Cait was impatient to go outside, but Jordan hadn't been able to make a dent in the snow-drift outside the door.

But the sun was out now, and it looked as if he'd be able to try again soon.

"I won! I won!" Cait jumped up. Then she added, "But you did really good, Jordan."

Cait's expression was so serious, Laura had to laugh. "Well, he certainly did better than me."

Jordan got up, too. "I think it's time to work off some energy. Get your coats on and we'll tackle the snow again."

An hour later they had a small path from the back door to the yard. The first thing Cait did was to shovel out the snowman from the day before. And then they created the rest of the snowman family. By the time they finished everything, including a makeshift igloo, the sun had dropped behind the mountain and, even though it was only four o'clock, it seemed much later.

"We should buy a place like this," Cait said as she packed another snowball. "We could have this much fun all the time."

Laura nearly choked. "As nice as that would be, it takes money to buy a place like this," she said, lowering her voice so Jordan didn't hear. "Lots of money."

Cait kept patting the snowball. "We have money. The money in the brown package."

Laura's heart dropped. It was three years ago. How could Cait remember? She glanced furtively at Jordan, hoping he wasn't paying attention.

"No, we don't." She turned, grabbed some more snow and tried to look busy.

"But I saw it in your room. I...I opened it just a little. It must be ours if it was in your room."

"It's not ours, and that's that." Laura gritted her teeth. "And I don't want you to talk about it ever again."

Tears welled in Cait's eyes. Oh, Lord. She never talked to her daughter that harshly, and she regretted it the second the words left her mouth. She reached to hug Cait. "I'm sorry. I didn't mean it the way it sounded." She kept her voice to a whisper. "I just meant the money isn't ours to spend. You know, like the money I get in grants to pay for the shelter." It wasn't exactly the truth, but it wasn't a lie, either. The money wasn't theirs to spend. She was aghast that Cait had ever come across it.

When she looked up, Jordan was watching them. Had he heard what she'd said? Would it matter if he did? He wouldn't have a clue what they were talking about. She *could* have gotten money for the shelter from a benefactor, or she could've saved it. She put an arm around Cait's shoulder. "Come on. I think it's time to go in and have dinner." She waved at Jordan and called out, "We're going inside now."

Jordan didn't follow. Instead she watched him get

out the snowblower and start clearing the driveway. After a few minutes, Laura poked her head out and asked, "Shall I make something for dinner?"

At first he didn't seem to hear her, but finally he stopped and turned off the motor. "There are frozen dinners in the freezer and plenty of food in the fridge. Make something for yourselves. I'll catch a bite later."

"Are you sure? I can make something and save you a plate."

"I'm sure." He started the motor again, the growling roar made louder as it echoed off the mountains.

His tone had seemed harsh. Maybe he was simply frustrated about not getting back to L.A., to his job. Lord knew he'd wasted enough time getting her settled. And then the snowstorm prevented him from leaving. If it snowed again tonight, all his work would be wasted. She'd be frustrated, too.

When Jordan came in two hours later covered in snow, Laura couldn't help but laugh. "You look like one of the snowmen."

"I bet." He shrugged off his jacket. "Where's Cait?"

"In bed. She practically fell asleep in the tub." She took his boots and set them in the coatroom. "I made spaghetti, there's some left in the fridge. I can warm it up when you're ready."

He looked surprised. "Spaghetti?"

"I found some Ragú sauce and a box of angel-hair pasta. Shall I warm it up for you?"

"Thanks, but I can do it after I shower. I need to warm *myself* up first."

"Okay, when you're done, then."

He gave her a half smile. "You can't quit mothering, can you."

"Is that a bad thing?"

His smile widened, revealing even, white teeth. "Not at all. I'm just not used to it."

She eased onto one of the rustic pine stools at the counter. "Want something warm to drink? Cocoa? That'll warm you."

He came over and took her by the arms. "I'm fine. I'm used to taking care of myself. You should enjoy having a break from catering to others all the time."

Maybe, but this was different. He'd helped her and Cait so much, she could never repay him. It wasn't even just that. She wanted to do things for him. It felt good. "Actually, except for Cait, I don't get to wait on others too much. Mostly I teach people how to do things for themselves. So, it's kind of fun to switch it up."

He touched her cheek. Was he going to kiss her again? Lord knew, she wanted him to. Her palms suddenly felt moist, her heart lodged in her throat. She wanted him to kiss her as he did last night—only this time, she didn't want it to end in a kiss.

"I'll eat later," he said, and then left to take his shower.

Oh, boy. She needed a shower, too. An icy one.

JORDAN TOWELED OFF, STILL thinking about what he'd overheard outside. Money in a brown package. The mention of it had significantly upset Laura. What was that all about?

Had someone given her the money? Was it her ex-husband's? Was it payment for something? Why had she reacted so harshly when her daughter asked about it? He'd never seen her even talk loudly to Cait, much less raise her voice in anger.

But the more he thought about it, the more he felt

like an ass. This was Laura, a woman he respected. The woman seemed to have everything together, a strong work ethic, gritty determination and a solid sense of who she was. So many women he'd been involved with were only interested in a meal ticket, a guy who could support them in the manner to which they wanted to be, or stay, accustomed.

He lathered his face with shaving lotion and scraped off yesterday's growth. Realist that he was, he couldn't blame everything on the women he'd been involved with. He'd always been drawn to women he could protect, women who needed him. He had to take the rap for some bad choices there. Had to examine his own motives.

Pulling on a cable-knit sweater and a clean pair of jeans, he realized he might've hit on the reason he was drawn to Laura. She was nothing like the women in his past. Protection wasn't something she wanted. And she didn't seem to have a needy bone in her body. Not even when she should.

Well, there was a fine line between independence and bullheadedness, and this was one of them. When he went back to L.A. he'd get all the information he could to cement his case. The name of the guy in the black car would be a good start.

His stomach growled. Spaghetti was sounding better and better.

As he walked into the living room, the scent of cedar wafted through the room. A fire was just starting to flame in the fireplace. He grinned. She certainly wasn't afraid to make herself at home.

"Hi. You're just in time," she said when he came into the kitchen.

"Something smells good."

"The spaghetti's in the microwave." She went to the refrigerator. "I made a salad, too, using some of the stuff you bought for sandwiches. Nothing fancy. Just some lettuce, tomatoes and onions. And I found some vinegar and oil."

"Sounds too healthy."

She brought a plate of spaghetti to the table where she'd already laid out the flatware, a napkin and a glass of water. "I guess it's healthy enough except for the carbs."

As he sat, she dropped into the chair next to him and leaned forward on an elbow, her chin resting on her palm.

He narrowed his gaze. "You're not one of those diet health freaks, are you?"

She tipped her head back and laughed. "Not a chance. I'm the quintessential junk-food junkie. But I have to do the healthy thing for Cait and the girls. At home, I have to keep my stash hidden."

She never failed to surprise him. He twirled the spaghetti on his fork and took a bite. "It's good." He kept eating as she continued to watch him.

"Do you think you'll be able to get back to L.A. tomorrow?"

"I'm counting on it. But I'll be back as soon as I can."

She tapped her fingernails against the tabletop. "We'll be fine."

"I have no doubt."

"Do you think you've run into a dead end on the black car?"

He caught her gaze. "Maybe. Maybe not. Can you think of anything you didn't tell me before? Anything that might identify the car or the driver? Any clue about the passenger—how tall, what she was wearing, her hair color, a bumper sticker...anything."

She looked away—guiltily, he thought.

He nudged harder. "Many times witnesses remember things later when they've had a chance to think about what happened."

Her back went rigid. She looked straight at him, steely determination in her eyes. "When did I become a witness?"

Wrong choice of words. "You know what I mean."

"I'm afraid I do."

CHAPTER TEN

LAURA LOUNGED CURLED UP ON the couch watching the fire pop and snap. She felt as if her nerves were about to snap, too.

Well, if Jordan thought she knew more than she was telling, he was right. But what good would it do to tell him it was Alysa who'd gotten out of the black car?

If the man in the car was Alysa's former pimp, which Laura suspected was the case, telling Jordan could turn this into an ugly situation and send the teen on a downward spiral. What she'd wanted when she'd told Jordan the license number was for Jordan to pick the guy up, scare him off—without involving Alysa. That would solve both problems. The pimp—aka stalker—would be out of commission. She'd deal with the teen's problems herself later.

God knew, it wasn't easy for any of the girls to stay on track. With deep insecurities and rock-bottom self-esteem, it was all too easy to fall back into their old patterns. The need for love and acceptance superceded all else, and they looked for it in all the wrong places, taking whatever scraps of affection they could get. A life of childhood abuse and emotional neglect didn't disappear with a few counseling sessions.

"I picked a hearty pinot noir this time," Jordan said, coming in from the kitchen.

"Thank you."

Sitting beside her, he leaned back and let out a deep breath, as if he was glad to finally rest. She could relate. She'd been tired before they'd finished making the snowmen.

"I'd forgotten how relaxing it is up here," Jordan said. "I almost don't want to go back."

"But you have to."

"Yep." He glanced at her. "I have other cases to work on, besides the black car."

"Are you getting any closer to finding a suspect in Anna's case?"

"I've got a person of interest to check out. But he's a ghost. I don't have a name, just a description. Apparently he and Kolnikov saw each other frequently before she died. If I knew where Kolnikov grew up, I might have a chance of finding him. Apparently he lived in the same town."

Laura sipped her wine. "Wouldn't her birthplace be in your records? On the death certificate?"

"It is, but she didn't grow up there." He frowned. "You mentioned that your ex-husband had sold her some real estate. Do you know if he kept records of those transactions?"

"Of course. For tax purposes. But I imagine the police confiscated everything in his place after he... died."

"Well, if they did, I didn't see anything."

"What would they do with the records if the case isn't solved?"

"They might keep them if they're important. If not, they'd return them to the nearest relative."

"That would be Eddie's mother. She passed away last year."

"Do you know what happened to her estate?"

"She didn't have much. Some things went to Cait, nothing much. There's a box of stuff in my garage, but it's just odds and ends. I doubt she'd have reason to keep his tax records."

"I'd like to look at it."

"Sure." Laura didn't know when he could, though, not unless she called the shelter and gave the okay to let Jordan investigate. "Where did you hear about this…ghost?"

"From a woman who worked for Kolnikov."

"What did she say?"

"He was tall and blond and quite a few years younger. She seemed to think he was a boyfriend, but he could just be another john. That would make him harder to track down."

Tall and blond. Younger. Jordan's "person of interest" might be the guy Laura had seen Anna with at Tucci's restaurant when she and Eddie went there to work out their divorce. Anna had introduced them, but Laura hustled away from the woman out of her past as quickly as possible. "I think I might've met him."

Jordan turned so fast to look at her she was surprised he didn't get whiplash.

"Well, I don't know if it's the same person, but he fits the description. It was at a restaurant. Eddie and I ran into Anna, and she introduced us to a man…Nick. He was tall, blond. A lot younger than she was."

"Nick? No last name?"

"Not that I remember."

"But you *do* remember meeting him."

She nodded.

"Does this mean you actually knew Kolnikov as an acquaintance? In fact, more than the couple of times you mentioned?"

Her stomach knotted. The lies were catching up with her. "Maybe it's like you said, things come back later."

He smiled. "So how long ago was this, when you met Nick?"

Eddie had been dead for three years, they'd been divorced for a year before. "Almost five years."

Jordan arched an eyebrow. "Not too long before she died, then."

"I guess so. Does that help at all?" She'd love to see Anna's murderer get what he deserved. In trying to forget her past, Laura hadn't had any contact with the woman for ten years before she married Eddie. And then she'd only seen her a few times after that.

"I'm hoping once I resurrect Kolnikov's records, it'll help."

Laura caught her breath. "She kept records?"

"Tax records. I heard she also had a proverbial black book, but no one has been able to locate that, either. But—" he stroked her cheek "—right now, I'd like to just enjoy the fire and your company."

She snuggled back into the pillow, her emotions at war. She could think of nothing she'd like better…and she knew nothing good could ever come of it.

They passed the rest of the evening relaxed in front of the fireplace, and now the two of them were sprawled out on the floor finishing up a game of gin. As she laid down her last card, Jordan took her hand. "I'll be leaving early in the morning, probably before you get up. Do you have any questions on how to do things around here?"

"You mentioned the security system and snowmo-bile."

"Let's do it now," he said. "It's really easy."

He got to his feet and helped her up. On the way to the garage, he gave her the rundown on the security system as they put on jackets. Staring at the two snowmobiles, Laura said, "They look like fun. I think I'd like to try this."

"I'm sure Cait would enjoy it, too." He lifted the seat. "The key is here. It starts just like a car except the gas and the brakes are on the handles. You turn the right handle to accelerate and the left to brake. It's simple."

"Can I do it?"

"It's very loud. Might wake up Cait."

She liked how he always thought about Cait. "Right."

"Go ahead, sit on it. Get the feel."

Hoisting one leg over the seat, it reminded her of getting on a motorcycle, something she'd done many times as a teen. As she wrapped her fingers around the handlebars, she felt Jordan's warm body sink in behind her. He reached around to place his hands over hers, his cheek against hers…his full lips close enough to kiss. Desire ignited inside her. She was going to burst into flames if he kept this up.

"The motion is subtle," he said. "Otherwise you'll take off like a shot and fall backward."

"Subtle. You mean like this?" She cranked the handle, but it didn't move.

"It's the other way. To accelerate, turn down on the right side, and to brake, turn up on the left." He demonstrated the movement and his body pressed even closer. "But neither works when the motor isn't running."

Who cared if it didn't work? She was, as he'd said before, *in the moment.* She moved her hands in the direction he described to show she knew what he meant.

"Great." He eased back, and as he did, his face brushed her hair. He stopped, inhaled deeply, not hiding his response at all. After a moment, he said, "I think…we'd better get back inside. It's cool out here."

Cool? She was burning up. She stood to get off the snowmobile, but her right foot caught on the seat. She swayed back and he caught her.

"Whoa. Easy does it."

Seconds passed, but neither moved. Her breathing deepened. Her pulse throbbed at the base of her throat.

His lips met hers, and in that one mind-spinning moment, her last barrier collapsed. Right, wrong or foolish, she was falling for Jordan St. James. And she wanted to enjoy the feeling for as long as she could. She felt weak, unable to do anything but kiss him back, long and deep and with all the passion that had been building in her for so long.

"Sweet," he murmured, his mouth still against hers. "I knew your kiss would be delicious."

And his was intoxicating. She lifted a hand to his cheek, feeling a connection she'd never felt before… and the feeling infused her with passion. She hoped he felt the same. When he lifted her in his arms and started to go inside, she knew the answer.

"My bedroom?"

"It's either that or the snowmobile." As she said the words, his mouth was on hers again, soft and warm and insistent. As commanding as he was. Her arms around him, she kissed him back and then he turned and carried her off, just like in the movies.

If she hadn't been drunk with ecstasy, she might've

looked to see what the room was like, but all she saw was Jordan. The rest was a blur. He placed her gently on the unmade bed. The sheet smelled like Jordan, woodsy and sexy, and she wanted to wrap herself up in it. When he lowered himself beside her, she wrapped her arms around his neck and pulled him as close as she could get him. This was her moment, hers and Jordan's, and she shut out all the voices telling her this wouldn't work.

He rolled on top of her, or maybe she pulled him there, but the next thing she knew he was straddling her legs. She felt him, hard, pressing against her, and she throbbed with desire. Her hands went to his shirt and slipped it over his head. He did the same for her. She reached for his belt and he watched as she unbuckled it, his breathing deepening. Then, impatiently, he stood and pulled the rest off himself. He stood there for a moment, letting her look at him—and she did…all six feet of him…all sinew and hard muscle, and so different than her soft, unathletic curves. She wondered if he'd be pleased or horrified when she undressed. But the second he climbed back in bed with her, she forgot every self-conscious thought she'd had.

She started to undress, but he stopped her. "Let me." He barely touched the front of her bra where it fastened and the lacy garment popped open. On his knees, he unsnapped her jeans and tugged them, inch by inch, down over her hips and her legs, one leg at a time. The deliberate slowness was like an aphrodisiac, until every nerve, every muscle quivered with need, her desire so intense she almost couldn't stand it.

When she was naked, he ran his fingers down her breasts and the delicate skin on her sides, then down her hips and the inside of her legs until he reached the bottom of her feet. "You're beautiful," he said, his voice low and husky.

"I want to make love with you so much," she said, pulling him to her.

"All in due time, sweetheart."

"I don't know if I can wait," she said, taking him in her hand. His groan told her he might not be able to wait, either.

"Well, if you keep doing that, it'll be over sooner than you'd want." He moved her hand to his chest and kissed her long and deep.

She ran her hands down his back, feeling the ridges of muscles, each stroke a type of pleasure she hadn't really known before. He caressed her breasts and her backside and then between her legs. It took only two strokes before she exploded, her body thrusting and tightening in orgasm. She felt as if it went on forever and she was drifting away, in another dimension. Somewhere in that foggy state, she heard a drawer open.

"Protection," he whispered.

She looked up, trying to focus. "Here, let me do it."

He smiled. "Be my guest."

When they were ready, he kissed her again. "You sure you're up for this?"

She smiled. "I've never been so up for anything in my life."

He laughed. "Just making sure."

"Be sure," she said, and pulled him into her arms for another kiss.

Jordan couldn't wait any longer. He spread her legs and slowly entered her. She flinched a little, but within seconds, they found their rhythm, a pulsating beat that coursed through him, building in intensity until he felt her release coming again and again, and he exploded inside her.

They lay there, side by side, his arm around her waist, for what seemed a very long time. She ran her fingers over his chest.

"I can't stay," she finally whispered. "Cait might wake up and find us in bed."

"Right. That wouldn't be good. But it doesn't mean I like it." He grinned. "What I like is you, right here in my bed."

"I like it, too. Too much."

"Stay a little longer."

When his lips went from her mouth to her breasts and lower, she couldn't have left if she wanted.

Later, back in her own bed, Laura stretched out, feeling more mellow than she had in, well, she couldn't remember how long. Everything about being with Jordan felt so normal, and she wanted the feeling to last forever.

CHAPTER ELEVEN

IT WAS STILL DARK WHEN Jordan got out of bed. He wasn't going to examine what had happened last night, because if he did, he'd either feel like a jerk, or want to stay and make love with Laura all over again. He gathered some fresh clothes, showered and headed out the door.

But even driving on an icy road in the dark couldn't keep him from thinking about Laura. He'd never felt as good as he had when he was with her. And he'd never felt so unsure. Take away the fact he was investigating issues concerning her, take away the fact she felt she was in danger and wouldn't tell him why, take away all that and then what did he feel?

He cared about her, damn it. This wasn't supposed to happen. Not when he didn't know where the case was going to end up. Still, they fit so perfectly together. Talking with her was as natural as breathing. Making love was, too. She'd dispelled any reservations he'd had the second her lips met his.

But why was this…relationship…whatever it was, so different from any others? He didn't have the answer. All he knew was that despite his vows not to get involved, he was. And if he continued to pursue the relationship, he'd only hurt her in the end. How could he ask someone to be a part of his life when his life was a lie. He wasn't Jordan St. James, the son of L.A. socialites Harlan and Mary St. James. And his brother Harry, Harlan Junior, wasn't his brother. Jordan was a bastard whose heritage was questionable. Harry had made the point every day from the time he learned Jordan had been adopted.

He'd come to grips with Harry's jealousy long ago, and Harry had, too. But it'd taken even longer to come to grips with his own need to belong. He'd done all the right things, was a decorated officer, the best at whatever he did. But nothing changed the fact that he was a bastard his own mother didn't even want. How could he ever father a child when he didn't know what he might inflict on that child? Though he'd learned to live with his own questionable DNA, he wasn't going to drag anyone else into his quagmire.

When he reached a point where he thought his cell phone could catch the satellite, he checked his messages. One from Luke sounded garbled. Was he drunk? He hadn't been drunk since last year on his son's birth— Damn. He'd vowed to be there for him this time.

He punched in Luke's number. No answer. He left a message telling Luke he was on his way to headquarters and he'd see him there.

Three and a half hours after he'd left Big Bear, he pulled into the police garage. Luke's car wasn't there. Heading into the RHD, he noticed the floor was nearly empty and stopped at Mary Beth's desk.

"Another Studio Killer homicide," she said.

Jordan was glad he'd missed it. He had work of his own to do and he could do it a lot faster without interruptions. He checked the Delores Matthews file. Rita Valdez said the woman mentioned Hawaii, but he found no references to the island in the file. But he did note that she'd been married once in Hawaii.

He set up a search for her former married name, and within the hour he had what he was looking for. Hilo, Hawaii. Her ex still lived there. It's possible he'd know where she is. If she was still alive. But that was a whole other investigation. Then he remembered Rico was in Hawaii. He hated to disturb a guy on his honeymoon, but if anyone would understand, it would be Rico. He wanted DeMatta as much as the rest of the RHD. He punched in his partner's number at the hotel where he and Macy were staying.

After making arrangements with Rico to contact the ex, and then finishing up his reports, he called Luke again. No answer. Damn. If Luke wasn't home, or at the station, he was probably at Bernie's.

Jordan piled up his work and headed for the bar. By the time he arrived it was getting dark outside. It was even darker inside.

The place was nearly empty. Luke sat at the bar, his glass shoved toward the bartender. "Hit me again," he said loud enough for the handful of patrons to hear.

"You sure you haven't had enough?" Dylan, the barrel-chested bartender, said gruffly.

Luke glanced up, squinting at the neon lights above the bar. "Not today."

The bartender took the empty glass. "Okay, but give me your car keys first. You're not driving home."

Just then someone slid onto the stool next to Luke, who turned to look at the man. Jordan walked closer, but couldn't identify the guy from the back and wasn't sure if he should interrupt. He sat at a table behind the two men.

The other guy ordered a shot, and when he got it, he turned to Luke and said, "I've got a message for a friend of yours."

Jordan took a second look at the guy. Fortyish. A burly man, wearing a dark suit. Nondescript, except for a mole on his left cheek.

"Yeah?" Luke said. "Well, I don't have any friends."

"Detective St. James."

Jordan's attention spiked.

"He's no friend," Luke said before he knocked back another shot. "Who's the message from?"

"Someone who could have your friend's job in a heartbeat."

"Go screw yourself," Luke snarled. "You got something to say to him, tell him yourself. Who the hell are you, anyway?"

"I work for someone who thinks your friend should leave well enough alone."

Jordan bolted to his feet, but before he could act, Luke had grabbed the guy's shirt collar and lifted him off the ground. "You slimy bastard."

"Your friend could get hurt. The girl could get hurt—" The creep gurgled, his words cut off by Luke's hand against his throat.

Within seconds, Luke had flipped the guy around and flattened him against the bar, pulled his hands back and cuffed him. "Call it in," Luke ordered the bartender. He shoved his face next to the guy's ear. "You got some more threats from your boss?" Frisking the guy, he removed a .38 Magnum from an inside holster. "You can tell me at the station."

The big man laughed. "You're wasting your time, pork chop. The only person I'm talking to is my lawyer, and he'll have me out before you get me there."

Jordan sidled up next to Luke. "Nice work, partner."

Luke didn't seem surprised to see him. "Just another day in the life of…" Luke mumbled something Jordan couldn't make out, adding, "You win some, you lose some."

It was obvious Luke was in no shape for business. Jordan knew how to take care of it.

Less than five minutes later, two officers entered the building. "Detective St. James," he said quickly, to cover for Luke.

"What's the problem?" one of the blues asked.

"Disorderly conduct." Jordan knew they wouldn't take the guy downtown because he'd made a couple of threats.

"He's lying," the suit said.

One of the officers pulled out the suspect's identification. "Dutch Greene. So, am I going to believe you or my fellow officer here?" He laughed as he said it. "You got anything else to say, you can tell us on the way downtown."

Jordan watched them leave. Dutch Greene was a name he'd heard before. One of DeMatta's men.

He turned to Luke. "Come on, buddy. I'm taking you home." ·

THE NEXT MORNING, as Jordan pulled into the garage across the street from headquarters, he had two things on his mind. Laura and Cait's safety. He had to get the guy in the black car. And then he had to talk to DeMatta about last night.

When Jordan walked in, heads turned his way. As he passed the row of desks, Ralston said, "The captain's gunning for you, big guy."

Jordan heard Ralston chuckle under his breath but

didn't acknowledge him. As soon as he reached his desk, the light on his phone flashed. He picked up.

"In here now, St. James."

What the hell? Jordan got up and crossed to Carlyle's office. "Nice vacation?" McIntyre called after him.

Jordan got the feeling Mac knew where he'd been. But it wasn't possible. No one knew. "Perfect," he shot back.

He palmed open the door of the captain's office. "Good morning."

"The hell it is."

Okay. This was about more than Jordan taking an unannounced day off. He sat across from the boss. "That bad?"

"I hope you know what you're doing reopening the Kolnikov case, because I've got the chief and the mayor on my tail."

"Why should they care?"

"They didn't say."

Jordan shrugged. He knew exactly what the captain *wasn't* saying. Too bad. He didn't give a crap about the private lives of the chief or the mayor or any of their friends. If they were dumb enough to stick out their... respective parts, that was their problem. "I'm not looking for the woman's little black book, if that's what they're worried about. I want to solve Kolnikov's murder, and I want to nail DeMatta."

"You uncover one thing and more pops up. I don't want this coming back to haunt me."

"What are you saying?"

"I'm not saying anything. I want you to wind it up."

"They must really be tightening the screws," Jordan said, disappointment grinding in the pit of his stomach.

The captain had always done what he believed was right, never kowtowed to the powers that be.

"I've got three years to retirement."

"And I've got a new lead."

The captain stared at Jordan, as if weighing the possibilities. "Tell me."

"The boyfriend no one mentioned before. His name is Nick. Apparently he had contact with Kolnikov right before her death."

"You got somewhere to go with it?"

"I do." It was a lie, but he was in so deep it didn't matter. He just hoped the captain didn't have to pay for it in the end. "And I got a new lead on Delores Matthews."

The captain steepled his beefy hands, placed his fingertips against his lips. "A good lead?"

"Better than nothing."

Jordan waited.

Finally the captain said, "You need help?"

"Not right yet."

Carlyle nodded. "Then do it."

As Jordan got up to leave, he reached out and shook the captain's hand. "You've restored my faith in the system."

"Get out of here." The captain waved him off.

Back at his desk, Jordan saw Luke coming in. Damn, he looked like crap. His clothes were the same ones he'd worn last night and looked as if Luke had slept in them. His hair was just as bad.

Jordan caught his buddy near the door and pulled him back into the hall, the alcohol fumes overwhelming. "Let's take a leak."

They headed for the john, where Jordan checked to make sure they were alone. "I'm sorry I wasn't here yesterday."

Luke's eyes resembled road maps. "No problem."

"I'm your friend. It's my problem."

"Then give me a break."

Jordan crossed his arms. "Okay. Only you need to get washed up. There's a razor in my locker and a clean shirt."

Luke rubbed his eyes as he slumped against the wall. "He would've been eight years old."

Jordan's heart ached for his friend. But he couldn't let Luke wallow in self-pity, not if he wanted to remain in the department. "I know. And next year he'd be nine."

Luke's head snapped up.

"You can't bring him back, Luke. No matter how much alcohol you siphon into your body."

His friend stood there, as if trying to absorb what Jordan had said. Finally, he straightened. "Right. You're right. I'll get cleaned up."

Luke started to turn but stopped. "The guy at Bernie's last night, I'm kinda foggy about what happened."

"He lawyered up and split."

"Who are we talking about?"

"Dutch Greene. One of DeMatta's crew. Same lawyer."

Luke rubbed his eyes again. "I've got to get something to wake me up."

As he remembered the threat—the threat toward not only him, but Laura and Caitlin—Jordan's chest tightened in anger. He turned to leave.

"Where are you going?"

"I'm going to the source," Jordan spat out. "Frank DeMatta."

"If you wait, I'll go with you."

Jordan clenched his hands into fists. "Thanks, but I need to do this alone."

LAURA WORKED ON THE Victory House budget for the next year, homeschooled Cait for a few hours and spent the rest of the day outside with her daughter. She marveled at the quiet; the only sounds were their laughter and snow crunching underfoot. She was awed by the majesty of it all, the almost perfect symmetry of the trees, the pristine snow. So different from the Valley. Snow covered everything like a layer of spun cotton.

That night, the stars glittered like diamonds against a black-velvet backdrop. It was so clear, so unlike the city. Cait had pointed out a couple of constellations she knew and Laura helped her identify what she could. Maybe she was biased, but Cait seemed smarter than other almost eight-year-olds.

After tucking Cait in bed, she went back downstairs, set the security alarm and built a fire. After pouring a glass of wine from the bottle they'd opened the night before, she wandered to the den to get a book. They all appeared to be leather-bound classics—Hemingway, Shakespeare. It felt a bit pretentious.

Then she came across a photo album, stuck haphazardly in with the books. Odd.

She pulled it out and went into the great room by the fire and flipped it open to the first page. A family portrait stared back at her. A model family that could've been from the pages of *Good Housekeeping*. Mother, father and two small boys both the same height and about five years old, one dark, one blond. The caption on the photo read 1975. Curious, she flipped another page. More photos from the same time period. As she turned the pages, she watched the years pass. The blond boy looked oddly familiar, a devilish glint in his eyes. The two boys didn't look alike and neither resembled the parents all that much.

She took a sip of wine, thinking she shouldn't be snooping, but couldn't help herself. Photo albums were meant to be viewed. She passed over the next section and reached 1985, finding a photo of the two teenage boys fishing. Her jaw dropped. That's why the blond boy looked familiar. His hair was darker now, but there was no mistaking who he was. Jordan.

No wonder he felt at home here. He'd been coming here with his friend since childhood. But that didn't make sense. If he was just a friend, he wouldn't be in *all* the family photos.

Awareness dawned on her. This wasn't Jordan's friend's cabin, it was his family's cabin. No wonder he knew his way around so well, seemed so comfortable. She clenched her jaw as she turned page after page and the photographs revealed the truth.

Jordan had lied to her.

It was obvious his family was wealthy, and it was also obvious he didn't want her to know it. He'd made love to her, the most intimate act between two people, but he couldn't confide in her. Did he want to keep his family separate from his job? She might believe that.... If he hadn't said he'd brought her here as a friend— hadn't said this *wasn't* part of his job. And he'd been pretty convincing.

What did he think, that she'd try to shake him down?

The thought seemed ludicrous. Jordan had whisked her out of a dangerous situation, done everything he could to make her comfortable, and at this very moment, he was trying to find the guy who was stalking them. She had no business questioning his motives. And who was she to do that, anyway? She hadn't been honest with him, either.

But she had good reason.

A loud rustling noise outside jerked her attention to the window. Probably just an animal. Jordan had said she should be watchful if she went outside, especially at night. The occasional mountain lion sometimes wandered down. Racoons looking for food. Bears.

She put the photo album on the coffee table and picked up a book she'd also brought from the den. The noise again. She froze. For the first time since Jordan left, she was aware of how isolated she was in a cabin miles away from anyone or anything. With a phone that might or might not work. What should she do?

Nothing. She was letting her imagination run amok. Her house in L.A. was a much more dangerous place to be, and if she were there, she'd simply go to the window, put the lights on and look outside.

Maybe it was the unfamiliarity. The feeling that she was a stranger here. Besides, it was quiet now. No noise.

That's what you need, Laura. Noise to quiet her runaway imagination. She clicked the remote for the television. Nothing. Jordan had said the cable satellite reception wasn't always the greatest. How about not at all?

She glanced at the French windows, where ice crystals were forming in the corners, and saw more snow falling outside. As pretty as it was, she hoped it didn't snow too much or Jordan might not make it back tomorrow. And right now, she wanted him back more than anything.

The wind howled through the trees, an eerie, mournful sound. A loud scratching at the window behind made her jump. Just a tree branch. Well, that was it. She picked up Cait's CD player from the table.

Music would help—even if she had to listen to a former Mickey Mouse Club cheerleader.

She put on the headset and sat on the soft leather couch with her book. As she finished the second chapter, she caught movement outside the window in her peripheral vision. A shadow. Her heart raced.

Immediately, she got up, walked to the door and flipped on the outside lights. The whole yard was lit up. If any animals were out there, the lights should scare them away for sure.

Finally, she decided she'd feel better in her room where the windows had coverings and she wouldn't get freaked out by every shadow and every scrape of a twig against the windows. She was in a new place, it was natural to think the noises were strange. At home she had every house noise memorized, every squeaky step, every creaking door.

She picked up the book, the glass of wine and, on second thought, took the rest of the bottle of wine along, too. There was an Almond Joy candy bar in her suitcase. Perfect. A good book, fine wine and chocolate. What could be better?

At around three in the morning she awoke sweating like a bricklayer in the desert sun. Still half asleep she realized she'd drifted off long before she finished the wine. And with sleep came the dreams. Wonderful dreams she immediately allowed herself to drift back into. Jordan making love to her. Jordan helping her and Cait make snowmen. Jordan kissing her, holding her, Jordan standing with the other boy in the photo and with his family. But suddenly the movie in her head switched. They were all laughing, but the laughter became louder and louder, their faces morphing into clowns with fire-engine-red gaping mouths. They were laughing at her. But Jordan wouldn't laugh at her. He wouldn't. Suddenly she was propelled into a dark, narrow corridor, like a house of mirrors at a carnival, and all the faces and bodies turned into distorted macabre caricatures of themselves.

She tried desperately to pull herself from the dream, but her body felt weighted down by a sudden and intense loneliness, and bone-deep despair. No matter how hard she tried to wake up, she couldn't pull herself from the black hole. She had no one. Jordan didn't love her. He'd made love to her because she wanted him to and now he was laughing at her. His wealthy family laughed at her, too, and her heart shattered into a million pieces.

A loud crash pulled her from the nightmare. She bolted upright in bed, shivering. Her blankets and sheets had fallen to the floor. It took her a moment to realize the noise was real, not part of the dream. Or was it? She lurched from the bed and ran to Cait's room, and taking her cell phone along, she punched in 911 as she went. Damn it, the phone was dead.

Reaching Cait's room, she saw her daughter curled up in the Barbie doll quilt, pillows piled high around her. Laura went over and tucked her in even though she didn't need it. Cait could sleep through anything. She stood there listening. Everything was quiet.

But what would make such a loud noise? It was too cold for thunder. A tree falling? An earthquake? She returned to her room, put on a robe and went to the window. The yard around the cabin was lit like a football stadium. She could even see animal tracks in the snow. Deer tracks, maybe. And...footprints? *Footprints*. The falling snow would've covered any prints they'd made earlier. Blood suddenly roared in her ears. She jerked away from the window.

Had someone been there? Had the loud noise been someone knocking? No, the noise had been louder, like a crack of lightning…a sonic boom…or a gunshot.

She swallowed, mustered her courage and peered out the window again, this time from behind the curtain. She scanned the yard below. The wind still howled through the pine trees, shaking the snow off the boughs and to the ground. The drifting snow gradually covered the footprints. She shifted her gaze to the left, then right, to where they'd built the snowmen. That was weird. The snowman family looked as if they'd had something dumped on them…something dark… dark red.

Oh, God! Fear sliced like a knife down her spine. She took out her cell again and punched the on button. No signal. Not even static. Her heart slammed against her ribs.

Cait. She had to protect Cait.

JORDAN PARKED BEHIND A black sedan in front of Vincento's Italian Restaurant in Studio City, DeMatta's favorite meeting place. From previous cases, he knew most of DeMatta's hangouts. The whole department knew. He glanced at the license plate. Nothing familiar, but he made a note to check later.

He glanced at his watch. It was 10:00 p.m., DeMatta's dinnertime, according to Al "Squeaky" Milano, the department's Mafia snitch. Jordan had been here before. From the outside, the place looked like every other little Italian restaurant in the Valley, and made claim to the best Italian food in L.A. Having been inside before, he knew the layout—a long rectangular room, elegant. White linen tablecloths and napkins. Most important, he knew the location of the exits, two doors, one on the side and one in back.

Buttoning up his suit jacket, he strode inside.

Apparently it wasn't a busy night; most of the tables were empty. Or else the four men at the back were having a meeting and had kicked everyone out. Jordan saw DeMatta right off.

The mobster saw him immediately, too, and waved him over.

"Detective, what can I do for you this fine evening?"

"I'd like to talk to you. Alone."

One gesture from DeMatta and the other guys left the table.

Jordan sat across from him. A tall man with wide shoulders and dark hair graying at the temples, he wore a designer suit and a crisp white shirt with a purple tie. He looked like a Donald Trump clone with better hair. If Jordan didn't know better he'd think DeMatta was the CEO of a major corporation. Jordan flipped out his shield.

"I know who you are, Detective."

"Then you know why I'm here." Jordan held the man's stony gaze.

"Refresh my memory."

"I heard you have a message for me, but your messenger had a problem getting the job done last night."

DeMatta's expression altered slightly. Questioning, now. The man almost seemed surprised.

"The problem being?"

Given DeMatta's response, Jordan wasn't sure he wanted to say. Was it possible DeMatta didn't know? If so, that meant someone else in the organization was giving orders without the boss's knowledge. It could mean problems within the mob.

The only thing he knew for sure was that someone wanted Jordan off the investigation and that Dutch Greene worked for DeMatta. On the other hand, DeMatta might be blowing smoke. "He got pinched before he could give me the message. Fratianni got him out on bond."

Jordan could see the wheels turning. "Ask Dutch," he suggested.

"Dutch!" DeMatta yelled out. When Dutch came over, DeMatta said evenly. "I hear you have a message for Detective St. James you weren't able to deliver."

The big guy stepped back, his gaze darting. "I'm in the dark here, Frankie."

"Tell me about last night."

Dutch shrugged. "I got in a bar fight with some drunk cop. He called the screws and I called Fratianni." He glared at Jordan. "No big deal."

Yeah, no big deal. If DeMatta believed the creep.

Just then the bells on the front door jangled. Jordan looked up. Another one of DeMatta's thugs.

He sauntered toward their table.

"You're late," DeMatta said, his displeasure undisguised.

"Traffic." The guy looked at Jordan.

"Nicholas here is from New York—" DeMatta looked at Jordan "—and he's still getting used to the urban sprawl. Thinks we're not as organized as the Big Apple."

The subtext in DeMatta's words told Jordan there was unrest in the ranks. He was well aware of the rivalry between New York and L.A. mobsters.

He studied the man. *Nicholas.* "I didn't get the last name."

The other man smiled. "I didn't give it."

Tall, blond and good-looking, he fit Rita Valdez's description. Not to mention his name was Nick.

"Detective St. James was just leaving," DeMatta said, then dismissed Jordan with a wave of his hand.

Not likely. Jordan leaned forward, hands flat on the table. He locked eyes with DeMatta, anger boiling inside him. "If your thugs have any more messages for me, tell them to deliver them to me, not my partner."

In his peripheral vision he saw one of the goons at the other table lumber to his feet. DeMatta signaled a negative and the guy dropped back in the chair. Nicholas didn't flinch.

Still looking at DeMatta, Jordan said, "I'm reinvestigating the murder of Anna Kolnikov." He took a photo from his inside pocket and handed it to the other man. "You ever meet her, Nick?"

Jordan watched for subtle signs of recognition, but Nick barely blinked.

"Never saw her before."

"You sure?" Jordan wanted him to know he didn't believe it. And he wanted DeMatta to know he wasn't going to run scared from a threat. "I have a witness who says differently."

DeMatta shot to his feet and, standing shoulder to shoulder with Jordan, said, "You're full of crap, St. James, and we both know it."

"Am I?"

The mobster stuck two fingers in his tie to loosen it at the neck. "Well then, bring her on."

Jordan smiled. "I didn't say the witness was female."

LAURA'S HEART RACED as she again punched 911 on her cell phone. Still nothing. She couldn't go downstairs to investigate because she couldn't leave Cait up here alone. But if someone wanted to hurt them, why leave such a cryptic warning in the middle of the night? They'd been there alone all day, outside for a good part of it. Plenty of opportunity.

The rationalization didn't quell her terror. She glanced around the room, searching for something to serve as a weapon. Finding nothing, she hurried down the hall and went into another bedroom and turned on the light. It didn't look like a guest room though, because there were personal things lying around—a Dodgers baseball cap, a pair of hunting boots. And the bedding was rumpled, as if someone had slept there recently.

She crossed to the walk-in closet. One side was lined with shelves of sweaters and sweatshirts. The other side was filled with drawers. She pulled open one after the other, lifting up the socks and underwear as she shuffled through, hoping to find something to defend herself and Cait. A gun, maybe.

Nothing. Her panic grew as she opened the last drawer and lifted up some T-shirts. Damn!

Shoving a hand through her hair, she switched off the light and charged from the room—right into a solid mass of flesh. Male flesh.

The man grabbed her arms, squeezing so hard so she couldn't move. "Can I help you with something?" His voice was sharp. Menacing.

Overpowering terror ripped away any reserve she might've had. A scream started low in her throat, but he slammed her against the wall, one arm pressed against her throat, cutting off all sound. She couldn't breathe, much less scream.

Every bone, every muscle in her body went into

fight mode, but when she tried to move, he increased the pressure against her neck.

"What are you doing here?" he spat out.

It took her a second to realize he'd asked a question. But she couldn't answer with his arm cutting off her air supply.

Just as she thought she was going to pass out, he eased his hold a fraction. "Answer me."

"I—I'm a guest." A whisper was all she could manage.

He flipped on the lights and she recognized him immediately. Jordan's friend at the airplane hangar. Then, looking more closely, she realized he was the other boy in the photographs, now an adult. He had to be Jordan's brother.

"Jordan brought me here."

He snatched his arm away and backed up, staring at her, recognition dawning. "What the hell." He took a step back, then forward, as if he didn't know where to go. "I'm sorry. I really am." He turned away, then turned back again. "I didn't know it was you… Jordan could've told me…. Damn him."

Laura swallowed. Jordan didn't tell him because he didn't tell anyone. And she couldn't tell him she was hiding out. "My daughter is sleeping in the other room. If we make too much noise we'll scare her."

"Yeah, sure." He lowered his voice, shoved his hands into his pockets and started pacing. "Where's Jordan?"

"He'll be back tomorrow."

He stopped, rubbed a hand against his chin, eyes narrow. "What were you doing in here? This is my room."

She braced against the wall, feeling some of her tension dissipate, but not entirely. "I heard a noise outside. I was looking for something to protect myself."

His unchanged expression said he didn't believe her.

"If Jordan brought you here, why would you think you needed to protect yourself?"

She shrugged. "I heard a really loud crash. I didn't know what it was. I think I kinda freaked." The second she said it, she realized it was partly true. She'd freaked—about everything. *Everything but the snowmen.*

After a couple of uncomfortable moments in silence, Harry said, "Sounds magnify in the mountains. A car backfiring sounds like a war zone."

"Thanks. That makes me feel better." She smiled at his attempt to assure her everything was fine. Jordan would've done the same.

He tilted his head from side to side, as if getting out a kink. Then he said, "I'm going downstairs for a drink. Want to join me?"

It was the last thing she wanted to do, but maybe it would show goodwill on her part. "Okay. I'll be there in a minute."

After he went downstairs, she checked Cait again, then went back into her room and threw on some sweats instead of her robe and nightshirt.

On her way downstairs, another thought hit her. It was 3:00 a.m. What was Harry doing arriving here in the middle of the night? Something didn't feel right. But right or not, it was his house and she was glad to have another human being with her. A strong man. He was Jordan's brother, he had to be trustworthy.

Downstairs, she glanced around. Everything seemed in place. Harry must have turned off the alarm system, she realized. Before heading into the kitchen, she went to the window in the great room and looked out. The wind had blown drifts over the snowmen and she couldn't see any markings. She wondered if she'd really seen what she thought she had. She'd check later, and until she did, she saw no reason to confide in Harry.

When she walked into the kitchen, he was sitting at the center island on a barstool, two glasses of wine on the counter. She slipped onto the stool beside him and took the glass he offered. "Thanks."

"So," Harry said. "I didn't know Jordan was involved with anyone."

His comment was unexpected, and she hesitated to answer. Even though she and Jordan had been intimate, they weren't *involved*. "Jordan brought me here because I was…having some problems and needed a place to get away. We're just friends."

"Oh." His eyelids lowered seductively. "That puts things in a different light." His gaze roamed over her and he surprised her by gently slipping a hand over hers. "You mentioned a daughter. Are you married?"

With his face so close to hers, his eyelids at half mast and reeking of alcohol, she realized he was drunk. She pulled her hand away. "No. I'm a widow."

He sloshed down the rest of his wine. "I'm sorry."

"It was a few years ago. I've gotten on with my life."

"But not with Jordan."

It wasn't a question, so she didn't answer.

"I'm surprised. Jordan rarely lets the good ones get away."

The implication wasn't lost. She shifted her feet. Half joking, she said, "Are you saying Jordan is a ladies' man?" Not that it mattered. Just because they'd had some intimate moments didn't mean she had a lock on his heart.

Harry laughed. "*That* would be an understatement."

Her chest constricted. She cleared her throat. "Well, I guess that's his business, isn't it."

"Sometimes," he drawled, bitterness heavy in his voice. "But not when he gets it on with his brother's wife."

The hairs on the back of her neck stood on end. "I'm sorry. I don't think I want any more wine. I'm going up to bed."

He laughed. "Just like all the rest. Jordan can do no wrong. Well, I've got news for you. He's not the up-standing guy you think he is."

Her nerves bunched. Instinct told her to defend Jordan from the verbal assault, but then how much did she really know about him? He'd lied about the cabin. What else had he lied about? It was obvious Jordan and his brother had problems, problems that needed to be solved between the two of them.

"I don't think anything, one way or the other. And you might want to have some caffeine instead of more liquor."

He gazed at her with a puzzled expression. Finally he said, "Okay. Can you get me some?"

She gritted her teeth, went to the counter behind her and lifted the coffeepot. Still some left.

What he'd said bothered her. More than it should. Well, it was probably just the booze talking. He couldn't mean Jordan had had an affair with his own brother's wife.

She poured coffee and stuck the mug in the micro-wave. "How long are you staying?" The thought of being here for any time at all with Harry made her nervous.

"As long as you want me to, sweetheart."

"And if I don't want you to?"

He shrugged. "I'm gone."

"Jordan will be back tomorrow. Did he know you were coming?"

"Nope. Doesn't know a thing. I needed a quick break. Tomorrow, huh?"

"Yes. Tomorrow." Laura turned to go back upstairs, but felt a warm hand on her shoulder stop her.

"I didn't mean all the stuff I said about Jordan earlier."

Without turning, she said, "I didn't believe it, anyway."

He was suddenly quiet, as if he hadn't expected her curt response.

She pulled away and started up the steps.

"But I meant the part about him and my wife."

Laura stopped in her tracks, her grip tightening on the rail.

Harry gave a croak of a laugh. "I guess I should say my ex-wife, shouldn't I. Thanks to Jordan."

She turned.

"Surprised to hear the upstanding Jordan St. James has some flaws?"

She felt as if a tight band had formed around her chest, making it hard to breathe. "We all have flaws, Harry. And what's the old saying…people who live in glass houses…?" She took a deep breath and put a foot on the next step. "I'm going to sleep now."

"Sure," he mumbled, "ignore the truth—just like everyone else…." His voice trailed off.

Laura hurried upstairs and went into Cait's room,

closed and locked the door. She stood there for a moment, her mind a kaleidoscope of questions. Was it Harry who'd dumped something on the snowmen? But what reason would he have to do such a thing? And, fact was, she didn't really know what had happened to them. It could be nothing, or something easily explained.

Most of the questions she could shrug off, except one—had Jordan slept with his brother's wife? Was Jordan the cause of Harry's divorce as he'd said?

Was she ignoring the truth?

What was the truth?

CHAPTER TWELVE

THE INSTANT JORDAN pulled into the driveway he saw the thick tire tracks in the snow. Someone had been here. Someone with a big vehicle, like a Hummer. As he drove closer, all his senses went on red alert. Ahead, the side door to the garage was open...no, not open, it looked as if it had been bashed in. What the— *Oh, God. Laura. Cait.* His heart pounded.

He cut the engine and sprinted toward the house, drawing his .38 on the way. He stepped into the garage, gun raised and scanning as he went. The lock on the splintered door hung half off. A crowbar lay on the floor. Cold fear gripped him. *Control. Keep the emotions under control.*

He crept along the side wall toward the door to the coatroom, turned the knob and then burst inside, both hands on his weapon in ready stance.

Laura stood in front of him, her eyes blown gigantic with fright.

He glanced behind her and kept moving forward. When he reached her, he pulled her behind him but kept the gun at ready. "Are you okay? Where's Cait?"

"I'm fine. And Cait's upstairs studying. What's going on? Has something happened?"

After taking another look around, he lowered his weapon. "You tell me. The garage door..."

"The door? What do you mean?"

He pulled her out to the garage. "What happened?"

She raised a hand to her mouth. "Oh, my God!" She stepped back. "I bet that's what I heard. The loud noise."

"What?"

"Last night I heard a noise like nothing I'd ever heard before…like a bomb going off. I thought maybe a tree had fallen or…I don't know what I thought."

"You don't know how this happened?"

"Oh, I think I do now. I just didn't know it at the time."

He holstered the .38. "Enlighten me," Jordan said as they went back into the kitchen. He noticed two wineglasses in the sink and an empty bottle on the counter.

She sat on a stool, her expression tight. "Why don't *you* enlighten *me?*"

"Excuse me?"

"Why didn't you tell me this place belonged to your family?"

He squared his shoulders. "It isn't important."

"And was making love with me unimportant, too?"

He took her hand. "What does one have to do with the other?"

Lowering her gaze, she pulled her hand away. "Honesty."

Honesty? He was confused—about the door, the wineglasses, and what the hell she really meant. "If you're thinking it was just a one-night stand, you're wrong."

"What was it, then?"

"It was a wonderful night with a woman I'm beginning to care a great deal about."

"So why didn't you tell me the cabin belonged to your family? What did you think would happen if I knew?"

He shook his head. "I don't know. I didn't think. I'm just not used to telling too many people about myself. I've been burned a few times."

Her back went ramrod straight. She got to her feet and grabbed the coffeepot as if she wanted to throttle it. She poured herself a cup, but didn't bother asking him if he wanted any.

"So, what did you think? That I was some money-grubbing gold digger who'd sleep with you to get at your family's riches?"

He stood in front of her, blocking her path and forcing her to stay in one spot. "I never thought, that's what. I'm not used to spilling my guts and there's no more to it. No ulterior motives. I brought you here to protect you and Cait."

His muscles were still tensed for action. "Besides—" he waved a hand in the air "—they're not my real family. I was adopted."

"Well, gee, that explains everything," she said facetiously, her gaze narrowed.

"You're right. It doesn't have anything to do with anything. I should've said something and I didn't. But I don't think it's the important issue here. I tried to call all morning and couldn't get through. Then when I drove up and saw the door, I was...scared to death that something had happened to you." He ran a hand through his hair in an effort to calm his ragged nerves. "What did happen?"

With a deliberate sigh, she said, "Long story short, Harry was here."

Jordan felt a jab to his solar plexis. "Harry?"

"Yes, the guy at the airport. Your brother. Remember him?"

"Harry broke down the door?"

"I'm guessing now that he did. I was hearing lots of strange noises, the wind and all—you know how it is when you're in a strange place. After I'd been in bed a while, I heard a horribly loud noise. I was searching upstairs for something to defend myself when a man grabbed me. It was Harry and he thought I was trespassing."

"Are you…did he—" He reached for her, but she quickly held up a hand.

"I'm fine."

Jordan swung around, clenching and unclenching his hands. "What did you tell him?"

"Nothing. Just that you brought us here to stay for a while."

"Did he say why he was here?"

"He was drunk and he said a lot of things. But he never said why he was here. He was gone when I woke up this morning."

A truly awkward moment passed between them.

Jordan took a breath, then, keeping his voice even, asked, "What things did he say?"

She moistened her lips, then said softly, "He said you slept with his wife."

Crap. They were back to that again. "It's not true. I was helping her, just as I'm helping you." Damn it. His inability to stay away from women in distress was going to ruin his life one way or another.

"Harry has some major anger issues. When he's drinking, he gets…aggressive with women. And he blames others for his problems. I've always been the closest target." He looked away. "When he's not drinking, he's a good guy."

She cast about the room for someplace to look other

than at him. "Well, that's between you and him, isn't it."

"You don't believe me?"

"I don't know what to believe anymore. But something else happened here that you should know."

He saw her hands were trembling.

"And I don't think Harry had anything to do with it."

Laura suddenly felt more vulnerable than she'd felt in a long time. Her choices kept narrowing and Cait seemed more at risk than ever.

Jordan stood there waiting for her to continue, but, Lord, she didn't even know how to start. Pacing, she went through the night's events.

"When I was downstairs, well before I heard the loud noise, I heard other sounds. I thought I saw something move outside, so I turned on all the outdoor lights, figuring if some animal was out there, the lights would scare it away. A loud crash woke me up a few hours later, so I got up and looked out the window and...I saw the snowmen we'd built had been...they were covered with something. Something dark red." She took a breath, her heart pounding violently.

He strode over to the window.

"You can't see now. It snowed again early this morning and the drifts covered them over. Anyway...I told you all the rest about Harry. I didn't tell him what had happened. I thought there might be some explanation. And now that it's daylight, things seem...more normal."

"Are you sure about what you saw?"

"Yes, but I didn't get a good look and I don't know what it was." She pursed her lips. "I wasn't hallucinating."

Jordan smiled—trying to make her feel better, she supposed.

"I just want to be sure of the facts," he said, then headed for the door. She followed on his heels, both of them grabbing jackets on the way. Jordan snatched a shovel.

Outside, the sun was shining, and the snow was starting to melt. She pointed. "Over here." They crossed the yard, footsteps crunching as they went, and when they reached one of the mounds, Jordan picked at the snow with the tip of the shovel, stopping when he reached red.

Laura fell to her knees and started gently scooping with her bare hands, careful not to disturb anything.

Jordan crouched down next to her. "It looks like paint," he said as he tunneled to the part where the color showed most vividly. "Anything else wouldn't be so bright."

Anything else...she knew what he meant. "Well, thank God for that."

Jordan gave a half grin and touched her cheek. "Let's cover this up so Cait doesn't see."

After they'd finished, they passed through the broken door in the garage and, once inside, Jordan prowled the perimeter. "Here," he said, calling her over. "One of the paint cans is missing."

A gasp tore from her throat. "Which means the person who did this came into the garage...before Harry got here."

"Probably. And if Harry ruined the door, the other person got inside another way."

"But...how? I had the alarm on." Laura covered her face with her hands, her fragile emotions ready to crack. She felt trapped. Cornered.

"It's all speculation," Jordan added quickly. "Maybe it was Harry, but…we don't know anything for sure, and I'll have to talk to him. Let's go inside."

Though he'd said the words, he didn't move, he just kept looking at her. He shifted his weight from one foot to the other, placed his hands on her arms, and said, "Please tell me what you're really afraid of. It might help explain some of this."

Laura stiffened. Keeping the secret meant Cait would be safe.

Only she wasn't sure that was true anymore.

Jordan led her to the den, then drew her onto the leather couch. This was the room where she'd discovered the photo album. Her guard went up again.

Why should she tell him anything now? How could she trust a man who'd lied to her? A man who thought she was a—a gold digger.

He took her hands, forcing her to look at him. "Let's put this in perspective. Someone is stalking you…but you've had stalkers at the shelter before and you've never run away. You ran and brought your daughter along, too, so it's apparent you're worried about her as well as yourself. What is it that you're not telling me?"

She shook her head.

"I can help," he said with conviction. "Whatever it is, I can make sure nothing happens to either you or Cait."

Listening, her resolve weakened. "If a whole police force couldn't protect Eddie, what makes you think you, one person, can protect the two of us?"

"That's what this is all about, isn't it? Eddie's murder."

Oh, God. Did he know? And if he knew, how could he help her escape from the prison of secrecy and lies she'd been living in?

He tightened his grip. "If you know something, you'll never be safe. Do you want to live in fear for the rest of your life?"

She shook her head. Swallowed the acidic lump that had formed in her throat.

"Do you want Cait to live like this? Running from place to place? *I* can help." He moistened his lips. "But I can't help if you're not honest with me."

She gritted her teeth. "*You're* talking about honesty?"

"Okay, I guess I deserved that. But we're talking about you and Cait. This is your life. Your future. Do you want to have one or do you want to always be looking over your shoulder?"

She closed her eyes.

"What suddenly changed to make you so afraid? What happened, Laura?"

She drew a deep breath, the raw emotion and fear that'd been bottled up inside her for so long threatened to explode. Maybe if she told him part of it... "I don't know what specifically happened. It all started about the time you came to the shelter asking questions."

Surprise registered in his eyes, but he kept them on her. "What started then?"

"The black car. And Cait saw a man by the house."

"And he hadn't been around before?"

"No. At least I never saw him."

"Were you wary right away?"

Confusion clogged her brain. Too many questions. Too much to think about. What if she said the wrong thing? "I don't know. No, I don't think so. I thought maybe it was someone for one of the girls. A parent, an old boyfriend..."

Standing, Jordan raked a hand through his hair. "So you didn't think anything of it at first. What made you change your mind?"

She told him about the break-in and the shredded quilt.

His eyes darkened.

"I thought it…seemed personal," she said. "Because Eddie had given Cait the music box, and his mother had hand stitched the quilt. And then there were the phone calls. The last one in particular."

Jordan's lips thinned, but he nodded for her to go on.

God, she wasn't sure she could.

"How was the last call different?" As he said the words, he sat beside her again and held her hands.

She knew he was trying to reassure her—and it worked. The comfort she felt in his touch nearly overwhelmed her. God, she didn't want to go through this anymore…the uncertainty…the never-ending fear, old fears, new fears. Would it ever be over?

No, she realized. It would never be over. Not unless Frank DeMatta died or was in prison for life.

She swallowed, cleared her throat. "The first calls were silent, just breathing and then a hang up."

"I've had some of those, too. One when we were together."

"Does that mean something?"

"Maybe." He gently pushed her hair from her eyes, brushed his fingers against her cheek. "But I don't know what. Maybe someone wanted me, or you, to know he knew we were together. What was different about the last call?"

Her heart raced, and she suddenly felt nauseous. "He s-said if—"

Before she got out the words, he pulled her into his

arms and held her, and as he did, she felt as if some of his strength transferred to her.

"He warned me to stay away from the police. He said my daughter's life would be in danger if I didn't."

Laura heard footsteps and pulled from Jordan's arms.

"Jordan. You're back!" Caitlin ran into the room, came over and threw her arms around him.

"Hey, squirt!" He ruffled her hair and then sat back. "Are you having fun here?"

"Uh-huh." Cait's face beamed—until she looked at Laura. "Mom? What's wrong? You look sad."

Jordan nodded to Laura, then mouthed, "We'll talk later."

Laura pasted on a wobbly smile and touched her daughter's cheek. "Nothing, sweetheart. Nothing's wrong."

JORDAN PACED THE CONCRETE floor in the garage while he punched in Luke's number on his cell phone, praying for a connection. He'd fixed the door as best he could, taking a door from inside the house and replacing the broken one. It didn't fit exactly right, but it served the purpose. He wanted to leave as soon as possible, but he was determined to get the whole story from Laura first. He couldn't make a plan if he didn't know what he was getting into.

Someone wanted her to stay away from the police... DeMatta's man had given *him* a warning about her. The phone crackled. Bad reception. He clicked off and redialed.

What did Laura know that might be threatening to someone if the police knew? It had to involve her husband's murder. What else could have such dire consequences? He'd thought from the moment he'd met

Laura that she was withholding something. Now he was certain.

He was also certain she was doing it to protect her daughter.

And whoever was threatening Cait probably knew Laura and Cait were at the cabin. They couldn't stay there any longer.

"Coltrane," a gravelly voice finally answered after several rings.

"Luke. Glad I got you."

"You back?"

"No. Who knew I was coming up here?"

"No one besides me. Why?"

"Laura's cover's blown. Someone knows and I need a backup plan."

"My house is available if you need it."

"Thanks. I'm not so sure that's a good idea, either."

"You find out why she ran?"

"Some of it."

"What can I do?"

"Check to see if the photo composite we did on this Nicholas guy produced anything. We're heading back before it gets dark."

"Sure thing."

Jordan disconnected and went into the living room where Laura and Cait were watching a DVD. He motioned to Laura to follow him into the den.

"I'll be back in a few minutes, Cait. I need to talk to Jordan about something."

"That means it's private, doesn't it?"

Laura smiled tentatively. "It does."

When Laura came in, Jordan said, "Sit. Please."

He closed the door. "We need to finish our conversation."

She sat on the edge of the chair, as if ready to bolt at any second. He stood in front of her, but far enough away not to crowd her.

"If I'm going to help you, I need to know everything."

She blinked. "The pictures I looked at were in the album over there. They're nice family pictures."

"Don't change the subject."

As if he hadn't said a word, she asked, "Have you ever tried to find your biological mother?"

His stomach knotted. "No. Now, tell me what you're so afraid of."

"I told you about the threat."

Nodding, he dropped into the chair directly across from her and leaned forward, elbows on his knees. He reached to take her hands, but she pulled back. "You didn't tell me why you're being threatened. What gives someone so much power over you?"

For a long moment she just sat there, fear and uncertainty battling in her eyes. "Power over me?"

"Yes. You're hiding out because someone has threatened you. Threatened Cait. That's power. You take that power away by telling the truth."

She launched to her feet. "I told you the truth."

"Yes, but not all of it. I can't leave you here alone again. You know that. It's time to stop letting this creep direct your life."

Her mouth opened, but nothing came out. She turned to look at him, realization in her face. "That's what he's doing, isn't it. Directing my life."

He remained silent.

After a few moments, she said, "As much as I hate being a pawn, it doesn't matter. If I say anything, I'll truly be putting Cait's life in danger. If something happened to her because of—" The words caught in her throat. "I can't do it."

"Or maybe just the opposite would happen. Maybe we'd arrest the guy and you'd release yourself and Cait from his control."

"'Maybe' isn't good enough."

"*Maybe* is life. Laura, there are no guarantees. What you're doing doesn't guarantee Cait's safety. You've seen that already. So, forget about what happened to your husband. One day later, safely under witness protection, and he'd be alive today. I'll do everything in my power to protect you and Cait. Whatever it takes, I'll do it."

She fell back into the chair and pinched the bridge of her nose with two fingers. "You say that with a lot of certainty."

"I have to be certain or I couldn't do my job. And more important, I'm not about to put the people I care most about in danger."

Her expression was surprised, then she frowned as she struggled over what to do. Would anything change if she told him? Could he really protect them? She'd be a fool not to wonder all of those things. Because he did, too.

He knelt in front of her. "If you tell me what it is, I can't guarantee the outcome, but I can guarantee that I'll do everything in my power to keep you and Cait safe. And…I can guarantee nothing will change if you don't give me the opportunity to find out what can be done. This isn't the kind of life you envisioned for her, is it?"

Tears welled in her eyes. "No. Not at all."

"I can help. Trust me."

She wrenched away, paced some more. Finally she

blurted, "Cait was in the house the night Eddie died. She saw a man there."

Jordan felt as if he'd been punched in the gut. Had she said what he thought she did? He'd imagined she might have withheld some information about her ex's gambling debts, or the names of people he owed money, someone she'd seen him with or...or something. *Not* that her child had been there during her father's murder.

"Cait was there the night of the murder and you didn't report it?"

Her head bobbed up and down.

"But if she was there—" He couldn't believe what she was saying.

"She was staying overnight, but she didn't see anything happen. Thinking her father was sick, she called me on the phone and I went to get her. That's when I discovered Eddie was...dead."

"You withheld information?" He couldn't disguise his shock. His judgment. "It's a criminal offense. How could you do that?"

Her face paled. "I—I thought if whoever killed Eddie knew Cait was in the house, he might think she saw him and come after her...th-that she'd end up like her father."

"What exactly did she see?"

"She saw a man there earlier talking with Eddie."

"Can she identify the person she saw?"

Laura hesitated, her arms crossed over her chest. "I don't want her involved."

"But," he said incredulously, "she is involved. And if she can identify the man, we may be able to solve the case." They might've solved it years ago, if they'd had this information.

She swung around, her expression hard. "I don't give a damn about solving the case. I only care about my daughter. If they knew—"

He placed a hand on her arm. "But someone does know. He knows enough to be threatening you."

She muffled a sob with her hand. "I—I thought we were okay…and the only way…anyone…would find out she was there was if I said something. And then…" Her shoulders began to shake, tears rolling down her cheeks.

Jordan felt her pain as if it were his own. He enveloped her in his arms, crushing her tight against him. He kissed her hand and her cheeks to dry her tears. "Shh. It's okay. We'll work it out."

Suddenly she pulled back, nearly stumbled. "No, it's not okay. Whoever has been calling me knows Cait was there. I can't think of any other reason for the threats. He knows we're here, too, and I can't see any way to fix any of it."

"There's only one way to fix it—if Cait can identify the person at Eddie's that night."

Laura looked at him, her face chalk-white, eyes filled with trepidation. She fell into the chair again, boneless, as if all the energy had drained from her body.

"The thing is," Jordan said, "if this person wanted to harm her, he'd have done it by now. But instead he's telling you to back off. That means it has to be someone who doesn't want to hurt you or Cait if he doesn't have to. But I can tell you right now, when pushed to the wall, he will."

The breath she took was so deep, he thought she might break down completely. Then, in a whisper, she said, "When we were at the funeral, Cait told me the man she saw at her father's was standing across from us."

"Someone you know?"

"Frank DeMatta."

He caught his breath. He couldn't believe she'd kept this from the police. If she'd told the truth, DeMatta would probably be on death row by now.

"But just because he was there doesn't mean he—"

Yeah, right. He stuffed his hands into his pockets to contain his agitation, to make himself think clearly, not on emotion. It was true that being there wasn't an indictment. At best it was circumstantial. They had no weapon, no other hard proof. "What did you tell Cait when she told you?"

"I said it couldn't have been Mr. DeMatta because he'd been out of the country. I said she must've dreamed it. She never brought it up again. I can't imagine she'd remember anything now."

Even if she did remember, the testimony of a seven-year-old child, three years after the fact, would likely make her an unreliable witness. But it did clear up a lot of things. Damn. If the person Cait had seen was anyone other than DeMatta, Jordan would have no reservations about what to do. But knowing DeMatta had a mole in the department changed everything.

"We need to go back," Jordan said, a plan developing. "It's not safe here."

"What about the threats?"

"I'll take care of it. Trust me."

THE HUM OF THE TIRES on the asphalt soothed Laura's frazzled nerves. They'd left the snow behind them and Cait slept soundly in the back seat with her earphones on. It would be another couple of hours before they reached L.A., during which she had to think of some way to keep her daughter safe. Her stomach churned along with her rampant thoughts.

Trust me, Jordan had said. Well, it wasn't a matter of not trusting *him,* although she did have reason to doubt his truthfulness. It was a matter of not trusting anyone other than herself. Every time she'd gotten close to someone, put her faith in another person, she'd been betrayed.

The only people she truly trusted were Rose and Phoebe. Even though she'd made amends with her father, and he'd helped her through a tough time, in the end, he'd betrayed her, too. But she'd been so needy she made herself believe he really cared.

It wasn't until years later when she was taking college psychology classes that she realized the truth about herself. She'd vowed then and there not to be bound by her own neediness ever again.

She glanced at Jordan, who was off in his own world. He'd been helpful beyond the call of duty, and though she didn't want to care about him, it was too late. She didn't want to love him, either…but she did.

Taking their relationship into the bedroom had been the biggest mistake of her life. They were poles apart; he from a wealthy cultured family, she a trailer-trash street kid who'd made more than her share of mistakes. She wasn't the kind of woman he'd be proud to introduce to his family, so why fantasize? She'd found her place in the world, and she liked it just fine.

While she was studying him, he turned to look at her. "I have a plan," he said, his voice low. "I think it'll work."

"Does it require my participation?"

"Not immediately. I'm going to take you to a friend's house for a while until… When I'm done, I'm hoping it'll be safe for you to go back home."

"How long is a while?" Lord, she sounded like Cait now.

"I don't know—as long as it takes."

She glanced back at Cait. She was awake now and listening to music again. "What are you planning to do?" she asked, keeping her voice to a whisper.

"I'm going to shut down the Kolnikov case."

She did a double take. "How will that solve anything?"

"The Kolnikov case is what brought me to you. And it's obvious my presence in your life is a threat to the person who's been stalking you. So, if I remove the threat…" He glanced over at her.

"But—"

"You said it started right after my first visit to the shelter. My guess is that this person is worried that if you know something, you might divulge what you know to me."

"Why would anyone think I know anything? And if he did, why would he wait until now to do something about it?"

"My guess is he didn't find it necessary before now. Things changed once I started questioning you about the Kolnikov case."

"But the Kolnikov case doesn't have anything to do with Eddie—" She turned to Jordan. "Or does it?"

He placed a warm hand over hers. "This isn't the time to talk about it. We'll talk later."

Oh, God. What had she gotten herself into? All she cared about was Cait…trying to protect her…and now *she'd* put her child's life in danger. "I'll do whatever I can."

He squeezed her hand. "You can help by authorizing me to get your phone records and by telling my partner everything you know, from beginning to end and not leaving out a single thing."

"Your partner?"

"I'm taking you to his house. When I'm not there, he'll be there—until we get a resolution."

"But why tell him? I already told you everything."

His shoulders tensed. "He might see something I don't." Then he paused, his brows drawn together. "I want to make sure my personal involvement isn't coloring my judgment."

Her pulse quickened.

"It's just a double check. We do it all the time."

CHAPTER THIRTEEN

LAURA WAITED IN THE CAR while Jordan knocked. The door opened and a large man appeared. She couldn't see him very well, except that he was about Jordan's height and had sandy-blond hair. Jordan stepped inside and seconds later came back out.

"Come on. This is where you're going to stay for a couple days."

"Are we still on vacation?" Cait asked. "I want to go home and play with my friends."

"Soon, sweetie," Laura said, getting out of the car. She was at a loss over what to tell the child. She didn't want to lie to her, and Cait was too smart to think they were just visiting one of Jordan's friends.

He led the way inside. "Laura and Cait Gianni, meet Luke Coltrane, one of the crankiest guys I know."

Cait giggled, then looked away as if embarrassed.

"It's true," Luke said, making a snarly face. "Some people think I gobble up little children."

"It's nice to meet you, Luke." Laura smiled and shook his hand. He was a detective; she recognized his name from one of the conversations she'd had with Jordan.

Cait glommed onto her mother's leg.

"He's just kidding," Laura said.

"No, I'm not. But I'll refrain this time."

"Ignore him, Cait," Jordan said. "He's harmless. Now, let's get you two settled." Jordan took their luggage and started toward the back of the house. "Where do you want them?" he asked Luke.

"There are only two bedrooms besides mine, so take your pick."

The stairway was at the back of the narrow two-story home. Despite the fact that the place needed a good cleaning, Laura liked the antique furniture, the dark wood, old leaded-glass light fixtures and the eccentric architecture. The house definitely had a personality of its own.

Cait clung to Laura's side as they went up the narrow stairwell and down an equally narrow hallway. Jordan stopped at one of the three doors and flung it open. He reached across to the other side and opened another. "Both bedrooms are small. Take your pick."

"I want this one, Mom." Cait indicated the bedroom on the left. "I can see the ocean from the window."

"I think we should share a room," Laura said. "Otherwise Jordan won't have a place to sleep."

He shook his head. "Not a problem. I like the couch downstairs just fine. And that way I'm in a better position to keep an eye on things."

"What things?" Cait looked at Jordan with big eyes.

Laura glanced at him, too, hoping he wouldn't say anything to frighten Cait.

"Actually, it's the refrigerator I want to keep an eye on. I like my midnight snacks."

"You're lucky. My mom won't let me have snacks."

Laura took a stance, hands on her hips. "Not true. You have snacks all the time."

"Fruit. Fruit's not a snack. It's food."

"It's good for you," Laura said. "Now, let's get you unpacked and let Jordan go about his business."

He smiled, then said softly, "I'll need about ten minutes alone with Luke."

She nodded her understanding but felt awful about it. He wanted to fill his partner in, to tell him how she'd lied to the police, how she'd obstructed justice. Funny how she'd never really thought about it that way until he'd said it. But she'd do it again under the same circumstances.

"Can we go to the beach, Mom? I want to go to the beach."

"It's getting late."

"Can we go tomorrow?"

"We'll see." If this nightmare ever ended, maybe they could get their lives back. Do normal things. Truth was, she couldn't remember what normal was anymore.

Cait flopped onto the bed. "You always say 'We'll see' when you really mean no. You never let me do anything."

Laura sighed, lifting Cait's suitcase to the bed and taking out the child's pajamas. "That's because you're seven years old."

"Almost eight. Shannon gets to go places all the time."

"Well, we just came back from the mountains. That's someplace."

Cait smiled. "Yeah, I guess, but—"

"No buts," Laura said. "None of us are going anywhere."

Cait's face crumpled. "You never want to talk about other things, either."

Laura felt Cait's frustration. And there wasn't a

damned thing she could do about it. "This isn't the time or the place to talk, but we will when we get home. And I promise I'll listen."

"I want to go home now. I don't like staying away so long."

"Neither do I, honey." *Neither do I.*

JORDAN FOUND LUKE IN THE kitchen holding a drink. "You can't be alert if you're drinking," Jordan said.

Luke frowned, then held up the glass. "Pure tonic water."

"You get anything on the composite?"

"Not before I left. If there's anything, it should be there by now."

"You tell anyone?"

Luke shook his head. "So, what's going down?"

Walking over to close the kitchen door, Jordan said, "A lot." He proceeded to tell Luke everything Laura had told him, including the events at the cabin...except the personal things.

"What the hell...if we'd known when we were investigating... She had to know she could go to jail for obstructing the law, didn't she?"

"She didn't care about anything except her daughter's safety. But she's willing to help us now. Only they need a safe place. I figured this was better than most."

Luke nodded. "She could still be in trouble for obstruction of justice."

"I know. I'll try to get her immunity if she testifies." Jordan felt edgy, couldn't stand still. "But I don't want it to go that far."

"You sound involved."

"I am involved. I think I started this whole thing."

"That's bull. She started it when she withheld information."

"Technically true. But she was doing just fine until I showed up."

"Yeah," Luke said, cracking a grin. "You've got it bad."

Jordan glared at him. "I'm trying to solve a case and keep two people safe."

"All good intentions. But you've still got it bad. So, what's the plan?"

"I'm going out. But when Cait's in bed, Laura's going to tell you the story from start to finish. I still don't know if she's given me everything and I just need a double check. See what you can do."

"Gotcha."

A half hour later, Jordan, on his way into the RHD, stopped at the front desk. "Hey," he said to Mary Beth. "Got that information I asked for?"

She looked up, her expression teasing. "What's it worth?"

He wasn't in the mood for joking around. He was on a mission. "Do you have it or not?"

She gave him a nasty look and shoved her hair out of her eyes. "Well, sort of."

"Sort of? Either you have it or you don't."

"I have this." She handed him a printout.

"Thanks." He snatched it from her hand and headed back to his desk.

"Hey, partner."

The two-pack-a-day voice grated on Jordan's nerves. Howie Ralston was the last guy in the department he wanted as his partner. Jordan turned. "Yeah. What's up?"

"That's what I was going to ask you. You get anything on the Valdez case?"

"I talked to the daughter, told her about her mother." Jordan laid the printout on his desk, then sat to read it, hoping Ralston got the message.

"How about the Kolnikov case?"

"What about it?"

"I heard you're honing in on a suspect."

"You heard wrong. In fact, it's just the opposite. I'm shutting the case down." He went back to the printout.

Ralston came around the desk to stand in front of him, apparently wanting Jordan to look up. "Why?"

"Because we've exhausted all leads. We're wasting our time."

Rubbing a beefy hand across his chin, Ralston turned to leave. "Okay. I've got better things to do, anyway," he said over his shoulder.

Before Jordan could respond, the guy was out the door. Hell, he couldn't have planned it any better. If Ralston knew they were shutting down the Kolnikov case, the whole department would know. And hopefully DeMatta's mole.

He shoved back his chair and glanced at the papers, flipping pages. He stopped on an entry, his heartbeat quickening. The Belzar Corporation was owned by a Nick Stanton. Quickly he punched the name into NCIC.

His phone rang and Mary Beth came on the intercom. "The boss wants to see you."

Damn. He let the program run, got up and went to Carlyle's office.

The captain sat behind the desk, his face drawn, dark circles under his eyes. "I heard you're giving up on the Kolnikov case."

Jordan grinned. "That was quick."

The captain eyed him from under his brows. "What

aren't you telling me?" It was tough to get anything by the boss. He motioned to Jordan to close the door. "Continue."

Jordan took a piece of paper and wrote on it, *I have information to suggest a particular person was at Eddie Gianni's house the night he died.*

The captain nodded, flipped on the radio and motioned Jordan to the window. Keeping his voice low, Carlyle said, "Anyone we know?"

"Yep. But no positive ID," Jordan whispered back.

"Can you get it?"

"I will." He didn't know how, but he would.

"You need backup?"

"Not yet, but soon. I don't want any leaks." Jordan knew the captain would readily agree if it meant solving one of their biggest screwup cases.

"Let me know. I can't wait to get the mayor off my ass."

Jordan went back to his desk and checked NCIC for the composite photograph he'd fed it earlier. Four pages of photographs popped up, each one bearing a resemblance to DeMatta's new man. He paged down, mentally eliminating those in jail and those who really didn't look like him at all. On the last page, a familiar face stared back at him. *Nicholas Stanton.* The guy who'd been at Vincento's with DeMatta was the same guy listed as the owner of the Belzar Corporation.

Stanton worked for DeMatta. Was the corporation a front for something else? According to Rita Valdez's description, Stanton was likely the man she'd seen with Anna Kolnikov. It made sense Stanton would know the woman if he was doing business with DeMatta. Laura had seen a blond guy with Kolnikov, and if she could identify him… Jordan's thoughts spiraled. Stanton's corporation owned the black car

that had been following Laura. But that didn't make
sense. Was Stanton one of DeMatta's new hit men?
Brought in from New York to take out Rita Valdez *and*
threaten Laura? Maybe take her out, too. The MO for
Kolnikov's murder was similar to Valdez's. Had he
been in L.A. four years ago, too?

Jordan went back to the computer, checked for any
and all information on Stanton, nerves pulsing under
his skin as he waited for the information to material-
ize. When it came, he sat on the edge of his chair, his
legs bouncing with nervous energy as he read. Stanton
had a couple of felony convictions, but with short jail
time. Last paroled in October 2000, not long before
Kolnikov died. But he had a New York address at the
time. DOB, December 24, 1965, New Paltz, New York.
Born on Christmas Eve. Jordan smiled. Stanton's
mother had a sense of humor.

He wasn't familiar with the New York town and
pulled up MapQuest on his computer. His blood rushed.
New Paltz was about twenty miles from Poughkeepsie,
the city where Kolnikov was born. Rita Valdez had said
the man she saw with Anna had been from the same
hometown. Had Kolnikov grown up in New Paltz?

But what would be the connection? There were too
many years between Nick and Anna for them to have
known each other as children.

Another completely unrelated thought popped up.
Kolnikov probably had parents and maybe brothers and
sisters who still lived in New Paltz. Possibly they could
tell him something about the woman. But would the information help him find her killer? He doubted it.

He sighed, resting against the back of his chair. He
didn't need to know anything more about Kolnikov. If
he found her killer, it would be enough. Justice would
prevail—and that's all that mattered.

LAURA HAD WATCHED LUKE'S expression change from understanding to incredulity during their conversation. Afterward, she couldn't tell if he was appalled or just plain disgusted.

He sat across from her on an old frayed couch in the living room. The piece of seventies furniture looked at odds with all the antiques, and she suspected he kept it around for comfort. He scratched his head. "Is that everything?"

"Yes."

"Did the person Cait identified at the funeral know she recognized him?"

"No." She wiped her hands on the thighs of her jeans. "Maybe...I don't know."

"Did you have any conversation with him at the funeral?"

"Not really. He gave me money. Said he takes care of his own."

"Do you know what he meant by that?"

"I didn't know what to think. Maybe he knew Cait was there and thought he was paying me off? Maybe he figured we would have a hard time financially? He is Eddie's family. Cait's great-uncle."

"And you didn't think any of this should be reported?" He shook his head, his expression as incredulous as Jordan's had been.

Anger tightened her throat. "I'm sorry, Luke. I did what I thought best for my child. If that means I'm a lawbreaker, then so be it."

"I'm not standing in judgment."

"Yes, you are. Both you and Jordan! But then I wouldn't expect you to understand. If either of you had children of your own you'd know what I'm talking about. A caring parent will do whatever it takes to protect her child."

Luke stared at her, his expression hard. She saw an undercurrent, something dark and dangerous simmering, which made the veins in his neck pop. He stood. Slowly. Deliberately. "Well, thank you for the parenting lesson. We're through with this conversation." He turned and walked down the hall.

She was still sitting there, stunned at his abruptness, when she heard a knock at the front door. She tensed. Had Luke heard the knock? No way was *she* going to the door. But as she sat there, the knob turned. Her heart raced. And then Jordan entered.

He looked surprised to see her.

"It's you," she said on a sigh of relief.

"A good thing, I hope."

"Considering the alternatives, yes."

"Where's Luke?"

"He just left." She pointed. "Thataway."

Shucking off his suit jacket, Jordan came over and sat next to her. "Cait in bed?"

"A long time ago."

"Did you and Luke talk?"

"We did. Until he got angry and stalked off."

He frowned. "He got angry? Why?"

She stood, feeling her own bottled-up frustration rising. "During our discussion—which really wasn't a discussion since I was doing all the talking—he seemed…well, like you, he seemed to be judging me for what I did. I got annoyed and told him I don't think either of you have any idea what being a parent means. That's when he left the room."

Jordan bowed his head, pressed his fingers against the bridge of his nose. "Yeah. He's got some issues." His voice was so low she could barely hear him. "Five years ago he lost his son. The ordeal was devastating.

It became too much for the marriage and he and his wife divorced because of it. I don't think he's ever gotten over either one."

Laura dropped down next to Jordan, her spirits deflated. "Oh, Lord. I had no idea." She leaned forward, hands over her face. Then she felt a warm hand on her shoulder.

"You couldn't have known."

She sat up. "I feel so horrible. I need to apologize."

"There'll be plenty of time for that. In the meantime, I've got a couple more questions for you."

Silent, she nodded.

"Do you know where Kolnikov grew up?"

"No."

"Can you remember anything more about the people in the black car when you took down the license number?"

She looked away.

"You've got to help me, Laura. I need to know everything. Even things that don't seem important to you."

The sharpness of his words went right through her.

"We're on the verge here. The car belongs to the Belzar Corporation. Have you ever heard of it?"

"No."

"The president of the Belzar Corporation is Nicholas Stanton. I believe he's the same guy you met with Kolnikov." He pulled out Stanton's photo.

She pulled back, astonished. "What does it mean? Why would he be following us? Why would he—"

"He works for Frank DeMatta. I think we know what it means."

She slumped against the back of the couch. "Oh… my…God."

Jordan's gaze locked with hers. "What?"

"Alysa," she whispered. "It was Alysa who got out of the black car."

She saw his jaw twitch. "And you didn't think this was important enough to tell me?" He jerked to his feet, every muscle in his body rigid.

"I thought she might be hooking again. I wanted to work it out with her. I thought when I got the license number, you'd find him and I could get a restraining order. Then both the stalking and Alysa's problem would be solved. I had no idea he worked for anyone, much less DeMatta."

He took a second before he asked, "What made you think she was hooking?"

"That night, I suspected something wasn't right and I went after her. I parked near the place where she said she was going. A strip mall. Some other girls were standing on the sidewalk and at first I thought they were just hanging out. Then a car pulled up and one of the girls got in. Then it happened again and I realized what was going on. When the black car pulled up and Alysa got out, I was stunned."

"Did you talk with her?"

"Uh-huh. She said she'd been devastated over her parents' rejection and thought it didn't matter what she did anymore. But she realized later she'd made a mistake and she was only hurting herself, not them. I think she's back on track."

Jordan shook his head in what seemed to be more disapproval. "But we know differently now."

Damn it. She was tired of his judgments, tired of finding herself in the wrong all the time. She stood. "I'm sorry if you don't agree with my decisions. The fact is, in my line of work I come across illegal activities all the time and I'm bound by the laws of confidentiality. I have to make decisions, and as long as I don't believe a person is a danger to herself or others, I'm doing what I'm supposed to do. So stop judging me."

Oddly, he smiled. "I'm not. Come sit back down."

Her agitation was too great. "I don't want to sit."

"Okay. Then we'll both stand." He stepped closer and said softly, "The thing is, I've found connections between the car, Kolnikov, your ex and some other things I can't mention. Now you're saying there's a connection between Alysa and one of DeMatta's men. That's huge. Every single piece of information is important here. Don't you agree?"

The air left her lungs. "Yes, of course." For the first time she fully realized how what she'd been doing had only made things worse. And the fact that she knew more about Anna might be important, too. She didn't know how, but if it could be... "Now that I know what's involved, everything seems important."

"And so is what we do from here."

"What's that?"

He shook his head. "I'm still figuring it out."

Laura took a deep breath. If she told him about her past, he'd probably never want to speak to her again. But wouldn't it be best, anyway? And if there was something, anything, he might think was important...anything that might help make them safe again, give them a normal life, it would be worth it. "There is something else."

He clenched his hands and squared his shoulders. "Tell me."

She couldn't look at him anymore. "I didn't think this was related in any way, but since I've been so wrong about everything else, I'll let you be the judge." She turned, kept looking down. "I was a runaway once myself. I lived on the street for a while supporting myself—any way I could. I got arrested with…a client one night along with some of Anna's girls and she took me in. I wanted to work for her, but I was only fifteen so she wouldn't let me. Except to clean her house. That's where I first saw Eddie. He came to her place every week. I didn't know what he was doing and the only communication between us was an occasional hello. Later, I—I became pregnant, and when my boyfriend split, Anna let me stay with her. She took me in, no questions asked."

He raised his head. Stared at her with blank eyes, waiting for her to go on.

"I planned to give the child up for adoption, but I had a miscarriage. When I was feeling better, I contacted my father and made arrangements to go stay with him. I didn't meet Eddie again until I was in college."

Jordan looked at her as if she were a stranger, confusion and disbelief in his eyes.

"I didn't say anything because no one knows. It's in my past and none of it seemed to be important…except that I knew Anna and I want to see her killer brought to justice. That's why I agreed to tell you anything in the first place. I had no idea how much trouble talking to you would bring me and Cait."

His mouth formed a thin line. "And if you'd known, would you have said anything at all?"

Jordan's animosity radiated through the room. Just looking at him made her heart ache. What else could she say? Nothing would make this any better. Tears began to well. She blinked them back and took a deep breath.

"I can understand if you despise me. I've done things you find unconscionable. But I've never claimed to be innocent. I've never claimed to be anyone other than who I am. I haven't done terrible things to anyone except myself. I also don't expect you or anyone else to understand."

Jordan, his back ramrod straight and his expression unchanged, seemed impervious to anything she'd just said.

He didn't even want to acknowledge her. God, she wished she could fix this somehow. "So, what do you think we should do now?"

He looked at her, his eyes dark with emotions she could only imagine. Anger. Disappointment. Hate.

He threw up his hands. "I have no idea."

"Well, I have some ideas."

Laura turned at the voice. *Luke.*

Jordan pried out his next words. "Any and all ideas are welcome." He glanced at Laura, then back to Luke and said, "Later, when we're alone."

That wrenched Laura's heart. He didn't trust her enough to even include her in the discussion. But how could she blame him?

"You'll be alone now. I'm going to bed." She started to walk away, then stopped, directing her comments to Luke. "I'm sorry for what I said earlier. I made an assumption and I feel like a fool because of it. I'm truly sorry."

Luke didn't breathe a word but nodded his acknowledgment. She left the room.

AN HOUR LATER, Jordan had shucked his suit and changed into a pair of jeans and a sweater. Laura had dropped another bomb on him. Oddly, he could understand why she'd kept the information about Caitlin being at her father's a secret, especially when her ex was supposed to be protected. But the rest of it hit him on a personal level. She wasn't the person he believed she was.

She'd been going to give up her child. The only reason she hadn't was because nature stepped in. He snatched his leather jacket from the front closet and yanked open the front door.

Luke's voice stopped him. "Have you got a plan?"

Jordan turned to his friend. "I need to go out for a while. I have to talk to some people."

"To see if their stories gibe?"

"Something like that." Jordan glanced at the clock. "You okay here for an hour?"

"I'll hold down the fort, but when you get back, we talk."

"Sure."

As Jordan headed for his car, a stiff sea breeze blew in from the shore, and he breathed it in deeply. He had to have a clear head, stay focused on the job, not on his personal life—not on how Laura was a chameleon, how she'd fooled him. What might she spring on him next?

Within the hour, he pulled up at Vincento's. This time there were more than a half-dozen cars in front. Either the place was busy or the mob was having a conference. He should be wary about going inside, but instead he felt numb.

The place was filled to capacity, mostly neighborhood types. Italian music and a cacophony of voices filled the air. He spotted DeMatta and Stanton immediately at the same table in the back. As he headed toward them, he heard nothing but his heart drumming in his ears. No fear? Yeah, right.

Reaching the table, he spoke directly to Stanton. "We need to talk privately."

DeMatta's face pinched. "Whatever you got to say, you can say it right here."

Ignoring DeMatta, Jordan directed his words to Stanton. "Either we talk privately here or I take you downtown. Your choice."

Stanton glanced at DeMatta, who nodded.

"Let's go out front," Jordan said, and together they walked outside.

Stanton was taller than him by a couple of inches and probably had a few pounds on him, as well. He looked to be in great condition and Jordan hoped this didn't develop into anything ugly.

"What can I do for you, Detective?"

The guy had manners, sounded well educated, at least if his diction had anything to do with it. For a guy from New York, he had no accent whatsoever. "You can answer some questions."

"If I can."

"What were you doing with the kid from Victory House in your car last week?"

"She needed a ride. I gave her one."

The guy never flinched, never hesitated, never registered emotion of any kind. "We both know that's a lie."

"Prove it."

"I intend to."

"Is that it?"

"Tell me about Anna Kolnikov."

He saw something flash in Stanton's eyes, but he wasn't sure what it was. Concern? Not likely. Recognition? Maybe.

"I told you, I don't know the woman."

"Did you use your hometown connection to gain her trust?"

Stanton crossed his arms. "Whatever you're getting at, Detective, either say it or get the hell out of here."

"You were observed at Kolnikov's place on several occasions. And the two of you were seen at a restaurant having dinner."

He shrugged. "So, okay. I met her a couple times and had dinner. That's no crime." He smiled at Jordan, almost as if he were playing a game of chess and he'd made a strategic move. Now it was Jordan's turn. "Are we done?"

"Two words," Jordan said. "Belzar Corporation."

Lines formed around Stanton's mouth.

It was a bluff, but it was all he had. He wanted to plant the idea they had more information than they did.

"That's it?" Stanton asked.

"Yes, it is—for now."

CHAPTER FOURTEEN

LAURA WENT TO BED emotionally exhausted. So many thoughts raced through her head, she felt as if she'd go crazy. What was Alysa's connection to one of DeMatta's thugs? It didn't make sense. Unless the guy was setting up another business like Anna's. Or maybe he was trying to get to her and Cait through Alysa.

She shivered as a cold chill ran through her.

Was it DeMatta who'd killed Eddie? Or did he just happen to be there that night? Had he sent one of his thugs to do the job? Or was it someone else altogether? Eddie certainly had his enemies. So, how would she ever know?

If someone wanted to hurt her or Cait, he hadn't made an effort to do it.

Luke had had the same negative reaction to her story as Jordan, and now she almost regretted that she'd said anything. Mostly she couldn't shake the devastation she'd felt when she saw the look of shock and disgust in Jordan's eyes.

But in a way, she was relieved she'd told him everything. She didn't have to carry all her dark secrets any longer. What would come of it all was the million-dollar question. And in the end…she knew she trusted Jordan would do whatever he could to protect them. And just maybe, she and Cait could someday live like normal people.

It was 5:00 a.m. when Laura awoke. She rolled over in bed and wrapped the sheet around her. Another day of interminable waiting. Waiting and wondering what was going to happen next. God, she was tired of it.

She sat up in bed, reached over and turned on the lamp on the night table. Sitting there, she noticed for the first time a photograph on the chest across from her. She slipped from the bed and took the photo back to look at it under the light.

It was Luke with a beautiful dark-haired woman and a child, a towheaded boy about four years old. The same age Caitlin had been when her father died. A pain twisted in Laura's chest. How awful it must've been for Luke to lose a child. She simply couldn't imagine. She set the photo back on the chest, her heart aching for Luke and the family he no longer had.

Or was it for the traditional family she'd wanted and never had.

Was there ever a time when life might've been different?

No, she realized after a moment. There was no going back. So, okay, maybe life hadn't turned out exactly as she wanted. But she had a beautiful daughter and her life was full. That should be more than enough.

Three years ago, she'd made a necessary decision. And that decision had changed her life. Right or wrong, she didn't know. She'd felt helpless for so long. But Jordan's words came back to her, "You can go to the police."

Yes, she had to go to the police and tell them everything—but not before she had assurances that Caitlin would be safe.

She rolled out of bed and slipped on a pair of

sweats. Everything was still when she opened the door. Still and dark, except for the sliver of moonlight that shone through the small window above the front door. From the top of the stairs, she could make out Jordan's form on the couch, one arm over his eyes. She tiptoed down the stairs and stole across the room, careful not to make any noise. But just as she reached the end of the couch, she felt a hand grab her wrist.

"Going somewhere?" Jordan said it so softly she had to strain to hear him.

"To the kitchen."

"It's very early."

"I know. I couldn't sleep."

"Okay, but don't make any noise." He turned away from her and jammed a pillow over his head.

In the kitchen, she found a glass, poured herself some milk and then sat at the Formica table in the middle of the room. The 1920s stove and the old glass cabinet doors made her feel as if she'd been transported back in time. No renovations here…which was probably a good thing. Renovations would've spoiled the essence of the room.

She noticed a pile of dirty dishes in the old cast-iron sink, got up and started to run some water. A noise behind her caused her to whip around so fast, she dropped the cup in her hand and it clattered against the tile counter. Her hands shook as she fumbled to keep the delicate cup from falling to the floor.

"Sorry if I scared you. I thought you heard me coming in."

She leaned against the counter, could feel her pulse beating in her throat. "I guess I was preoccupied."

"That looks good," he said, indicating the milk on the table.

238 AND JUSTICE FOR ALL

"I'll get you some." She went to the sink and washed out a glass. "I think your friend needs a maid."

"Maybe. Guys aren't the greatest housekeepers."

"Maybe not. But I'll bet your place is neat as a pin."

His mouth lifted at the corners but didn't quite make a smile. "You'd be wrong."

After she poured him some milk, they sat at the table, silent, as if there was nothing left to say. But she did have something to say, and she wanted to get it all out there.

"I know what I told you before was probably a shock. I'm sorry about that. But I can't change the past…and I'm proud of what I've done with my life. I've also come to realize you were right. I can't go on like this. And if you can make sure Cait and I are protected, I'll go to the police and tell them everything."

Thoughtful, Jordan lingered over his glass of milk. Finally he said, "There was a time when I thought going to the police was the best thing to do…but—"

"But what?"

"I still think it's the right thing to do, but it might not be the safest thing to do."

"I don't understand."

"I know, and I can't tell you anything more, except that we have to work this from another angle."

"Because?"

"Because I've found out some things that need to be kept quiet until we have hard evidence. If you go to the police, it'll become public information, a feeding frenzy for the media."

"So, what do you want me to do?"

"Wait."

"And what happens while we wait?"

"I'll work on it."

"Fine. But I'm going to wait at home."

He did a double take. "Excuse me."

"I believe you were right. If someone really wanted to hurt me or Cait, he's had plenty of opportunities. Since he hasn't, he must have another agenda."

"Maybe so. But since we don't know what his agenda is... I think it's too dangerous to take that chance."

"I'm going back to the shelter later today. I'm tired of running, letting this person pull all the strings. This has to stop. If you want me to go to the station and tell them everything, I will. If I can do something else, tell me what."

He rubbed his chin. "If you insist on going back, maybe you can talk to Alysa. Find out what she was doing with Nick Stanton."

"I already talked to her about it. I don't think she'll tell me anything new, but I'll ask."

"Thanks. If it doesn't work, then I'll talk to her."

"Do you have any other plans?"

"I'll need to make sure you and Cait are well protected. I know a few people."

"And other than that?"

"I'm working on it."

JORDAN HATED THAT LAURA had decided to go back to the shelter, but she was stubborn and there wasn't a damned thing he could do about it. Well, if he couldn't convince her, the least he could do was make sure she had protection. He checked his watch. Was it too soon to call? She'd only been back home an hour.

"Hey, buddy." Luke came over and slapped a printout on Jordan's desk. "Something for you." He glanced at Mary Beth. "From you know who."

Jordan scanned the paper. Apparently Mary Beth had done more research on Stanton, research he hadn't asked her to do. Was she trying to ingratiate herself? Or find out more about what he was doing? The second he thought it, he felt foolish. Sheesh. Now he was second-guessing the admin assistant. As if she could be a mole. Stupid.

He glanced at the printout. No history from the time Stanton left New Paltz in 1987, when he'd have been about twenty-two, until the time of his incarceration at Attica in 1995. Eight years missing.

Hell, Stanton's history was probably the most insignificant piece on this case. All he really wanted to know was if he was the guy DeMatta hired to take out Kolnikov and Valdez. For DeMatta to have been at Eddie Gianni's on the night of his murder, it was possible the mobster even managed a few hits of his own.

He needed to start from the beginning, draw a time line. He picked up the Kolnikov file one more time, scanning the list of personal effects. One tiny shred of evidence could make the case—the right piece of evidence.

The paper with a date on it flashed in his mind. Like the birthday card from Rita Valdez, there'd been no follow-up. What was the date? Did it have any significance? Had the paper been tested for fingerprints? Was it Kolnikov's handwriting or someone else's? He flipped through the file and found a smudged copy of the note. He read the date. *December 24, 1965.* Damn. He shoved papers aside to find the report on Stanton and compared. December 24, 1965, was Nick Stanton's birth date.

Why would Kolnikov have written that specific date on a piece of paper? *If* it was her writing. Was she trying to find out if Stanton actually did come from her hometown?

"Good stuff?" Howie Ralston's voice came out of nowhere.

Jordan turned to find the guy standing directly over him, obviously reading the file. "No. Nothing new."

"I thought you stopped working on the case."

He didn't have to explain anything to Ralston. But if he didn't... Hell, at this point he was suspecting everyone. He swallowed his irritation. "I did. Just wanted to make a final note in the file."

His answer seemed good enough for Ralston and he walked away. After packaging up the note with the date and a sample of Kolnikov's handwriting for comparison, Jordan handed it to Mary Beth to send to the science guys in SID. It wasn't much, but it was a start.

Then he headed for the evidence room. On his way downstairs, he pulled out his cell phone and called Laura. Phoebe answered.

"Hi, Phoebe. Is Laura around?"

Seconds later Laura came on. "Hello."

"Just checking. Everything okay?"

"We're fine. Cait's at school and everything is back to normal. Well, except for the bodyguards you have surrounding the house and Cait's school."

"They're not supposed to be seen."

"They're discreet, but *I* know they're there. I doubt anyone else does."

He wanted to say more, but felt the distance between them ever widening.

"Thank you for doing this," she finally said. "I'm grateful, and I know the police department isn't paying for it. When this is all over, I'll pay you back...only it'll have to be in installments."

"Forget it." He wanted to say he'd do it for anyone, but it wasn't true. He was doing it because he cared about her and Cait. *He loved her.* "Repayment isn't necessary."

So, if he loved her, why couldn't he put what she'd told him out of his mind? The thought of Laura willing to give up her child, the thought of her selling her body made his stomach churn. How could he love someone and yet hate what she'd been?

"I'll call later," he said. He disconnected and kept walking, his anger growing. The pain of her deception hurt like nothing he'd ever felt before. He was a fool. He'd fallen in love with one woman and then found out she was another. Some judge of character he was.

The smell of stale tobacco hit him about ten yards before he reached the storage room. He went to the desk and signed in with a request for the evidence collected in the Kolnikov case.

George Federovski, a blue on his last year with the force, stubbed out his cigarette and shoved the ashtray under the counter. Smoking had been banned from the department a few years ago, but some diehards ignored the rules. Which was probably why George was in the basement.

The man studied the registration book, then scratched his balding head. "I think it's gone. Yeah, someone checked it out earlier."

"Someone? You got a name?"

His sausage fingers ran down the pages. "Here it is. But I don't recognize it. Walker Davis."

Jordan didn't recognize the name, either.

"And there's no date or department listed. I don't know how it happened." George shrugged.

Unfortunately, Jordan did. George was counting the days until retirement and only did as much work as he had to. Back at his desk, Jordan pulled up the computer file of officers on the LAPD. Twice he scanned the list, but found no one with the name Walker Davis. He got up and walked over to Luke.

"Yo," Jordan said as he sat on the corner of his buddy's desk. "You know an LEO named Walker Davis?"

"Nope. Someone new?"

"I don't know. Never heard the name and he's not listed with the LAPD. He checked out the Kolnikov evidence."

"You need it?"

"Yeah, but it's like it disappeared into thin air."

LAURA WAITED IN THE LINEUP of vans and SUVs along the street outside Cait's school. It had been a week since they returned from Luke's and every day Cait complained bitterly over not being able to walk home by herself anymore. But Laura simply wasn't going to take chances—no matter how many people Jordan had on watch.

She'd explained to Cait about looking at some pictures that Jordan was going to bring over sometime, and the child hadn't flinched. And then she'd scampered off as if none of it had any significance to her. Had Laura known it would be so easy…

But she couldn't go back.

At three o'clock the children started spilling out the door, running to their parents' cars, some to the playground and some walking home. Laura saw Jenny and Shannon and expected Caitlin to be with them. But she wasn't.

She bolted from the car and caught the girls before they got away. "Hi, there. Either of you know where Cait is?"

They looked at each other, then back to her and shook their heads.

"But she's usually with the two of you."

"I think she might've had to stay after school," Shannon piped up.

Kids didn't stay after school in Caitlin's grade, and if they had problems of any kind, a parent was always notified. "Are you sure?" Laura crossed her arms.

The guilty look in Shannon's eyes told her the child was lying. "Tell me the truth," she ordered, while casting about for Cait. "You two stay right here. I'm going in to check with Cait's teacher. And if I find out—" She rushed off before finishing the sentence.

Lunging up the stairs, she saw Cait's teacher standing just inside the door directing the children out in single file. But Cait wasn't among them.

"Mrs. Gianni." The teacher smiled. "How nice to see you."

"Where's Caitlin?" Laura blurted. "She's not where she's supposed to be."

"Really?" The woman glanced around, her attention caught by children trying to run instead of walking or joining in line. "She was here just a while ago, talking to Shannon." Her gaze darted from right to left. "I thought she was right here."

"Did she have any problems today?"

The woman drew back in surprise. "Of course not. Caitlin's one of my best students. And I would always call a parent if there's a problem."

"But you don't know where she is?"

"I'll call someone to look in the bathroom. She may have gone there without permission, though that doesn't seem like her."

"Please do," Laura said, then ran out the door, scanning for Cait's curly hair and pink jacket. She didn't see Cait, and the other two girls weren't there, either. "Oh, God." She ran back into the school to the principal's office and barged through the door. "My daughter is missing. Please call the police."

The man behind the desk stared at her for a moment, as if not comprehending. Then he stood. "I'm Mr. Clancy," he said, and held out a hand.

"I know who you are! Didn't you hear me? I said my daughter is missing."

"What's her name?"

"Caitlin. Caitlin Gianni." Laura's heart pounded with fear. "Please call the police immediately." She lifted his phone, pressed 911 and handed him the receiver.

He shook his head. "I can't just call the police without know—"

Laura got on the phone. "My daughter's disappeared. I'm at her school, Highland Elementary at Sixth and Dover."

"What's your daughter's name, ma'am?"

"Caitlin Gianni. Please come right away."

"When did she go missing, Mrs. Gianni?"

"Just now. I came to pick her up and she's not here."

"How long has she been gone?"

"I don't know. All I know is that she's not here."

"Perhaps she's with a friend. Or her father."

Laura couldn't breathe. "Her father is dead and this is not helping. I need you to send someone right away. The longer you wait—"

"Ma'am, please take a breath."

Laura threw the phone at the principal. "You talk to her. Tell them to get out here right now." She ran outside, and seeing most of the kids had left, she sprinted to the playground. Nothing, just some boys playing basketball. She ran to the other side of the building but didn't see Cait anywhere. She ran to the car across the street where one of Jordan's men held watch. "Caitlin's not here. Did you see her?"

The man immediately clicked on a microphone inside his jacket. "No, I didn't. I saw you here and thought everything was fine."

He repeated the problem to whoever was on the other end and was still talking when she ran to her car. On the way, she pulled out her cell phone and dialed Jordan's number. "Cait's missing," she said as soon as he answered. "I came to pick her up from school and she's not here."

"Where are you now?"

"Getting into my car to look for her." She saw the bodyguard jump out of his car, apparently to search.

"I'll be at your place as soon as I can. Did you tell any of the guys on watch?"

"I did." She started the engine and took off driving down the street, searching as she went. "Apparently they weren't doing their jobs, or if they were—"

"The important thing is to find Cait. Stay near your phone. I'll be there soon."

Laura turned the corner and saw Cait's friends walking slowly, laughing and cajoling with each other and some boys ahead of them. She screeched to a stop, jumped from the van and planted herself in front of the girls. "I want the truth, you two. Or I'm taking you home to your mothers right now."

The sweet, innocent faces didn't look so innocent all of a sudden.

"I didn't lie," Jenny said. "Shannon lied."

"You lied, too. You told me to say it and that's the same as lying yourself."

Laura eyed Shannon, hoping to scare the truth from her. "What did you lie about?"

Shannon looked at the ground. "When I said I didn't know where Cait was."

"Well, where is she?"

"She said she wanted to walk home with us, so instead of going out front, she went out the side door so you wouldn't see her. She was supposed to meet us back there, but she didn't come. I thought you found her and gave her a ride."

Laura's blood drained from her face. She felt dizzy. "Is there another way that you girls walk home?"

They both shook their heads. "Maybe she's already home," Jenny said.

Was that a possibility? Laura climbed back into the van and gunned the engine. A tiny glimmer of hope. If Cait *was* at home, she was going to strangle her...or she just might hug her to death.

CHAPTER FIFTEEN

WHEN LAURA ARRIVED at the house, she saw a squad car parked out in front and an officer was just getting out of the vehicle. She pulled up next to it. "Are you here about Caitlin?"

"No, ma'am." The officer started for the house.

"Excuse me. I'm the director of this shelter and my daughter is missing. I called 911 to have someone come out."

"I'm sorry, miss. I'm here to talk to Alysa O'Connor."

Laura stepped back. Oh, God. What now? "Can't it wait...until after you've found my daughter?"

As Laura reached the door, Rose pushed it open from the inside. "What's all the ruckus?"

"Caitlin is missing," Laura said, rushing inside. The officer followed her in and flashed her badge.

"I'm Officer Jensen. I'm here to see Alysa O'Connor."

"Sorry, she's not here," Rose said, then turned to Laura. "What happened?"

Laura fought back tears. She had to stay strong. Had to think...find a solution. "Caitlin ditched me after school and told her friends she'd meet them behind the building so she could walk home with them. But she wasn't behind the school and she didn't meet them. Something has happened to her. She wouldn't just go off—" *Or would she?* She'd been making all kinds of protests lately about doing things on her own.

Just then, Jordan came into the house. Walking past the police officer to Laura, he placed a hand on her shoulder.

She'd rather feel his strong arms around her. But *her* feelings weren't at issue here. Caitlin was gone. And they had to find her.

"Any luck?" he asked.

"I just got here."

"Did you look in her room?"

"I didn't see her come in," Rose said.

Laura hurried down the hall—Jordan and Rose on her heels. They checked Cait's room. Not a sign. Laura checked the bathroom and in her own room, as well. Nobody. Standing in the hallway, she started to tremble, her fears threatening to overwhelm her. "Where could she be? Do you think someone—"

This time Jordan did put his arm around her. "Don't speculate," he said. "Let's sit down and think logically."

They went back to the living room. The other officer now had a pad and pen in her hand. "A team is on the way," she said, glancing out front again. "But I'll call them off if the child coming up the walk is your daughter."

Laura ran to the front door and saw Cait dawdling on the sidewalk. A torrent of emotions coursed through Laura. Anger. Relief. Her heart hammered erratically. "Caitlin Elizabeth," she ground out. "Get over here this minute."

The child looked up, as guilty as a thief. "I'm sorry. I forgot."

Laura tapped her foot, her stomach churning. Not if what the other girls said was true, she didn't forget. Which also meant she was lying. Cait had never lied to her before. Laura said evenly, "I was very worried, and I'm hugely upset. Go to your room and I'll be there to talk to you in a few minutes."

Cait's mouth pursed, but apparently she knew she'd better do as asked and stomped down the hall to her room without a word.

"I'm so sorry," Laura said to Jordan and the other officer. She was going to tell the uniformed officer it wasn't necessary for anyone else to come out, but the woman was already on the phone taking care of it.

When the officer left, Rose said, "Well, I'll leave now. I've got to take the girls to the store."

Alone with Laura, Jordan felt as if they were two statues staring at each another, neither able to speak. Jordan wanted to comfort Laura and could only imagine what she'd gone through today thinking something had happened to Cait. "Don't be sorry. Under the circumstances you did the right thing. The next time it could be real."

He hated to be so blunt, but if it made her realize how dangerous it was to stay here, he didn't care. He hadn't been around for the past week, but he'd received reports several times a day. How Cait had managed to get off by herself with so much cover boggled his mind.

"What can we do?"

"You can go talk to Cait before she thinks the worst."

"She should be thinking about what she did…the worry she caused."

"But she doesn't know the danger. Maybe it's time she knew the truth."

Her mouth fell open. "You can't mean that."

"I do. Wouldn't it be easier if she knew?"

"Easier for whom?" She turned, eyes wide. She shoved her hair back from her face and stared at him. "I—I can't tell her the real reasons," she said incredulously.

"Why not?"

"Because she's only seven."

"She's almost eight, and from what I've seen, she's more mature than most twelve-year-olds."

"But what would it prove?"

"It would keep her from finding out about it somewhere else. It would prove that telling the truth is important. It would prove that you trust her enough to tell her. And then, she probably wouldn't be taking any jogs off by herself if she knew."

"It's a lot for a child to comprehend."

He shrugged. "Make it simple." He hesitated, wondering how far he should go with this. Finally, he decided he couldn't put it off. "Do you ever plan to tell her about her father?"

She gazed down the hallway. Moistened her lips. "When she's old enough to understand."

"And when might that be?"

She didn't answer. "If Cait knew your concerns, she might be able to explain what she saw at her father's. She might have seen more than she told you."

Laura's eyes flared with anger. "Is that why you think I should tell her, so you can get more information?"

He flinched at the accusation. "That isn't why," he said, fighting the urge to shake her, to tell her this wasn't about the case. It was about telling the truth. It was about Cait.

He stepped closer, looked into her eyes and said softly, "I'm sorry you think that. I was concerned about Cait. She could be suppressing what she saw…and that can't be a good thing."

She stared blankly, then gave a terse nod. "I'm a counselor. Don't you think I've thought of that?" She raised a hand to her forehead as if she might be fighting a headache.

"It's such a big step." Her voice was a whisper.

He reached out, held her by her arms. "I know."

Abruptly, she pulled away. "There's no way I want her to testify at any trial."

"That's your choice."

"Eventually, it's going to come up."

He nodded. "It would help if she could identify the person she saw in a lineup. It might mean the difference in taking a killer off the streets."

The furtive look in her eyes said she was scared. "But you don't know if he's Eddie's killer. Just being in the house doesn't mean anything."

"True." Fact was, they had no solid evidence DeMatta had been involved in any of the murders. Which was why the guy was still on the streets. "But Cait's identification would give us reason to get a warrant and search his home. It might be all we need to find our killer."

"Eddie's and not Anna's?"

"Both, maybe."

Her green eyes darkened. He could tell she was considering it. "Think about it. That's all I ask. Think about how much better your life will be when all this ends."

Fatigue dulled her eyes, circled underneath by dark smudges, and she seemed thinner than the last time he'd seen her only a week ago. He hated this. He wanted to comfort her. But he'd only be asking for more trouble.

Finally, shoulders sagging, she said, "I'll think about it."

"Time is of the essence."

"I know."

LAURA COULDN'T BELIEVE she was considering Jordan's advice. All this time she'd done what she thought best for her daughter. And now he'd made her question it all. Their lives were falling apart and Cait was in the middle. Maybe Jordan was right.

Rubbing the tops of her arms, she shivered at the thought. Was her reluctance because of Cait or because she'd have to admit to Cait that she'd lied…and the reason they'd had to flee was because of her lie?

The dilemma weighed heavily on Laura as she walked down the hall and knocked on Cait's door. When she didn't get an answer, she edged it open. "Hi." Cait lay on the bed, looking up. Laura walked over and lay next to her, staring at the ceiling, too.

"I'm sorry," Cait said.

"I know. But sorry doesn't make lying and disobeying any better."

"I won't do it again."

"I know, because you'll be grounded if you do."

"I don't know what the big deal is, anyway. Why do you need to pick me up all the time? I'm not a baby and all the kids tease me about it."

Laura let out a long breath, exasperated. Jordan was right, she did need to tell Cait. She hoped he was also right about Cait being mature enough to hear it. "I understand. I really do. In fact, I felt the way you do many times when I was growing up. But there are a few things you don't know that makes this different."

"What things?"

Laura paused, thinking of how to phrase it. "I have a story to tell you about your father and it's important for you to listen to everything and try to understand that some things have been done for your own good."

"Are you going to tell me my dad was murdered?"

Laura bolted upright. She stared at Cait. "Where did you hear that?"

"One of my friends. Her brother told her."

"What did he say?" Laura's mouth was so dry the words barely croaked out.

Cait sat up and crossed her legs. "He said my dad was a criminal and he got killed because of it. He said it was in the newspapers."

Laura's thoughts raced. "Why didn't you say something to me?"

Caitlin shrugged. "'Cuz I thought it would make you sad."

Oh, Lord. "Well...I know about your father, and what the boy said isn't true."

"He said it was in the newspaper."

"The newspaper isn't always right, either. Your father was actually going to help the police. That's why he was...why he's dead. He put himself in danger to help the police and the bad guys found out about it."

"You mean the man I saw?"

Laura pinched the bridge of her nose with two fingers, her head beginning to throb. "No, I don't mean him...not exactly."

"But he was there the night when Dad was sick. Maybe he came back and killed him."

She realized then that for a seven-year-old this was

all some abstract concept. She was just repeating what someone had said and putting it with what she'd remembered. To her, the murder and her father being sick were two separate events. Laura had to clear up whatever misconceptions the child had.

"Just because he was there doesn't mean he did anything bad."

An hour later, she'd explained as best she could why they needed to be careful and why they should help Jordan. Cait didn't seem any worse for it, but then she couldn't be sure Cait actually understood it all.

"So, if someone wants to hurt us, why doesn't Jordan arrest him?"

"Well, they don't know who to arrest. But Jordan would like to talk to you about when you were at your dad's. Do you think you could do that?"

"Uh-huh. I remember lots of stuff."

Yes, her daughter had a mind like a steel trap for some things. She'd have to make sure she was really okay, get her counseling for sure. But for tonight, this seemed enough. "Well, then, maybe we should look at what homework you have to do and get busy."

"It's a crapshoot," Luke said, turning a corner on their way to Vincento's Italian Restaurant. "Do you think a guy like DeMatta would keep stuff around to incriminate himself?"

"No, but he might inadvertently." Jordan cracked his knuckles. "Besides, it's all we've got."

"And you want to tell him ahead of time before the kid even identifies him? That's screwed up."

"No it's not. I want to see his reaction. And I'm not going to say anything about Cait." Jordan's cell phone chirped. "St. James here."

"Hi," a female voice said. "This is Alysa O'Connor and I really need to talk to someone. I think I'm in big trouble."

"Can you talk now?"

"No. Can you meet me somewhere? Somewhere Laura won't know about?"

He hauled in some air. "Sure. Where and when?"

"Right now. It's got to be right now."

"Are you in danger?"

"I don't think so."

"Where are you?"

She told him and he said, "Stay put. I'll be there as soon as I can. I'm about a half hour away. Will you be okay for that long?"

"Uh-huh."

Jordan hung up. "Hollywood and Vine. One of Laura's kids is in trouble."

Luke turned the wheel heading for the freeway, but he looked at Jordan as if he was nuts. "Are we working for the shelter now?"

"It's the girl who was with Stanton."

"What about DeMatta?"

"DeMatta's been on hold for years, he can wait a little longer."

Once on the freeway, Luke said, "Speaking of Laura, what's happening with you two?"

"Nothing. Nothing ever will, so don't ask."

Luke snorted derisively. "What's up with that? I know you're crazy about her."

"That was before. Before I knew more about her."

"Ah, a dark past?"

Jordan exhaled. "Something I never imagined."

"Like?"

He clenched his teeth. Just thinking about it made

him angry. "She was a prostitute. She got pregnant and was going to give away her child. The only reason she didn't was because she had a miscarriage. She's just like…"

"Just like your real mother?" Luke finished for him. "But what if you're wrong. Maybe her circumstances were different."

Jordan eyed his partner with disdain. "She is what she is."

Luke let out a weary sigh. "Yeah, she's just like everyone else. We're all plagued with some kind of history we want to forget. Laura's nothing like Kolni-kov's women. I talked to her long enough to know that."

"And I think I know her better than you do."

"I doubt it. I don't think you know yourself, much less anyone else."

The words hit Jordan like a punch in the gut.

"You think because you discovered your mother was a whore, that somehow taints you. You think because of Laura's past, she's the same as your biological mother."

"Ridiculous. I don't think that at all. I had two won-derful adoptive parents who raised me to have integ-rity and to be honest, and Laura's—" He stopped, realizing Luke had manipulated him. "Let's drop it."

"Sure. But it's your loss."

They were quiet until they reached the exit.

"Well," Luke said, "I want to say one last thing, then I'll be quiet. I haven't learned much over these past few years, but I have learned a couple things. One, I can't blame my demons on someone else. And two, I have to deal with them myself because until I do, I'm always going to be searching for the next high, whether it's a drink or something else."

Jordan frowned. "What the hell is that supposed to mean?"

Luke gave Jordan a critical squint. "Deal with your own demons, buddy. Don't look for a place to hide or a place to lay blame. I've done it all and it doesn't work."

Within minutes they reached the corner where Alysa said she'd be waiting. Dusk fell in graduating layers after the sun set, the eerie time when it was neither dark nor light. When darkness fell, neon lights illuminated the streets as if it were Las Vegas.

During the day, the tourist-attraction factor kept the city clean…but at night, the disenfranchised came out to play. Or work, such as it was.

"Is that her?" Luke pointed to a young girl who looked like she'd been an extra for *The Walking Dead*.

"No. Alysa is tall and blond. Model material."

"How about we park and get out?" Before getting an answer, Luke pulled into an empty space next to a fire hydrant.

"You're gonna get a ticket," Jordan said facetiously. They got out of the car and stood next to it on the sidewalk.

"I could get a mega bust right here if I wait around a few hours," Luke said.

Jordan saw movement in the shadow of a doorway near a trendy restaurant. "That might be her." He walked toward the door.

Alysa huddled in the corner, her gaze darting four directions all at once.

"You want to come with us?" Jordan asked.

"I don't want anyone to see me with you," she said.

"I can make it look like an arrest. Will that help?"

She nodded.

Jordan pulled out his shield, so if anyone was watching, he was covered. Then he took his cuffs and turned the girl around to secure her hands. She kept her head down as he led her to the car. Luke was already in the driver's seat when Jordan got in. "Go."

"I'm on it," Luke said.

As they pulled away, Alysa said, "I didn't know you were going to bring along another cop."

"Detective," Luke said over his shoulder.

"He's cool," Jordan added. "Trust me."

"We're not going to the station, are we?"

"No. How'd you get my cell phone number?"

"I—I got it from the card you gave Laura. But please don't tell her."

"Can't make any promises until I know what's going on."

"Where are we going?"

"Luke's going to find a private spot to park and then we can talk." No sooner than Jordan got out the words, than Luke turned into an alley behind a warehouse. "Let's get those cuffs off," Jordan said.

She leaned forward so he could reach her. After the cuffs were off, she rubbed her wrists. "Those things hurt."

Something they heard all the time. "Good thing you have no reason to be in them for a longer period of time."

Alysa didn't meet his eyes.

"So why are we here?" Jordan asked. "You said you might be in trouble."

Her big blue eyes expanded. "I think so."

"Why do you think so?"

"There's this guy—"

"Start from the beginning."

She bit her lip, then flopped back against the seat. "Before I came to Victory House, about six months ago, I was a real mess. I was a mess for a long time afterward. Just when I started to get my act together, I had a setback." She chewed on her lower lip as if it was difficult to go on.

"A setback?"

"Yeah. It's not the same as a relapse. Anyway, this setback really put me down. I couldn't think or do anything, and when this guy offered me money for some information, I said okay."

Jordan and Luke's attention was piqued. "What kind of information?"

"He asked me get some information about the shelter, and the director. Laura." She glanced at Jordan, guilt in her eyes.

"Specifically her?"

"Yes. He wanted to know about her money, how she got funding for the shelter and all kinds of stuff I don't know about. I told him I didn't know anything and he said he'd give me even more money if I found out."

Luke eyed Jordan. "And did you?" Luke asked.

Tears pooled in her eyes. "I did."

"Did he say why he wanted the information?"

"He said something about taxes and being with the government, but I really didn't know what he was talking about. I copied the information from the records he asked for and then I told him about the hidden money."

"Money?" Jordan asked.

"Money in brown wrapping. Lots of money."

"What happened to the money?"

"Nothing that I know of. But last week when I met this guy and told him about the money, Laura was at the shopping center and she saw me getting out of his car."

"Did you tell her what you'd done?"

She was shaking now, tears flooding down her cheeks. "I told her I had a relapse." She sniffed and wiped her eyes—to no avail. The tears kept coming. "I didn't tell her I gave information to this man…a-and now I'm afraid I did something terrible and got her in trouble, too."

Laura had told him about Alysa's meeting with Stanton. Now he knew why. Damn! But what reason would Stanton have for wanting information about Laura's accounts? And where had the money come from? She'd mentioned money from DeMatta, but that was three years ago. Had he given her more? And why would she be hiding it?

LAURA PACED THE ROOM, waiting for Jordan to arrive. He'd called more than an hour ago and said he had to talk to her again. She definitely wanted to talk to him about her conversation with Cait.

She glanced at the time again. Jordan should be there any minute. It was after ten and Alysa wasn't home, either. And because Phoebe and Rose were on street duty, she didn't have any way to go looking for the teenager even if she could. She'd left a call on Phoebe's cell phone for them to keep an eye out for the teen. She felt helpless to do anything more and it irritated the hell out of her. Maybe Jordan would have some ideas.

She knew better than to call the police to report Alysa missing, not until twenty-four hours had passed. She had a history of running. It was normal to think the kid had run again.

But Alysa was different from other troubled kids. The child longed for the security she'd never had, and Victory House had given her that. Maybe not in the way she wanted, but enough to get her back on track. That's what bothered Laura the most. Alysa had to be in trouble. Something she couldn't talk about with her counselor. But maybe with a friend?

Deciding that would be her approach when the teen returned, Laura flipped on the television set for company. Then the doorbell rang. Still on edge, she went to the door and peered between the curtains. The outside light gave the night an eerie yellow cast… Jordan and Alysa stood on the steps.

What the— Quickly, she opened the door. "Oh, my God, Alysa, where have you been?"

Jordan held up a hand. "Let's sit. Alysa has something to tell you."

Laura listened quietly as Alysa told her what she'd done. With every word out of the girl's mouth, Laura rode a roller coaster of emotions…astonishment, disappointment, sadness—and the ultimate knowledge of betrayal. The raw truth twisted like a knife in Laura's chest.

Was it always like this? Did everyone in the world disappoint you at some time or another? As a counselor, she knew the answer. People were flawed. People made mistakes. God knew she'd made enough of her own, and some of them would have consequences that lasted the rest of her life.

Alysa apologized through a flood of tears. "I'm so sorry. I don't know what I was thinking. At first I thought I was doing the right thing, and when I found out it wasn't, it was too late."

"It's okay, Alysa." Laura took the girl's hand. "I'm glad you told me. Now we'll just go on from here."

Alysa's head came up. "You don't hate me? You're not going to make me leave?"

"I'm surprised and…hurt. But I'd no more ask you to leave than leave myself. We've made it this far, we'll get through the rest. Now, why don't you go upstairs and get some sleep. Things will be better in the morning."

The girl looked at Laura in disbelief, then hugged her. "I can't believe you don't hate me."

"I care about you, Alysa. I could never hate you, no matter what you do."

Alysa looked as if her world had just been resurrected. She swallowed, dashed at the tears on her cheeks with the back of one hand and gave a wobbly smile. Then she turned and ran up the stairs.

Laura knew the power of forgiveness, how it had turned her own life around.

"I'm in awe," Jordan said.

Laura glanced at him, her attention still on Alysa and the significance of what she'd revealed. "What?"

"I admire how you handled that."

Laura looked away. "I was honest, that's all. I care very much about Alysa and what she does with her life. I'm not going to throw away all we've done because she made a mistake."

"A mistake? I'd say it was more than a mistake."

She shrugged. "I don't believe a person's actions condemn them for life. We all have to own up to our mistakes and failings and deal with them. Alysa will have to deal with hers."

He rubbed a hand across the back of his neck, puzzlement in his eyes. "The big question for me is how does Alysa's contact with one of DeMatta's men fit into my investigation?"

Thoughtful, Laura nibbled on her bottom lip. "I don't know the answer. Why would anyone want to know about my finances? About any money I might have?"

"Tell me about the money. Where did you get it? Why are you hiding it?"

She pulled back. "I wasn't hiding it. It's the money Eddie's uncle gave me after the funeral. I didn't want to use his dirty money and, under the circumstances, I couldn't give it back. So I put it away."

Jordan frowned. "Which doesn't get me any closer to an answer." He stood, glanced at his watch. "The only way to get it is to go to the source."

"DeMatta?"

"No. Stanton. He's the one asking questions."

A loud banging at the front door nearly brought down the house. Both Laura and Jordan rushed for the door, Jordan with his gun drawn.

"Who's there?" Jordan shouted.

"FBI. Open up."

Jordan nodded to Laura but kept his gun leveled chest high. She'd only opened the door a fraction of an inch when it burst open. Four men rushed in waving badges. "Drop the gun!" The rest of the men moved in.

Jordan let his gun fall and another guy shoved him to the floor.

CHAPTER SIXTEEN

HER HEART RACING, Laura turned to look down the hall to see if Cait had heard. Apparently not. Thank God she slept like the dead. Within seconds, all the other girls were huddled on the stairs, fear etched on their sleepy faces.

"What's going on?" Brandy asked from over the railing.

"I'm Special Agent Martinez," the guy in front said. "Are you Laura Gianni?"

Numb with shock, she nodded.

"We have a warrant to search the house."

"For what?" Jordan growled as the other guy started to handcuff him. "And if you look in my pocket you'll find a badge. I'm with the LAPD."

The guy holding Jordan down found the badge and quickly let him go.

The special agent handed Laura some papers. Jordan brushed off his clothes and read the warrant over her shoulder. "It's legit," he said.

"This is ridiculous, that's what it is." She tossed the papers back at the man.

"I'm sorry, ma'am. Please step aside." The agent motioned to his men. "You two start upstairs, the rest of you down here."

Standing directly in front of them, Laura blocked

their path. "My seven-year-old daughter is sleeping and you'll scare her to death if you start going through the house."

Martinez asked, "Which room?"

"Downstairs, the room on the left at the end of the hall."

He nodded at the men. "Be quiet and do the kid's room last." He faced Laura again. "You may want to wake her up and take her someplace else for a couple hours."

God. What was going on here? "What should we do?" she asked Jordan.

"Let them do their job. You can go to my place and wait there if you want."

Confused as she was, Laura had no intention of leaving and letting anyone ransack her house without further explanation. "I *want* to know what's going on," she said to the man called Martinez. "I have a right to know what you're looking for."

When one agent came out of her bedroom with her ledgers and a brown paper package, her stomach dropped. "It's not what you think."

The man's lips thinned. "I don't think anything. But it's my job to find out facts. Ma'am, I'd like you to come to headquarters with us for questioning."

"Headquarters?" She edged back a step.

"The FBI field office headquarters," the agent added.

"She's not going anywhere, unless you're arresting her, and I'm pretty sure you might need an arrest warrant. And she'll want to call an attorney. Otherwise she can talk here."

The agent shrugged. "Okay. But it's just a matter of time then."

As if gathering strength from Jordan's words, Laura

held her head high. "When you're ready to go into my daughter's room, please let me know." Because she'd have to wake Cait and explain.

If she could.

JORDAN LEFT LAURA ONLY after the feds had gone and he knew the women would be okay. Laura had given Cait an explanation that the child apparently understood and she'd gone right back to sleep in Laura's room. The men he'd hired to guard Laura had backed off when the FBI came, and he couldn't blame them for that. He'd called them back and felt certain everybody at the shelter would be okay now.

As he hit the ramp and accelerated onto the freeway, he punched in Luke's number. When he didn't answer, he called the captain at home and asked to meet him at an all-night diner at a halfway point. While he hadn't gotten a full explanation from the agents, he had enough information to know the FBI had some kind of sting going with DeMatta and somehow they figured Laura was involved.

What he didn't know was if the LAPD was also in on the undercover sting and he'd been left out of the loop.

Sifting through every fact he could remember about the Kolnikov and Gianni cases, he was reminded how surprised DeMatta had seemed when Jordan told him one of his thugs had come looking for him. Were Stanton and Dutch involved in a takeover of DeMatta's so-called empire and had they set up their boss for the feds?

But that wouldn't explain why Stanton had chosen Alysa to get him Laura's financial information. Unless Stanton, like the feds, thought Laura was involved with DeMatta, too.

Bright lights glared in his rearview mirror, the car behind suddenly closer than it should be. Jordan changed lanes and kept watching. A few seconds later, the other vehicle changed lanes. His adrenaline surged. He was being tailed, but the lights were so bright, he couldn't identify the make. When he exited on Rosencranz, the car didn't follow.

Odd as hell. He found the diner, parked and got out. The captain's car was already there. Inside, the acrid scent of grease wrapped around him like a shroud. The overweight cook was frying something in a big vat, while across the room, the captain lounged in a booth looking as if he'd just rolled from bed.

"Yo, boss," Jordan said, walking over.

Carlyle leaned forward with both elbows on the table. "This better be good, St. James."

"It is." Jordan slid into the booth. "You know if the feds are involved in a sting with DeMatta?"

Carlyle's head came up. But just then, the cook came over. "What can I get you?"

"I'd like a shot of booze," the captain said. "But I'll have a bowl of vanilla ice cream instead."

"Nothing for me." Jordan smiled and leaned back. When the cook left, he said, "I was at Laura Gianni's tonight and the suits came banging on the door with a search warrant. I thought you might know something."

"Not a thing." A muscle jumped near the captain's right eye. Carlyle hated when other agencies impinged on his turf. To say he was territorial about his department was an understatement. "What's your assessment?"

After the cook dropped the ice cream in front of the captain, Jordan told him about Alysa and Stanton and everything leading up to this moment.

"So you think the feds have been working on this for a while?"

"Yeah. How else would they know about the money DeMatta gave Laura? It was three years ago."

"Marked money," Carlyle said sharply. "Damn it, I'm not going to let the stupid feds take credit for this. DeMatta is our collar." He shoveled nearly half a bowl of ice cream into his mouth.

"It's got to be something that's out of our jurisdiction."

"Did you ask?"

"I thought I'd leave that up to you, boss."

"Shit. Do we have enough to arrest DeMatta first?"

"I think so. I talked to Rico—he's tracked down Delores Matthews through her ex-husband in Hawaii. She's ripe to testify against DeMatta on Kolnikov's murder. But she's scared. I've also got a witness placing him at the scene of Eddie Gianni's murder. We get a warrant for DeMatta's place and snag him at the same time."

"He'll lawyer up before we get the cuffs on him."

"We'll have enough on him to stay bail. I can have both warrants in a couple hours."

"Who do you want on it with you?"

"Coltrane and Houston, for sure."

"Santini's back. How about him, Watson and McIntyre?"

Watson and Mac were the greenest detectives in the RHD, but he had no choice. "Okay. This needs to be done now, or we'll be blowing wind after the feds clean up."

"I'll set it up," Carlyle said. "We'll be on it by midnight."

They parted company and Jordan drove to headquarters, called Laura to see if Cait could do an official photo ID and said he'd bring the photos to her. A half hour later he was at Laura's with the book. When they finished and Cait had easily identified DeMatta as the man at the house the night her father died, he headed back to headquarters while Luke went for the warrants.

At the RHD, the rest of the crew drifted in within the hour. Luke was last to come with the papers. Just as Jordan was about to brief everyone, Carlyle shouldered through the door.

"Go ahead," the captain said. "I'm in, too."

Jordan outlined the plan, which wasn't complicated. He and Luke would go in with the arrest warrant while the others covered them from various angles. Once they had DeMatta secured, Jordan and Rico would take him in while the others did the search.

"Piece of cake," Mac said.

Jordan stared at the new detective. "No matter how simple an OP seems, it's never a piece of cake. Lives are at stake."

Mac, a good-looking kid in his late twenties, lowered his gaze.

Jordan knew he'd embarrassed him, but nothing could be taken for granted. He threw a jacket on over his Kevlar vest. "Any questions?"

It was so quiet one could almost hear the collective hearts pounding, hear the men breathe. Jordan's nerves danced under his skin. He took a breath to ease the tightness in his chest.

Everyone got jazzed before a bust.

"Okay. It's showtime."

By midnight, after they'd disabled the electrical alarm system and satisfied DeMatta's guard dogs with raw meat with tranquilizers in it, they had the exterior of the Bel Air mansion nailed down. Jordan and Luke banged on the door three times before the inside lights went on downstairs.

One of DeMatta's men appeared at the door, and it wasn't the butler. Jordan recognized him from police records as a former wrestler who towered over his own six foot two. From the looks of his mashed nose, he'd been in one too many fights.

He held up the papers. "We'd like to see Mr. DeMatta."

"He's busy."

"Tell him to get unbusy." But just then, DeMatta appeared at the top of the stairs still dressed in a suit and tie.

"Gentlemen. What can I do for you?"

"We'd like to talk to you. Either you come down or we come up."

DeMatta waited a moment, then started down the stairs. When he reached bottom, he crossed the room to Jordan. DeMatta clenched his hands, the gesture belying his otherwise cool-and-calm demeanor.

DeMatta gave a nod to his man at the door, then turned to Jordan. "What's this about?"

"We've got a warrant for your arrest, Mr. DeMatta. "For suspicion of murder. You have the right to remain—"

Suddenly the lights dimmed, then everything went dark. Jordan lunged for DeMatta and jammed his gun against his neck. "Don't move or you're dead." If DeMatta's men wanted a shoot-out, their boss would be first to go.

"I've got your back," Luke called out.

Somewhere glass shattered, then they heard a loud crash, as if someone was kicking down the front door, followed by shouting and spotlights crisscrossing the room. Jordan held his position with DeMatta as his hostage. "Call your goons off," Jordan ordered.

"Not my men," DeMatta croaked out.

Then the lights came on and a dozen men with masks and heavy-duty assault rifles surrounded them. A SWAT team. Jordan didn't move but kept holding DeMatta as a shield.

"Drop it!" one of the men shouted at Jordan. "FBI."

As the irony hit him, Jordan shouted back, "LAPD!" He tipped his head to Luke, who held out his shield.

The guy claiming to be FBI let out a string of curses. "The freaking LAPD is here!" he shouted to someone outside.

A short, stocky man in a bad suit sauntered inside. Damn. Phil Ledbetter. Jordan recognized the agent immediately from another case they'd worked on. Phil was the special agent in charge. "Hey, Phil," Jordan said, glad his own department had arrived first. "We seem to be in each other's way here."

"My jurisdiction," Ledbetter said. "Prostitution over state lines. Money laundering and extortion of a public official."

"Whoa. That beats my two tiny homicides all to hell, doesn't it."

"I want a lawyer," DeMatta snarled. "You got nothing on me."

Jordan tightened his grip around the mobster's neck. "I think an eyewitness who saw you at Eddie Gianni's place the night he died is good enough to take you downtown. And we've also got another witness who implicates you in Anna Kolnikov's murder. Does the name Delores Matthews ring a bell?"

"You got nothing. Kolnikov was a whore. Matthews is a whore."

Jordan's stomach churned. He squeezed harder. Suddenly it seemed important to defend Kolnikov. "She was a human being," he said through gritted teeth. He sucked in some air, willing away his fear, squelching his pride…to finally admit the truth. "And she was my mother."

Jordan's body shook with the admission. He glanced at Ledbetter, then shoved DeMatta toward the agent. "You take him. I'm getting dirt on my clothes."

In seconds, Ledbetter's men cuffed DeMatta, read him his rights and hustled him toward the door. On his way out, DeMatta cursed. "You're dirt then, too! You ever think about who your father is?"

Jordan swallowed hard, his throat squeezed tight. Yeah, he'd thought about it. A lot. And if he hadn't known the answer before, he did now. He stepped forward, his face directly in DeMatta's. "The man who raised me is my father. A sperm donor doesn't count." He glanced at his men, who, after hearing his great revelation, seemed frozen in place.

"All right!" Jordan yelled out. "We've got a search warrant here. Let's get this show on the road."

At headquarters after they finished, Rico came over and sat on the corner of Jordan's desk. "That took guts."

Jordan shrugged off his jacket and vest. "No, not guts. Just facing my own demons."

"It's about time," Luke mumbled.

"Hey," Jordan said to Rico. "Thanks for showing up. You and Macy must've just got back."

Rico shrugged, his dark eyes still glowing from the bust. "It's my job. Besides, if DeMatta was going down, I wanted in on it."

Luke paced around his desk and Jordan could see he was still jazzed, too.

"Let's get a beer," Rico said.

But just then Carlyle called over, "St. James, Ledbetter wants you at his office in the morning. Apparently he's got some issues."

Jordan stuffed his hands into his pockets. "Why doesn't he come here?"

"I asked the same thing. He said it was personal, between you and him."

LAURA JERKED AWAKE FROM a fitful sleep and glanced at the clock. It read 6:00 a.m. Time to get up. For the first time since she'd opened the shelter, she didn't feel like facing the day. She wanted to stay in bed and hibernate. Away from all her problems—and she seemed to have so many. Her worst fear was that she'd simply exchanged one problem for another.

After the FBI left last night with her books and DeMatta's money, she'd wanted to collapse in a heap. But she'd had to stay calm, had to assure everyone that things were okay.

That the FBI thought she was somehow involved with DeMatta was ludicrous. Jordan had said he'd help her work things out, but she didn't know how he was going to do it. He worked for the LAPD, not the FBI. As far as she knew, someone could knock on her door any moment and take her downtown. A possibility she'd already discussed with Rose and Phoebe, just in case. Rose said she'd stay at the shelter for the night.

Laura had been on edge ever since Cait had identified the photo of DeMatta—and even with the police doing double duty, the waiting was excruciating. Jordan's phone call in the middle of the night telling her DeMatta was in custody gave her a modicum of relief.

But he couldn't give her all the information right then, he said, and would come over in the morning and explain.

The phone rang, the sound seeming louder than normal, piercing her sensitivities. Her hand trembled when she picked up the receiver. "Hello."

"Hi, it's Jordan. Did I wake you?"

Relief untangled her nerves. "No, I was awake."

"Can I come over, or would you rather talk somewhere private?"

"Somewhere else." In just a half hour, everyone would be up, vying for the bathroom and complaining about not having time to get ready. "Name the spot."

After taking down the address, she got up, showered and threw on a pair of jeans and a baby-blue T-shirt with a black sweater over it. On her way to the kitchen, she heard a banging against the outside of the house. She peered out the window and saw a teenage boy who looked as strung out as she'd ever seen anyone.

It was the boy Brandy had been living with before she came to Victory House. Her drug supplier. The guy who'd pimp his own girlfriend to get more money for their habit. A story she heard all too often.

"Can I help you?" she said, opening the door.

"You! You're the reason she won't see me anymore."

Laura girded her reserves. "I will help you if you want me to, but I won't allow you to stand out here and disturb my neighbors."

He wavered on his feet. "D'ya think I care what you think? D'ya think I care what anyone thinks?" His voice rose an octave with each slurred sentence.

Laura might've been wary, but given his condition, she was sure she could push him over with one finger. "If you don't want my help, go home or I'll call the police."

He waved his arms. "I don't got no home to go to."

That was probably true. But she knew no one could help someone who didn't want to be helped. "Are you hungry? I'll give you some breakfast."

He stared at her. "Really?"

"Really."

He started inside just as Phoebe drove up. "What's going on?"

"He's hungry. I'm going to fix him something to eat."

"And then what?"

She took Phoebe aside. "I've got to leave to meet Jordan. If I fix him some food, can you call someone to help him? The men's shelter, maybe?"

Phoebe nodded. "I'll be back in a minute after I put my stuff away."

Laura hurried to make some scrambled eggs, enough for Cait, too, when she woke. The child had stayed up late last night watching girl movies with Alysa and Claire, so Laura didn't expect it would be soon.

As Laura finished scooping the scrambled eggs onto the boy's plate, he stared at her with bloodshot eyes.

"You're nice," he said. "I didn't think you'd be nice."

He was obviously too far gone to remember she'd sent him away before and had even called the police on him once.

"I didn't mean to wreck your stuff. I just got so mad when I couldn't see Brandy."

Placing the pan back on the stove, Laura stopped in her tracks. "Wreck my stuff?"

He shoveled a forkful of eggs into his mouth. "The blankets and stuff. I'm sorry. I just wanted to see Brandy."

Oh, God. *"You* ruined Cait's quilt?"

His eyes bugged out and he jerked to his feet. "I d-didn't want to. I just got mad because I couldn't see Brandy. You needed to be punished."

"You broke in here?" she repeated incredulously.

His eyes bugged out. He shoved to his feet and the chair scraped backward and crashed to the floor. The boy turned and, obviously panicked, stumbled toward the door and fell down the stairs. He got up instantly and started running.

"Wait!" Laura called after him. "It's okay." But he didn't stop and she didn't have time to go after him. What did he mean? Who told him she was keeping him and Brandy apart?

Phoebe came back into the kitchen. "Where is he?"

"Gone." Feeling incredibly weary, Laura sighed. "He said he was the one who destroyed Cait's quilt. All because he couldn't see Brandy."

Phoebe didn't seem surprised. "Lots of things are done in the name of love."

While Laura was relieved to know who'd broken in, she couldn't sit around and talk. She had to meet Jordan. "I'll be back in an hour or so."

"We're cool. Really. I can take care of things quite well."

Laura smiled. "I know. And I don't give you enough credit for all the things you do."

"Get out of here," Phoebe said, her discomfort with the compliment undisguised.

On the freeway, Laura got out the address Jordan had given her. His home, he'd said. It would be easier to talk there. She had to admit, she'd been curious about the other parts of his life, whether he lived as if he had tons of money, or as if he was an officer of the law? The Brentwood address gave her the answer… and made her realize just how far apart their lives were.

JORDAN ENTERED THE FBI field office headquarters building on Wilshire Boulevard and went directly to the screening desk.

"Special Agent Ledbetter will see you in the conference room on the fifth floor," the guard at the desk said after Jordan had signed in. He gave Jordan a visitor's badge.

Jordan hoped to hell this was quick. He had to meet Laura. In the few hours before coming here, Jordan had gone through every scenario Ledbetter might come up with. But none would be reason enough to get him down here. And he'd said it was personal. Jordan couldn't think of one thing he had in common with Ledbetter, personal or otherwise. Except that they both worked in law enforcement.

"St. James," Ledbetter said, when Jordan walked into the room.

Three other agents sat in chairs at the long mahogany conference table.

"Have a seat."

Jordan did as asked. "What's up, Phil? I know you didn't ask me here to chat about old times."

Phil gave a weak laugh. "No, you're right there." He cleared his throat. "This is not my deal. One of my agents made a request to talk to you, but since he's undercover, this is a high-security clearance issue. I want your assurance you won't mention it to anyone."

Though wary, Jordan couldn't think of any reason not to agree. "Okay. You've got my word."

"Good. Wait here." With that, the four suits left the room.

Waiting, for what he didn't know, Jordan drummed his fingers on the shiny table. His nerves twitched, and he got more tense as the minutes passed. He stood. After a few minutes of pacing, he finally heard voices outside, and then the door opened.

If ever there was a time he could've been knocked over with a feather, this was it.

Nick Stanton entered the room.

"Good morning," Stanton said.

Jordan's tongue felt glued to the roof of his mouth. Finally he managed to say, "You're an undercover agent?"

Stanton nodded. "On this gig for four years. Ever since the Kolnikov murder."

Jordan's hands went clammy. "Your meetings with her were part of the sting?"

He shook his head, his blond brows drawn together. "No. Something else brought me to see her initially."

"Something that will help my case?"

Stanton narrowed his gaze, as if debating some deeper issue. Hell, the question wasn't that tough.

"It's about what you said to DeMatta," Stanton said.

"What I said to DeMatta?"

"About Anna Kolnikov being your mother."

Jordan had already blocked it from his mind. He'd admitted it, then forgot it. He squared his shoulders. "If you're wondering if I have some kind of inside in-formation on Kolnikov and DeMatta because of that,

I don't. I only found out she was my mother after she was murdered."

"That's not it." Stanton sat in a chair and indicated Jordan should do the same. "I was raised by my father and stepmother in New Paltz, New York. The same town where Kolnikov grew up."

"I know where she lived and I know your history, or at least I thought I did. I guess your prison record was just a setup for your cover."

Stanton nodded. "True. But the reason I wanted to talk—" He cleared his throat. "Prior to meeting Anna Kolnikov, I'd learned she was *my* mother. I went to see her. It…it was a shock. I'd had all these fantasies about what she'd be like, what kind of relationship we'd have." His blue eyes darkened. "Later, when I heard she'd been murdered—well, that was another blow."

Jordan stared at the guy. It couldn't be. He searched the man's face for something familiar. He could see a resemblance to Kolnikov…even something of himself looking back at him. The eyes, maybe. Then he shook his head, reeling from the implications. "This is like some weird science-fiction movie where nothing is as it seems."

"You can imagine how I felt standing in my SWAT gear with a gun on you and DeMatta—and then hearing we were half brothers."

Half brothers. Jordan steadied himself against the boardroom table. "You were on the DeMatta case because of her murder?"

"No, the DeMatta sting has been on the boards for years. And now that we've finally got him, it's a bittersweet victory. Nobody can help the people he's murdered or their families."

Jordan knew the feeling. All his life he'd wanted to

know his real mother. Believed if he found her, she'd fill in the gaps he'd felt all his life because he didn't know who he was, never felt he belonged.

"What…what did you think when you met her?"

Stanton shoved to his feet. "At first? Disappointment. Disgust. Hate. A whole raft of emotions. But afterward, I realized I felt the way I did not because of who she was, but because of my own expectations. What I'd wanted her to be. No matter who she was, she couldn't possibly live up to my fantasy. When I came to grips with my own issues, I couldn't hate her." He reached into his pocket.

"This is a photo of Anna Kolnikov and my father."

Jordan hesitated. When he looked at the photo, his mouth went dry. The young blond girl in the picture appeared sweet and innocent, sixteen at the most. Just looking at her took his breath away. "She didn't look like that at all in her later years."

"I know. She didn't when I first met her, either."

Jordan started to hand back the photo.

"You keep it. I have another."

Jordan had thought solving Kolnikov's murder would be the end of it. That he'd be able to sleep at night knowing he hadn't let her down. But it wasn't the end of it, and Jordan's gaze was drawn to the photo again. He'd felt exactly as Nick had when he found out about his biological mother. Disappointment, disgust, hate, he'd felt them all. And still, he'd been compelled to know more about her. "What was she like?"

"We only met four or five times. And…"

Jordan knew the words Stanton had left unsaid. It was hard to reconcile the photo with the person she'd become. He cleared his throat. "In my investigation, I learned she helped some people."

Nick looked surprised. "Oh?"

"I heard it from more than one person."

The other man nodded. "That's good."

"And we found a witness. A former girlfriend of DeMatta's who'd gone missing. She used to work for Kolnikov and she's willing to testify about DeMatta's part in the murder."

Nick rubbed his hands together. "Justice does win out in the end."

A smile formed as Jordan looked at Nick—the man who said he was his brother—and as strange as that was, he felt a bond of some kind. They had a history. They had the same DNA. "Yeah, it does."

He wondered what Laura would think of what he'd learned today. But Nick Stanton was undercover. He couldn't tell anyone. Remembering that Nick still thought Laura was involved with DeMatta, he asked, "Why were you following Laura Gianni? And Alysa, why did you get her involved?"

"All part of the sting. I'm sorry, but I can't divulge the details."

Jordan understood. "Laura's never worked with DeMatta."

Nick's forehead furrowed. "You sound sure of that? We were at her husband's funeral when DeMatta gave her the money."

"Her ex-husband. And yes, I'm sure. The money DeMatta gave her was the stash you collected last night. She never spent a penny. I'll give you a copy of my report when it's completed."

Nick's eyebrows arched. "You sound involved in more than just an investigation."

Jordan drew a resigned breath. "Yeah. I've been on the case a while." Fact was, he was as involved as a guy could get.

He was in love.

Except he'd screwed up any chance they might've had to be together. She probably hated him for all his platitudes about justice, and then judging her in the process. He'd hurt her, unfairly.

LAURA PULLED INTO THE DRIVE and checked the address again. Her battered van seemed out of place in the ritzy upscale neighborhood. She gave a dry laugh. *Upscale* was an understatement.

Jordan opened the door before she even had a chance to knock. "Come on in. I'm glad you're here."

She forced a smile. Under other circumstances, she might be glad, too.

"Let's go into the living room."

She followed, her gaze drifting over the designer furnishings. A black leather couch with straight clean lines faced a flagstone fireplace. Two chamois-colored chairs flanked the couch, and the Oriental area rug in black and tan in the middle of the floor obviously cost a fortune. The same with the black lacquered coffee table. The room was immaculate, as if it had never been used. "Have you lived here long?"

"Since I graduated college. I guess that's long." He motioned for her to sit on the couch. "My mother finally got tired of seeing the place empty and just recently decorated this room. The rest of the house isn't so nice."

She sat, tried to find a comfortable position, but her body felt as stiff as a surfboard. "It's nice." Why was she so edgy? This was an informational meeting and nothing more. He'd tell her about DeMatta, then tell her what she and Cait needed to do…and then she'd go home.

"Before we get into other things," she said. "I have to tell you I discovered who broke into the house. It was Brandy's old boyfriend. He was angry at me for keeping them apart."

Jordan sat next to her, faced her with one arm slung across the back of the cushions. "Where did you hear that?"

"He told me. I caught him hanging around the shelter this morning."

His gaze lingered. "That's good to know. What about the phone calls? Did he make those, too?"

She shook her head. "I don't think so. He'd have no reason to say the things the caller said. But he did say someone told him I was to blame for keeping him from Brandy."

His head jerked up. "Who?"

"I asked, but he ran off."

"You think it was Brandy?"

She shook her head. "No, I don't. She wouldn't do something so destructive."

"Ever trusting." He smiled.

"Until I know otherwise."

He nodded. "Well, if things go as I expect they will, we'll find out soon enough if the phone calls were from DeMatta or one of his hired goons. The paint, too."

He kept looking at her, making Laura even more uncomfortable. "So, is Cait going to have to do anything else?"

"I don't know. Once we get all the evidence in place, we may be able to make a case without involving her. The black car belonged to the FBI. They were scoping you out because of your past contact with DeMatta." He reached into a gym bag on the floor and pulled out a tiny red tennis shoe in a Ziploc bag. "Do you recognize this?"

"Oh, God. That's Cait's. She wore the shoes to Eddie's that night. I must've missed it when I collected her things."

"It turned up in a search of DeMatta's office. It's prime evidence if you can identify it as Cait's."

"It is. They were new and when she discovered it was gone, she was heartbroken." Her chest constricted as the significance of it hit her. "That means he's known all along that Cait might have been there."

"Looks that way. And there's reason to believe someone in the department leaked him the information that I was talking to you—his motive for the threats." He slouched against the couch.

"Do you think he would've carried them out?"

"I don't know. He wasn't in any hurry and he knew where you were."

"Odd. Maybe he has a soft spot for kids?"

"Maybe. But it doesn't matter. With all the evidence we've got, DeMatta is going away for a long time."

Laura placed a hand to her mouth, as if what he'd said was too good to be true.

"I'm hoping it won't be necessary for you or Cait to testify, but if it comes to that, you'll have to be in a protection program."

She nodded. "If it means I can finally live a normal life, I'll do whatever it takes."

"We also have a witness who will testify about the Kolnikov murder."

"Oh—you found Anna's killer?"

"I can't discuss the details, but I think so, yes."

Laura blinked back tears of joy, but the darkness in Jordan's eyes said he didn't share her happiness. He'd made it clear early on what he thought of people like Anna.

How could she blame him, given the woman's reputation? And most of it being true. Still, her guilt weighed heavily on her. She had to set the record straight. "Anna wasn't the horrible woman you believe her to be, you know. Yes, she did illegal things, but for her, it was the only way to survive. She'd been on the streets since she was a teenager. She didn't have family or anyone to help her. Just people like DeMatta who exploited her from a very young age."

She attributed his silence to disapproval. "Anna helped people. She found my father for me and arranged for me to live with him and finish school. If she hadn't taken the initiative, I can't say where or how I'd be living today." She gave a wry laugh. "I learned later that she had to pay him to take me in. But I didn't know it at the time, and having a home base allowed me to get back on track."

Jordan's eyes went from steel-gray to charcoal.

"She never took underage girls. That's why she wouldn't let me work for her except to clean. My street time came before I met Anna. She only hired women who'd already made the choice and who wanted to continue making their living in that way."

Laura's voice began shaking with emotion as she said, "Anna was the only person who ever cared enough to help me. But she never had anyone to help her."

Jordan rubbed his hands together awkwardly as if he didn't know what to do with them. "I'm sorry. You obviously cared about her very much."

"I did. I wish she'd known it."

He frowned. "What do you mean?"

"I—I never told her I appreciated all she'd done for me. Instead I blamed her. If she hadn't paid my father to take me in, I would've known him for the bastard he was. I wouldn't have been so heartbroken when I found out. I was angry at her because she gave me false hopes, and I never kept in touch with her after I found out she'd made a deal with my dad."

She drew a shaky breath. "During college, I was ashamed of my past and wanted to put it all behind me, including Anna. It was only after she died that I realized my utter stupidity." The tears she'd forced away began to spill like rivers down her cheeks.

Jordan pulled her into his arms. "She helped you and now you're doing the same for other kids."

"I don't know what I would've done without Anna. Probably stayed on the streets." Her words were muffled against his shoulder.

"So, there you are. You're her legacy. What you do is part of that legacy."

His kindness and understanding unleashed another flood of tears, and then deep racking sobs shook her body.

Jordan simply held her closer, tighter.

As her tears subsided, she said through a sniffle, "If I'd not been so stupid…" Her breath hitched. "I'll never forgive myself for that."

"She knew you were running the shelter, didn't she?"

Laura sniffled again. "Yes."

"I'm sure knowing what you chose to do with your life, and knowing what a strong person you've become, was enough for her."

Laura looked at Jordan. The thought was a balm of sorts, soothing her ragged emotions.

As Laura's crying stopped, Jordan felt the tightness in her shoulders ease. Now that he knew more about Laura's past, he realized she probably felt he'd abandoned her, too, just like everyone else in her life. And truth was, he had. He'd been a first-class jerk. It probably wouldn't change things between them, but he'd never know if he didn't try to explain.

When she quieted, he held her at arm's length, then sat her on the couch beside him. "I have some things to say."

She sat there like a zombie, but managed to say, "Okay."

"Because of you, I've come to realize some things, too. My own stupidity, for one. Mostly, that I'm really good at judging others without understanding all the circumstances."

He itched to get up and pace to release the tumult inside, but he needed to stay near her. "When I told you I never tried to find my real mother...I lied. I lied because I was ashamed." He swallowed. "I was ashamed because when I found her, I discovered she was a prostitute." He closed his eyes. "Anna Kolnikov was my mother."

Laura's mouth fell open. "Anna was...I can't believe—"

"It's true."

"How did you find out? Through investigating her case?"

"No, before that. But it was after the murder. When I found out about her, I was horrified. Angry. Ashamed. I wanted to erase it from my mind. But I couldn't. I couldn't stop thinking about her—hating her. But I was compelled to find her murderer. I convinced myself it wasn't personal, that justice had to be served. I started to reinvestigate."

"That's when you came to talk to me?"

"Yes. I think I wanted to solve the case to prove to myself I could be objective. That my feelings about her, who she was and what she'd done, didn't affect me in any way. But they did. I despised her—not because she was who she was, but because she'd disappointed me. All my life I'd fantasized about finding my real family. My expectations were huge. I expected I'd discover some extraordinary reason why she gave me up, some reason beyond her control."

He shook his head. "She killed the fantasy. She'd given me away without a thought. I couldn't forgive her for that."

"Did you find out differently?"

"No, but it isn't important anymore. I know who I am. And it took finding her to make me face myself…and to realize what she'd done for me. Had she not put me up for adoption, I wouldn't have had the life I've had. I wouldn't have had the love and support from two wonderful people who have been parents in every sense of the word. What I regret the most is how I allowed my bitterness to creep into the rest of my life, how I allowed it to color my judgments." He lowered his head. "I judged my parents… and I judged you."

Frustrated, he stood, shoving his hands into his pockets. "My expectations clouded the truth. And the truth is that nothing has changed my feelings about you. I know what kind of person you are. I've known from the beginning. You're everything I wish I was."

She sat as still as a statue. And as silent.

Well, what did he expect? That she'd jump into his arms? He'd hurt her deeply. He didn't deserve her forgiveness, but he had to apologize, anyway.

He threw up his hands in a gesture of futility. Kneeling in front of her, he looked into her eyes. "From the bottom of my heart, I'm so very sorry for any pain I've caused you."

When she remained silent, he got up, shoved a hand through his hair. "I'm not asking for your forgiveness. I don't deserve it. But I had to tell you how I feel."

After what seemed an eternity, she said, "And how do you feel?"

Surprised she'd even asked, he dropped to the couch beside her and took her hands. "I love you. That's how I feel. I know that probably seems trite right now, but it's true."

Laura's heart leaped, but just as quickly her guard came up again. No matter what he said right now, no matter how sincere he believed he was at this minute, it didn't mean he'd be there forever. It didn't mean he'd love her forever.

"Laura, what I feel for you is something I never imagined possible. And more than anything I want us to have a chance. I'm hoping you'll give *us* a chance."

And then what? How could she be sure he wouldn't leave? If things didn't work out, she'd be alone again— and the hurt would be that much greater. She moistened her lips. "I don't know what to say."

"You don't need to say anything. I want you to know that watching you with Alysa, with Cait, and with all the people in your life, has given me something I never had before. For you, forgiveness is a big part of love. And loving someone means accepting the whole person, not just the parts that fit. You've taught me that self-forgiveness is as important as forgiving others. And it doesn't happen overnight."

She cleared her throat, her emotions on edge. He

was the most honest, most caring man she'd ever known. And now, even knowing the worst about her, he said he loved her.

And God knew, she loved him.

He traced her cheek with his fingertips, his touch gentle and reassuring, then with one finger he tipped her chin up. "You know what I think?"

"What?"

"I think you can forgive others without a thought, but you can't forgive yourself for things you had no control over. It took me a while to understand the significance of my need to find my mother. I needed to know who I am, but what I didn't realize is that who I am *is* my past—all of it."

He touched his fingers to her chest. "Your heart is full of love…and you are the person *I* love. All of you, past, present and—" He cleared his throat. "And I hope future."

She wanted it so much. Why couldn't she just let go?

"I want you in the rest of my life, Laura…but I know how much I hurt you. If you want me to go away, all you have to do is say so."

God, no! Her chest constricted at the thought. She didn't want him to go away. Ever.

"Do you love me, Laura?"

She looked into his eyes, filled with unconditional love and acceptance, and she loved him so much her heart ached with it.

She'd known when they first met that somehow her life would never be the same. And she'd been right.

"I love you," she whispered. "More than I could ever have imagined."

And when his lips again met hers, she knew her heart was his forever.

Turn the page for an excerpt from book three in the COLD CASES: L.A. trilogy by Linda Style. Coming from Harlequin Superromance in 2006.

"YOU CROSSED THE LINE." Julianna listened to the recorded message, the distorted voice, then heard the dial tone. She closed her eyes and waited for the next message. The recorder had indicated there were three.

Message two. "I told you before, if you don't stop, I'm going to stop you."

Her heart raced. The third article had run yesterday, and the fact that she hadn't heeded the caller's earlier message to quit writing had probably enraged him.

A second later, the next call came. Listening, a chill ran up her spine and she clicked off in the middle of it.

She hadn't told anyone where she was going—not even the managing editor at the magazine—and no one would think to look for her at her ex-father-in-law's ranch in New Mexico. As far as calling the police, that was an exercise in futility. They'd told her that with no other evidence, there was no way to track the e-mail messages she'd reported. They didn't have the manpower to do a stakeout based on a couple of crank phone calls. One officer suggested it might be easier if she simply stopped writing the articles.

Idiots. She heaved a deep sigh as she fell into Abe's recliner, its leather soft and cracked with age, and switched on her laptop. Three more articles and she'd be finished with this series detailing the case of a little girl abducted in California. It was one of many stories she'd written about missing children who'd met the same fate. Yes, it might be safer to stop writing the articles, but there was no way she could.

Apparently the caller felt threatened. What he didn't know was that his threats worked in reverse, stoking a powerful determination inside her.

She pulled up the Word program on her laptop, went to the last page and typed in, "Now he's threatening me. Why? Am I getting too close to finding out who he is? Someone out there knows something about this man. If you think you recognize the profile—if you know anything, call your local FBI, or call 1-800-CRIMETV. Help us find this killer and take him off the streets. Don't let this monster kill another child."

A noise outside jerked her from the story. Gravel crunching. An animal maybe? Abe had complained about the javelina disturbing his chickens. It certainly wouldn't be a visitor at two in the morning. Hell, her curmudgeon of a father-in-law didn't have visitors no matter what time it was.

The old man was asleep in the back wing of the sprawling territorial ranch house. He was a friend, a surrogate father—and he'd taken her in, no questions asked. Abraham Coltrane might be cranky and bull-headed, but she loved him dearly. Not even the divorce could take that away.

Something rustled near the window. Her pulse kicked up a notch. Except for the soft light of an old faux oil lamp across the room and the light coming from her laptop, the rest of the house was dark.

A coyote bayed in the distance, its lonely howl a faint echo decrying the vastness of the high desert, reminding her how much she loved it here. She felt a peacefulness she never enjoyed at home in San Francisco.

Julianna took a deep breath and kept on writing, the keys clicking loudly in the quiet. She hadn't known when she'd started writing the articles on abducted children that her research would show similar findings in diverse cases. Though many of the cases she profiled were from different states, there were similarities in some of the crimes, similarities that suggested either a copycat, or a killer who traveled the country in search of victims. A deviation from the usual profile for a serial killer, but the facts were there nonetheless.

The police dismissed her as a hack out for publicity. Yes, she wanted publicity, but only for the victims. How many were there? Why hadn't this monster been stopped? And could he possibly be…

No! As a journalist, she had to stay objective. The hard part was that…as a mother, as a human being, being objective in this instance was the most difficult thing she'd ever had to do. It was, at times, impossible.

She heard another noise that sounded like it came from the kitchen. She stopped typing, waited, listened. She heard it again. The doorknob in the kitchen rattled. Was someone trying to get inside? Oh, God!

She took out her cell phone. All she heard was static.

Her gaze went to Abe's rifle in the gun rack on the other side of the room. Retrieving the key to the case, she took out one of the rifles. The wood felt smooth under her fingers, probably from years of Abe's use. She was suddenly reminded that she'd never held a gun in her life. What the hell did she think she was going to do? She'd probably shoot herself.

Gun against her chest, heart pumping like a piston,

she stole into the kitchen and stood behind the door, her back flat against the wall. Just as she settled in place, the doorknob jiggled one more time…and then it stopped.

She held her breath. Oh, crap. The window in her bedroom. She'd left it open. She edged down the hall toward Abe's room to wake him. As she passed her bedroom door, she heard a loud thud from inside. She tightened her grip on the weapon. Now what? Think.

Her heart banged against her chest and just when she decided to run, the door creaked open and a large male form stood shadowed in the doorway. Trapped. Abe's room was beyond where he stood. On instinct, she raised the gun, butt end up, and mustering all her strength, hit the man over the head as hard as she could.

The man grunted…but he didn't keel over.

Oh, my God! She dropped the gun and turned to run. But he caught her, shoved her against the wall on the opposite side and pulled her arms back so she couldn't move. "What the hell are you doing?" the intruder said, his voice low and raspy.

That voice. She knew that voice.

"Move and you're history."

If you enjoyed what you just read,
then we've got an offer you can't resist!

Take 2 bestselling
love stories FREE!

Plus get a FREE surprise gift!

Since when did life ever tell you where you were going?

Sometimes you just have to dip your oar into the water and start to paddle.

THE
SUNSHINE
COAST
NEWS

KATE AUSTIN

Available February 2006
TheNextNovel.com

HARLEQUIN®
NeXt™

HARLEQUIN *Super*ROMANCE®

**Home to Loveless County...
because Texas is where the heart is.**

**Introducing an exciting new five-book series set in
the rugged Hill Country of Texas.**

Desperate times call for desperate measures. That's why
the dying town of Homestead, Texas, established the
Home Free program, offering land grants in exchange
for the much-needed professional services modern
homesteaders bring with them.

Starting in October 2005 with

BACK IN TEXAS
by Roxanne Rustand
(Harlequin Superromance #1302)

WATCH FOR:

AS BIG AS TEXAS
K.N. Casper (#1308, on sale November 2005)

ALL ROADS LEAD TO TEXAS
Linda Warren (#1314, on sale December 2005)

MORE TO TEXAS THAN COWBOYS
Roz Denny Fox (#1320, on sale January 2006)

THE PRODIGAL TEXAN
Lynnette Kent (#1326, on sale February 2006)

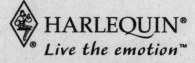

HARLEQUIN®
® *Live the emotion*™